APEX OF THE CURVE

Sacred Hearts PNW Chapter - Book III

A.J. DOWNEY

COPYRIGHT

∽

ISBN: 978-1-950222-27-8

Editing & book design by Maggie Kern @ Ms.K Edits

Cover art by Dar Albert at Wicked Smart Designs

DEDICATION

To Ben, for giving me more than a sliver of hope back. The least I can do is dedicate another book to you.

PROLOGUE

*F*enris...

The bar was hoppin'. I sometimes bounced at this cowboy bar out in Ravensdale, just north of Black Diamond. I lived out on the edge of Auburn in the Green Valley area, so it wasn't too long of a haul for me and it was something to do on a Friday night when the club didn't have anything going on.

It was a pretty okay gig – a flat rate of pay for the night, cash under the table, and it bought some goat or chicken feed for the farm on occasion.

Mostly, it gave me an outlet for some of my aggression when shit was otherwise calm around the club. There's nothing like pitching some drunk frat bros or wannabe cowboys out on their ass, or better yet, their face in the gravel lot.

This was one of my pop's first stops when he got out of the joint. His old high school buddy, Mitch, ran the place and always had a job for him when he got out. When my pops started getting up in years, after my sister died, I'd just naturally transitioned into the spot my dad had held down at the door.

He still came in and drank sometimes, taking up a stool at the end of the bar to shoot the shit with Mitch while I worked the door.

Not tonight, though. Tonight, it was just me, checking IDs as the citizenry's ladies and gents filed in.

Mitch had been making a killing ever since he'd put in the dance floor and sound system and added the mechanical bull in the corner.

He had a regular Texas-style roadhouse going on out here, and it was popular.

"Hey, Fen." Bobby, the junior doorman, handed me an ID. I shone my flashlight on it and double-checked it for him. It was legit. I looked at the picture and up at the girl who didn't look a fuckin' day over sixteen.

"Try not to stay too late, darlin'. Place gets pretty nuts after eleven," I said, handing it back to her. She smiled prettily and blushed, and it did absolutely nothing for me.

"I don't know, Lindsay… I don't think this is a good idea," I heard. I looked up into a beautiful set of green eyes, taking the two rectangles of laminated whatever the fuck driver's licenses in Washington were made of.

Lindsay was a brunette. The math told me she was twenty-eight, and she looked like a bitch. Her makeup was overdone, titties on full display – one of those types looking to hook up and ride a cowboy. She fit right in with the rest of the posers inside. Fake as shit, I had no interest in her or anyone else who came through these doors, typically.

The other license – the name, like her eyes, caught my eye for its uniqueness. Aspen. Aspen Lawson. I handed each lady their license back and let my gaze linger on Aspen.

She was beautiful in an unconventional way – thicker, with some real tits and an ass, a true hourglass figure in a thin sweater that clung to her over jeans and a pair of stylish knee-high boots. She looked cold standing out here waiting to get in. It wasn't exactly a night for going without a jacket, but a lot of girls did. It was warm inside the bar and it was one less thing to have to try and keep track of.

She had these luxurious blonde curls that framed her face, held back by a slim glittering line of rhinestones – some kind of headband that was hidden but for the evenly spaced stones in her hair. Simple, cute, her makeup, if it was there, understated and accentuating her natural beauty.

She was tall, too. Five foot nine, maybe? Still, not too tall when it came to me. I still looked down at her from my six-foot-five height.

"Thank you," she murmured, eyes wide when they met mine and I nodded. She plucked her license from my rough, tattooed fingers and I looked after her as she disappeared inside with her friend.

"Hey, man." I turned back to the half-jock, half-cowboy wannabe who was next in line in his polo shirt and scowled, taking his license from him and skimming it.

"Go ahead," I growled and let him through. I had some difficulty putting the pretty blonde out of my mind.

Hours later, the bar was closing and Mitch came to find me at the door.

"Hey, we got one that's drunk as fuck and I can't find her friend."

"On it," I growled and heaved myself off the stool at the door. It'd been a quiet fuckin' night. One near fist fight over a girl, but they'd all been pussies, and I'd thrown them out without incident. That'd been it, so far.

I headed into the bar trailing Mitch, and I didn't know what I would find. I can tell you, the absolute last thing I expected to find was the reluctant blonde, Aspen, drunk as fuck in a back-corner booth.

I mean, she was *gone*.

It was pretty impressive, actually.

I slid into the booth with her and cupped her cheek.

"Hey!" I called out. "Hey, Aspen!"

"You know her?" Mitch asked.

"No, I just remembered the name for some reason. Not one you see very often."

"Well, she's the last one in here. You remember if she came with a friend?"

"Yeah, a brunette, L-something," I answered absently as Aspen groaned.

"Shit, I'll have Becca check the ladies' room but looks like Aspen here got ditched."

"Don't bother. The bitch she came with probably got drunk and fucked off with one of these wannabe cowboys. Do me a favor and call my pops, have him bring the truck."

"You sure?" Mitch asked with an incredulous scoff.

"I'm sure," I said.

I leaned Aspen up against me and sighed. Wouldn't be the first time I'd brought a drunk back to mine and my pop's place to sleep it off, but it definitely was the first time I'd be bringing a woman as pretty as she was home with me.

It took my pops a good half an hour to get there, and he wasn't happy about it.

"What the fuck?" he demanded, and I scowled up at him.

"Shut up and get the fuckin' doors for me, old man."

"I am *not*—"

"You ain't doing shit except driving. I'll handle the rest."

He growled a rumbling noise of displeasure and I ignored him. I got her up, unsteady on her feet, groaning. It so wasn't happening. I got my arm beneath her knees and lifted her just as she passed out again. She had some weight to her, and while I wouldn't be able to do this forever, it was a straight shot to the front door and out to my dad's truck where he'd parked it. *Thankfully,* he'd had the presence of mind to keep the passenger side pointed this direction. I went out, Mitch holding the front door for me, and put her right into the truck.

My pop's closed the door when he knew she was clear and he wouldn't bang into her.

"Hope like hell you know what you're doing," he said, and I nodded.

"Just drive, I'm right behind you."

I waved at Mitch, who waved back, and I went over to my bike, mounting up.

The ride home was brisk, and when my dad pulled up, he did it right in front of the door, passenger side pointed the right way. He got out of the truck calling something or other out, but I couldn't hear it over the bike. I shut it off.

"What?"

"I said, you clean that shit up! I'm going to bed!"

"Fuck," I muttered.

Sure enough, I opened up the passenger door of his truck and the woman was an absolute mess. The vomit sweet and off-smelling, and I wondered if there was more than just alcohol at play here.

"Come on, darlin'," I muttered and helped her stagger out onto the gravel driveway. "I gotcha."

I helped her into the house, carried her up the stairs and sat her on the john in the upstairs bathroom. She was *out of it*.

I stripped her, got her cleaned up, helped her puke into the tub and spent the better part of an hour helping her into my room and into my bed where she would be more comfortable. Her clothes I put in the laundry across the hall. I got out some aspirin and a clean glass of water and put them on the bedside table for her. Finally, I wrote a long-ass note trying to cover all the bases and left that too.

I still had some proverbial miles before I could sleep, myself. I dragged my ass back downstairs and dealt with my dad's truck, which wasn't that bad seeing as she'd mostly nailed herself.

Finally, after all of that, I dragged myself in and onto my couch.

Tomorrow morning was going to be interesting. That was for sure.

CHAPTER ONE

Aspen…

I woke up, my head just *splitting*, and I didn't know where I was. I sat up in unfamiliar clothes in an unfamiliar bed and looked around.

It was creepy in here. The walls were rustic, rough-hewn boards on three sides, the wall behind me, at the head of the very large bed, stone. The bed itself was similarly rough-hewn logs, stripped of their bark and was not only high up off the ground, but was covered in what looked like animal furs.

An animal skull hung above the bed, vines twining through the eye sockets and around the horns, and I shuddered. On the bedside table was a tall glass of water and two round white tablets, beneath them, a note.

I picked it up with shaking fingers, letting the pills slide to the nightstand's surface, and read the neat printing in big block letters…

Don't Panic! You're safe.

Where are you?

You're at the bouncer's house. Your friend ditched you and we couldn't call anyone for you.

Where are your…

Clothes? In the dryer in the closet across the hallway. (You threw up. A lot.)

Phone? No idea. Maybe with your friend, maybe back at the bar. We'll look for it.

Jewelry? Bedside drawer.

ID? Also, the bedside drawer with your debit card. Found both in your jeans pocket.

What now?

There's fresh water and two Tylenol on the bedside table. Start there. There are clean towels in the bathroom if you want a shower, which you might. I don't think I got all the puke out of your hair.

When you come downstairs, we can give you a ride, call you a cab or an Uber – whatever you'd like. If no one is up when you get up, there's food in the fridge, Netflix on the TV in the living room, and the dogs love to be played with and loved on.

Main thing is, you're okay.

See you downstairs. I go by Fenris.

"Huh." I blinked several times, read and re-read the note as if there were more answers to be found in it.

I had left my phone in Lindsay's car because Charles had kept blowing it up. I didn't want to see my soon-to-be-ex-husband. Didn't want to speak to him. Lindsay, on the other hand, I would like several words with.

I threw back the blankets and furs and sat up, letting my feet dangle off the side of the bed. I opened up the raw and distressed rustic bedside table's drawer, and sure enough, there was my license, debit card, rings and necklace.

I took the Tylenol, drank the water all the way down, and sat breathing heavy for a moment, willing the throbbing in my skull down to a dull roar.

Donning my jewelry and tucking my license and debit card into the front pocket of the red-and-black checkered flannel I wore, I stood up slowly and found the bathroom. I took care of that bit of business and peeked out into the hall. It was quiet out here. Too quiet, and I didn't think anyone was up yet.

I crept down the stairs and halted in the entry way to the kitchen.

An older man was in the kitchen at the cutting board cutting up mushrooms. He looked up and squinted at me, his head clean shaven, his beard quite the opposite.

"Ah, she lives," he stated dryly.

I didn't say anything. I didn't know *what* to say. I heard a cough behind me and I jumped, turning sideways. It was an open archway at the bottom of the stairs. To the left, there were two steps leading down into the living room, the couch along the wall. Someone rolled off of it and loomed, standing like some great leviathan rising from the deep.

This man, I at least recognized. He was the man checking IDs at the bar last night. I remembered his eyes – sharp and very blue. The silver beads winked from his blond beard, his hair braided and twisted in a sort of modern rendition of a Viking warrior's mohawk. I shuddered as he loomed, the living room space quite diminished with his presence. He was *huge* at well over six feet and broad through the chest and shoulders.

"Morning," he grated in this bass rumble.

I looked back at the older version of him in the kitchen.

"Well, what's the matter?" the older man asked. "Cat got your tongue?"

I swung my gaze back to the younger man, Fenris, and he cocked his head, staring me down and I couldn't help it. I broke down, clapping first one hand, then the other over my mouth as a pitiful sob escaped.

"Oh, shit. Hey, now..." Fenris said, everything about his imposing presence softening, but it was too late. The flood gates were open and the tears just started to pour, and I couldn't stop them.

Too much! This was just too much!

Oh, shit was right.

I crumpled to the floor, sitting down *hard* on the edge of the landing at the bottom of the steps leading into the room, and hugged myself. I felt like such a freak, crying like that in front of these two strange men.

The older man in the kitchen turned his eyes away from me and grunted, jaw tightening, and I shoved both of my hands over my mouth to try and stifle the unpleasant noise coming from it.

The younger man, who had risen from the couch, who positively *towered* over me, grunted and came toward me. I scooted aside and pressed myself to the wall as it looked like he was going for the stairs and I wanted out of his way. He took a great step from beside me, skipping one of the stair treads and I tried to get myself together, but then his warmth hit my back and his boots appeared to either side of me. Strong arms went around my body in a stabilizing hug and he grated in my ear, "It's okay. Let it out."

I didn't know what to do for a heartbeat, but then the next wave of emotion hit, and I dissolved against him like sea-foam on the shore. I took his invitation and I let it all out.

CHAPTER TWO

Fenris...

She calmed down eventually. My pops moved around the kitchen unconcerned, fixing up some breakfast for the three of us. I just sat still and waited on her. I was in no rush. She fit inside the circle of my arms kind of nice, actually.

"Come on up here," I murmured when she'd settled down, and I stood, holding a hand down to her. She took it and I hoisted her up and onto her feet. She was an ugly crier, her face going all blotchy and red, all the way down her neck and across what I could see of her chest before she clutched the collar of the shirt, *my* shirt, she was wearing closed.

She looked damn good in it—the flannel hugging her breasts, the hem brushing just above her knees, the sleeves rolled back in this adorable way that made her look like a living doll. *Like she was wearing her boyfriend's shirt...*

I led her to the upstairs' bathroom and hit the light on the way in, then I turned and helped myself to a handful of her hips to either side, my hands sliding over her body covered as it was by the flannel of my shirt as I lifted her and sat her on the edge of the counter. She made a slight cry of surprised protest when I did it, her green eyes wide and her pale face draining of color even more, and I crooked a one-sided grin and apologized.

"Sorry."

Even sitting this high up, her feet dangling over the floor, I still had to look down at her, and she wasn't exactly a short or even a petite woman… just shorter than *me*.

I picked up a washcloth off the stack on the back of the john, within reach of the shower without looking.

"Take a deep breath," I said eying her, and she stared up at me, her green eyes still startled and wide, framed in her wild blond curls, the tinge of red around them from her crying making them somehow more vivid. Bright.

She jumped slightly when I smacked the arm of the faucet up, the cold spray a slight shock against my fingers as it soaked the washcloth I held under it. I wrung the square of rough cloth out, folded it in into a padded quarter of its original size and raised it up. She leaned back, and I gave her a look. I admit, it was stern at first, but it wasn't my goal to scare her into submitting – I was trying to help, in my own heavy-handed way and shit, I didn't want to make things worse.

"It's cool," I said and tried to keep my tone in check.

She stilled, and I carefully washed her face with the cool cloth as though she were a child.

She broke the silence first, leaning back when she'd had enough, grasping my wrist gently to pull my hand away, putting the other with its perfect, long nails, against the cloth to push it down along with my hand.

"I'm sorry," she murmured, and her voice was distressed.

"It's not a problem," I said neutrally, then asked a little more gently, "You want to tell me what that was all about?"

She stared at me mutely for several seconds and I could tell that, *yes*, yes, she *did* want to tell me, that she needed to tell *someone*, but she finally bit her lips together and stayed quiet.

"It's alright, you don't need to. Just thought it might help to get it off your chest."

At the word chest, she crossed her arms over hers, tucking her hands beneath her arms, and I smiled and chuckled.

"You're a strange woman, Aspen," I said.

"How did you know my name?" she asked.

"Driver's license," I answered, shaking out the washcloth, folding it in half once, and laying it over the faucet's neck to drip into the sink - if it was going to drip.

"Oh," she said softly, looking away.

"Couldn't find your clothes?" I asked.

She looked back at me and blushed faintly.

"I don't remember what happened," she said.

"You were pretty drunk."

"I only had one drink, maybe two, but I never drink more than that when I go out."

I grunted and gave a nod.

"Your friend left with a couple of guys, think one of them maybe slipped you something?" I asked.

"I don't know..." she looked on the verge of tears again and I shook my head.

"Doesn't matter," I told her with a sniff and she looked back up at me, those clear green eyes of hers slaying me every time they met mine. "You're safe, nothing happened to you last night. No one touched you but me, and only to get you cleaned up so I could put you to bed. I swear it."

She swallowed hard, hesitated and finally said, "Thank you."

"It's no problem," I reiterated. "I'll get you your clothes. You get in the shower and I'll leave 'em right outside the door. Uh, keep the shirt – your sweater was marked 'dry clean only' and I put it in an over-sized Ziploc until you could decide what you wanted to do with it."

"Okay." She nodded, wincing as she hit a rough patch in her hair, smoothing it behind her ears with her hands.

"Yeah, I couldn't keep it out of your hair, sorry."

"It's no problem," she said with a slight smile, and I gave her one back.

"What's your name?" she asked as I got half way out the door.

I looked back over my shoulder and said, "I go by Fenris."

"Yeah, but I mean your real name."

I smiled and I knew it was a bit feral, but I couldn't help it.

"Not to be alarming, but it's the only name I need."

"Okay," she whispered, her eyes a bit wide.

I shut the door and went up the hall to get her clothes out of the dryer.

"What the fuck was that all about?" my dad groused when I got to the bottom of the stairs.

"No clue," I said with a shrug. "She's getting a shower."

He grunted, slapped some scramble on a plate and set it in front of me at the breakfast bar. I slid into a seat and dug in, elbows to either side of my plate, taking a protective stance over my food. Some old habits die hard.

The squeaky tread on the stairs gave her away as she came down, and my dad and I were both stopped and looking to the mouth of the stairway when she peeked around the corner. She blushed, her hair, which had been full of body and a little wild before her shower, hung lank around her face, heavy with damp.

She put her hands in her back pockets, took a deep breath and emerged more fully into the room.

"Sorry, again, about earlier," she said shakily, and I shook my head.

"It's nothing."

"Come and eat." My dad echoed the dismissal of her apology and set out a plate for her.

"Oh, I'm not really that hungry—"

My dad snorted and cut her off, "I didn't cook all this so his big ass could eat it all, now sit down."

I smirked and shook my head. "Crotchety old bastard," I muttered.

"You're just like me, so shut the hell up, boy."

My smirk turned to a grin and I didn't say anything about it, just shoveled another bite of food into my mouth.

She slipped onto the stool beside mine, her face a study in beauty and confusion, and I tried not to stare. I didn't know what her deal was, but clearly, she had some shit going on. I thought back on my sister and shifted slightly in discomfort.

I hadn't pried back then. I should have, and by letting shit slide, I'd let *her* slide right into her grave. There wasn't a day that went by that didn't weigh on my soul. This chick right here, though? She wasn't my sister. I didn't even know her.

"Thank you," she murmured softly as my pops put a plate in front of her.

"Welcome," he grunted and started cleaning up between forkfuls off his own plate. I slid my empty one to the side and picked up my cup of coffee, swilling down some of the bitter brew.

"So, what's yer name?" he asked, drying off the cast-iron skillet he'd cooked up the scramble in a few minutes later. We'd all been silent for the most part – simply eating our food or drinking our coffee as the occasion called for it.

"Aspen," she said.

"Your parents some kind of hippy peace freaks?" he asked, and Aspen snorted a delicate little laugh.

"Guilty – at least my mom was…" she paused and took a fortifying breath. "Dad wasn't ever really in the picture."

"Oh, sorry to hear that." My dad sounded guilty to my ears, and I sat placidly. Didn't comment. Didn't have to. Our family dynamic was complicated on a good day. At least, it'd been a string of them lately. Good days, that is.

"Sorry, um, what's your name?" she asked.

"Oh, they call me Vyking."

"They?" she asked curiously.

"People. The club." My dad shrugged. He took a deep breath and sighed and changed subjects. "I cooked breakfast, why don't you go on out and feed the goats before you take Aspen home."

Before I could say anything, Aspen perked up, "Goats?" she asked, and it was the cutest damn thing.

My dad grunted with a secret smile. "Yeah. You're on a goat farm," he said. "Don't get too attached to any of 'em, though."

"Oh…" her excitement diminished some.

"Well, not exactly true," I said with a sigh, wanting that sparkle to come back to her green eyes for some reason. "There are a few you can get attached to. I'll show you which ones."

She finished the last few bites on her plate and my dad reached out and took it away from in front of her.

"You two kids have fun," he said.

"This way," I said and jerked my head toward the mudroom off the kitchen.

She'd donned her nice riding boots from the night before and I took down my newer farm jacket, a rusty brown Carhartt I'd bought recently to replace the dingy gray one I took down for myself, the elbow of the sleeve ripped out spectacularly, the padded ticking leaking out of it.

I held it open for her and said, "It's cold out there, better put this on."

"Thank you," she murmured, donning it. "How'd you do that?" she asked with wide eyes at the mangled sleeve of the coat I put on for myself.

"Barbed-wire fencing," I said, pulling down the old leather American outback crusher hat I used to keep the rain out of my eyes. I donned it and held open the back door, motioning for her to go on ahead.

The chill damp of the fall air rushed in to greet us and she ducked out into the fine misty crap sifting down out of a leaden gray sky to keep the damp and the cold from getting into the house.

I slipped out after her with a sigh. It was gonna be muddy as fuck and I hadn't bothered switching out my riding boots for my farm boots with the better tread. Too late now.

"Watch yourself," I cautioned. "Bound to be muddy as hell. I don't want you to slip."

"I'll be careful," she promised, perking up at the bleating of the goats out in their pasture.

"They act like they never been fed a day in their life," I groused.

"Poor creatures," she said lightly with a smile, an edge of teasing to her sweet voice. "They look absolutely starved."

I chuckled and looked across the yard to the split log fence of the first pasture and the small herd beyond the wire fencing lining we had just behind those logs. Sure enough, the goats were lined up begging at the fence line, waiting for my big ass to get in the barn and get their grain.

"They look it," I agreed, deadpan. "Just look at those ribs poking out."

Aspen smiled and I think it was the first genuine one I'd seen thus far, timid as it was.

She huddled in my oversized jacket and shirt and picked her way carefully in my wake through the muddy grass that squished beneath our feet as we made our way to the barn.

"You're in serious need of some stepping stones," she said mildly with a laugh and then finished up with, "The flat flagstone kind with the irregular edges would look fantastic with the aesthetic of the house." She turned back and looked at the weathered brown of my home. It was half log cabin, half weathered cedar shake tiles, and all rustic and as organic as the land around us.

"You might be onto something there," I said and thought about it. As much of a bitch as it would be to get them in place, it *would* beat wearing a muddy track in the grass. I'd see what my dad thought about it, but might just do it on my own anyway. He wasn't getting any younger and had a bad hip – anything to save the stubborn old bastard from a fall and breaking the damn thing. He was getting up there – had just turned seventy-three.

"Do they all have names?" she asked lightly when we ducked into the deep, permanent twilight of the barn. I liked it in here – the smell of fresh, dry straw and alfalfa.

"Breakfast, lunch, and dinner," I said. "The only named ones are Gunnar and Olaf, our two bucks and the girls who are the baby factories."

"How many mammas?" she asked.

"Seven," I answered.

"Oh, wow."

"It gets pretty hairy," I agreed. "Especially when they go dropping twins quite a bit."

"I can imagine," she said, moving a stray damp curl behind one ear.

"Wanna give me a hand? They'll be your best friend." I held a metal pail full of grain out to her and she *really* smiled then and it lit up her whole face with delight.

"Thank you," she said. "I'd love to."

I chuckled. "Famous last words," I said, and she laughed softly. I loaded up another pail for myself, then loaded up two big five-gallon buckets, and a third smaller pail for some of the goats that needed a little extra. I'd let her take care of the permanent stock while I took care of what my pops and I liked to refer to as our disposable little darlings.

Sometimes, it was tough. Once or twice, we had a goat come along that just had the right personality and sweet temperament that we couldn't do it. Those either got sold, or kept depending on the farm's needs.

Gunnar and Olaf bleated at us insistently and I stopped her at the gate, setting down my two five gallons and picking up the third pail off the top of one.

"Better let me get in there with the food. These two are around two hundred pounds of stank and attitude where a meal of grain is concerned."

"Okay," she agreed and handed one of the buckets over.

"Goats are assholes," I said with a shrug. "These two would bully you. They know they can't get one over on me – still hurts when they knock into you a little overenthusiastically, so watch yourself, okay?"

"Got it," she agreed with a nod.

She ghosted in after me, hanging back with the third bucket, and I smiled and called out, "C'mere, you two ungrateful fucks."

I hung one bucket on an exposed nail on the outside of their shelter and tipped the other one, emptying it half way while the moms and still-nursing babies trotted up from the lower end of the pasture. When I was sure the boys were engaged with their grain, I handed back the empty pail to Aspen while I took the full one from her and the third off the nail.

"Watch your footing," I warned, and we went over to the other, bigger shelter to pour grain into the troughs for the ladies.

"Oh my God, they're so cute!" she cried at the sight of the little babies, and I nodded.

"Yeah, they are. Think we're gonna keep that one," I said, pointing a black and white spotted little girl out.

"Have you named it, then?"

"Nope, not yet. You wanna?" I asked.

"Boy or a girl?" she asked, and I grinned.

"Girl."

She smiled and asked, "Can I think on it?"

"Sure can," I said and told her, "You can get in there and say 'hi.' They're still curious this young and could use the human interaction."

I watched her as she went over to the newish baby who wasn't more than a month old, her little tail set to wagging as she soaked up the pets Aspen gave her.

I couldn't help but find myself thinking that that was one of the things this place lacked – a woman's touch. Watching her unfurl, open up and flower with joy at the sight of the goats made putting up with the storm inside earlier worth it. It was like watching a damn rainbow arch across the sky real-time, watching her smile and laugh with the baby and I was almost sad to break it up, but I had to finish feeding the meat stock and get her home at some point today.

"So, what's your story?" I asked as we made our way to the second, larger pasture across the property.

"Oh, um, geez… where do I even start?" she asked.

"The beginning is as good as place as any innit?" I shot back.

"Um, well, my mom died about a month and a half or so ago," she said quietly. "Cancer, a long battle with it."

"Shit, I'm sorry to hear that."

"Oh, that's just the tip of the iceberg, I'm afraid," she said with a bitter chuckle.

"My brother died exactly a month after she did, a freak thing – car accident."

"Fuck, you kidding me?" I asked, looking back over my shoulder at her as I set down the buckets of grain just the other side of the fence.

Feeding these guys was easier, just had to dump it in the trough over the fence line. Didn't actually have to go in.

"It gets better," she said with a dubious tone. "The day after my brother's funeral, I caught my husband cheating… with other men… I'm going through a divorce right now." She sniffed and stared off over the rolling green grass and into the tree line of the woods that edged our property.

"The day after?" I asked, stopping and setting the first empty orange bucket down on the ground so I could pick up the other, full one.

"Yep," she said with a heavy and exhausted sigh.

"What the fuck?" I asked, looking her over. She was fucking *gorgeous* – why any guy on the planet would pass that shit up for a fuckin' sausage party was beyond me. He had to be crazy. "He bi and just didn't want to tell you or something?" I asked.

She pursed her lips and shrugged miserably.

"I don't know," she said softly. "I don't know if anything about our relationship is—" She stopped herself, stumbling over her words. "Or was true anymore."

"Shit, I'm sorry to hear that."

"You know, I didn't even want to go out last night," she confessed, covering her face with her hands. Her next words were half muffled when she said, dragging her hands off her face, "Lindsay practically dragged me out."

I gave a sardonic half-smile. "And ditched you like that?" I grunted. "You need new friends, baby girl."

She smiled slightly and bemused asked, "What did you call me?"

I chuckled. "Sorry, force of habit."

"It's alright," she said dismissively, and it was in that way that told me she'd sort of liked it – at least judging by the slight smile on her lips.

"Where you live?" I asked. "I'll run you home after I'm done here."

"Oh, I'm all the way over in Tacoma's north end," she said. "Um, you don't have to go to all of that trouble. You've already done so much."

"It's no trouble."

She gazed off into the distance again, her green eyes vacant as she thought about it. Finally, she gave me a wan smile and nodded, looking like she was on the verge of tears all over again.

"Okay, then," I said and gave a quick nod.

I TOOK HER HOME. THE NEIGHBORHOOD WAS A SHITTY ONE; HILLTOP. I didn't like a lot of what I was seeing, but I kept it to myself. This was the type of hood me and the boys belonged in, not someone sweet like Aspen.

"You got a way into the house?" I asked her when we pulled up to the curb out front. She stared at the dilapidated thing and gave a brittle nod.

"It's not even my house," she said softly. "It's my mom's."

"She leave it to you?" I asked and immediately wished I could take it back as I shifted my dad's truck into park. "You don't have to answer that," I said quickly. "It's none of my business."

"No, it's alright," she said. "She left it to me and Copper – um, that's my brother. I mean, *was* my brother. God, everything's so complicated!"

"Hey, breathe, one thing at a time, okay? Let's get you in the house."

She nodded and pulled on the door handle, sliding around in her seat so she could hop down. I picked up my cut off the seat in between us and shrugged into it as soon as my boots were firmly on the ground.

I hated driving cages of any variety, but it was too cold and too wet to expect Aspen to get on the back of my bike to get her here. She would have frozen her ass off.

She went to the rose bed in front of the house and looked around flipping over random rocks until she found what she was looking for with an 'ah ha!' She jerked her head for me to follow and I went up the path as she slid open the false bottom of the clever hidden key rock and retrieved the key.

"If you give me just a minute, I'll find my phone book, call Lindsay, and give you your shirt back."

"Sounds good," I said with a nod. I was in no hurry. She could call her friend first if she liked.

"Home sweet home," she said and followed it up before I could get through the door with a gusty sigh and a "Sorry, it's such a mess."

"Mess isn't the word I'd use to describe it," I said, stepping through the door and laying eyes on the scattered packing materials and piles of boxes.

"Oh, yeah?" she asked, rooting through one before shifting it to the floor and opening the one beneath. "What would you call it?"

I shrugged. "A state of transition, a moment of flux, you got a lot going on." I put my hands into my back pockets for a lack of anything else to do with them and to resist the urge I had to start going through shit. I found myself wanting to learn more about her.

She was on her knees going through a third box when she suddenly let out another triumphant, "Ah ha!" and held up a little black address book.

"Nice," I said.

"Let's hear it for being paranoid," she said, clambering back up onto her feet. "I hate to ask, but can I borrow your phone?"

"Paranoid?" I asked, digging in my inside pocket for my cell. I was having an 'oh, duh,' moment realizing she needed my phone to call her friend. The paranoid comment still threw me, though.

"Yeah, I write everyone's number down in my book in case my phone ever decides it wants to purge my contacts or something," she said, flipping it open and flashing through pages.

"Good idea," I said and nodded. She was having a hard time juggling the book and the phone to turn pages so I took the book from her and held it open. She found the page and frowned at my phone.

"Shit, sorry, it's five-four-seven-three," I told her so she could unlock it.

"Um, you didn't have to tell me that," she said with a nervous laugh.

"It's cool," I said with a wink. "I trust yah."

She blushed a bit and pulled up the keypad and entered her friend's number and I smiled as she turned her back and took a few steps away. While she waited for the call to ring through, I slid a pen out of the inside pocket of my jacket suddenly inspired.

I flipped through her book until I got to the 'F's and wrote my name and number on an available line, even threw the address for the farm in there. I put the pen back, slipped one of the farm's business cards out of my inside pocket and bookmarked the page with it, leaving it sticking out the top of her book.

If she ever needed anything, she could find me.

"I ended up at the bouncer's house last night," she said and there was hostility in her tone. I looked up to her hunched shoulders and had a quick moment of regret that quickly turned to pleasure at her next words – "And thank *God*, he was there to take care of me, because you sure weren't. I just want my stuff back."

There was a long pause, and she pinched the bridge of her nose.

"One of those yahoos put something in my drink, Lindsay. I'm glad *you* had a good time, but I really didn't." She turned and looked at me and said, "At least not until this morning. I just really want my purse and my phone back."

Another pause.

"I'm at home. I had a hidden key… Yes, that's fine. Okay. See you in a few. Bye."

I was proud of her. She wasn't taking any shit from her friend and letting her gaslight her. I held out her book when she held out my phone.

She took it, one eyebrow going up at the card sticking out the top.

"New number to add when you get your phone back," I said. "Just call if you need anything."

"Oh, thank you," she said with a light blush. "I don't want to impose any more than I already have, though."

"Hey, it was no imposition," I said. "Just glad I was there to catch you."

"Me too," she murmured, setting her address book aside on top of one of the boxes.

"I'll, uh, be right back," she said. "Just two seconds."

"Take your time," I murmured at her back. I would be lying if I said I wasn't checking out the rounded curve of her ass beneath the checkered flannel of mine she had on.

She disappeared into one of the bedrooms and I sighed, rocking back and forth impatiently between my heels and the balls of my feet on the area rug that covered the worn-down hardwood floor beneath it.

I could already tell, she was gonna be on my mind for a minute. I somehow hoped she would find an excuse to call me soon.

CHAPTER THREE

*A*spen...

I kept thinking about him – Fenris – long after he'd left and Lindsay had arrived. She was wholly unrepentant about things and genuinely didn't understand what the big deal was. She seriously thought it was just another rowdy night out with the girls. Like, I was fine and overreacting. I didn't think I was angry *enough,* but to be honest? I just couldn't muster up the energy for it.

Instead, I'd taken my things, had checked to make sure everything was there, and I'd ended the friendship. Done. Right then and there. No going back.

I was tired of being mistreated. Only thing I was more tired of was the fact that I'd been *allowing* it for so long.

I took a hot shower, a proper one with shampoo and conditioner this time. I hadn't used any of the stuff at the goat farm. I didn't want to dry out my hair and let it turn into a frizzy mess on me – so I'd just watered it down really, really, good until I got home. Now, I felt truly clean and that was saying something.

I'd washed a lot more down my shower drain than just dirt and used soap.

I made myself some hot tea in my favorite hand-thrown mug and settled into my favorite old chair of my mom's in the living room.

So much was up in the air, it wasn't even funny. I didn't know how long I had to live here with Mom still owing on the house and everything still caught up – even more tangled now that my brother had died.

I supposed I would have to sell it, which I didn't want to do, but I didn't see any other option. After paying the rest owed, I might get out with at least a decent down payment for a place of my own. I just didn't want to think about any of it right now.

I unlocked my mostly recharged phone and picked up my address book from the side table where I'd relocated it.

I couldn't imagine calling Fenris for anything else, but I couldn't deny I wanted to. Just… Jesus! How soon was too soon? My divorce wasn't even final. I'd only left Charles four months ago.

He was being an ass over the division of assets, trying to get me to talk to him, but I didn't want to.

I heaved a big sigh at the big fat mess in front of me and let my gaze un-focus, drawing up the image in my mind's eye of my unlikely savior.

He was unconventionally handsome – rugged, and those blue eyes of his… I shuddered to think of how they seemed to see through right down into my soul. He was massive, imposing, and downright scary but I couldn't help but realize how kind, gentle and how sweet everything he had done for me had been. He'd been a perfect gentleman, and it just didn't make sense to me, what with his rough exterior.

I plucked the business card out of my book and read it over again.

Fjordson's Family Farm

Fenris Fjordson, his address, and an office number. I wondered if Fjordson was his actual last name or if it was made up too. I mean, he'd already said that he *went by* Fenris, so that couldn't really be his first name.

I sighed and entered him in as a new contact, adding his mobile number that he'd written in my book and the business line under 'work' for good measure.

It was raining heavily outside the front window and I sat in the little golden pool of lamplight, cozy in my pajamas and robe, hands wrapped around the steaming mug in my hands and just let the sky cry for me, too spent to shed any more tears right this moment.

I wanted to, though. *Just how many losses am I supposed to take this year?* I wondered. First Mom, then Copper, then Charles, and now Lindsay – I didn't have many friends and so I was feeling the loss keenly.

I sniffed, sipped some tea, and closed my eyes, letting my tears match the rainfall outside my mom's window.

I missed them. I missed them all terribly.

God, I felt too old at thirty-eight to be starting all over again… but here I was, and that was just what I was going to do.

I sighed and tried not to let my misery swamp me which was a lot easier said than done. It felt like my mind was literally on fire. I had this funny feeling in my chest, and every time I looked around at the mountain of boxes around me, I felt overwhelmed.

"Get it together, Aspen," I murmured, staring out the front window and sniffing back more tears. This feeling… this loneliness had been around for a while, except now? Now it was raw and aching. The chasm left behind in the center of my chest at the loss of literally *everyone* I held dear was killing me slowly.

"One day at a time," I whispered. "You're doing the best that you can with the hand you've been dealt."

I repeated the positive affirmations the social worker had given me and they just didn't work anymore. I felt like I was drowning, like there was no more coming up for air and I didn't know what scared me more – the prospect that I had literally lost everything inside of a month's span, or the deep-seated feeling of apathy that was creeping from the darkest parts of me and had me so thoroughly bound up.

I sighed, struggling within myself and finally gave up.

Enough of this. I was tired, so damn tired. I set my tea aside, switched out the lamp and went to bed.

I wish I could have slept a solid twenty hours like I had a few times since, well, *everything*, but I had to work the next morning.

There were certain perks to owning your own business, but there were a lot of drawbacks, too. My biggest drawback right now was that I needed to be there.

I couldn't let my business crumble. I had to keep going, but it was hard, so unimaginably hard right now. I didn't have anybody who understood, or who I could talk to anymore. I'd been on my husband's health insurance and he'd switched jobs after the break up. I don't know if it had been just to kick me off of it, I mean, I don't think he was *that* spiteful.

I sighed and went to bed, waking up just as tired as when I had laid down.

The weather was better, at least. I mean, it was still crisp, but the skies were blue and the leaves were changing as fall battled it out with these last dregs of summer. It was so Pacific Northwest in that you needed to layer. Cold in the mornings, misty and foggy, but by the afternoon, highs in the seventies.

Plus, it was always warm in the back of the shop with all the kilns firing unfinished pieces.

If it was one thing my mother and I had been close on, it was for our mutual love of pottery. Otherwise, our relationship was fairly strained. Copper and I both agreed, it was like we carried too much of our father in us and for some reason… our mother *hated* him, but we never knew why, precisely.

It wasn't like he was around. He'd ditched us when I was just a baby and never bothered to look back. Copper was two, and pretty quickly it was apparent that he needed to become the quote, unquote man of the house.

He really came into the role when I was five and he was seven and he nearly shot an intruder when Mom was working a late shift at the diner. That was back when we lived in Colorado. She nearly had us taken away from her and she moved us to Washington to avoid it.

Her best friend, Annie, had lived out here which is what brought us this way back in the eighties. Annie had died of lung cancer back in 2014. She smoked a pack and a half a day from the time she herself was fourteen, so it wasn't exactly a shocker. It still sucked, though. Annie was like a second mom to me and Copper and had owned a bead shop. She'd left everything to my mother, which is how my mother had bought this place.

Copper had a home, a wife, and a daughter of his own when he died, so everything that was his was now theirs, which left me in quite a bit of limbo since half of this house was his. I didn't worry too much for right now. His wife, Christen, was a bitch but his son, Silver, was as sweet as could be – a little darling with his dad's smile and – God, I missed my brother.

He had always been the one to take care of the big things. I mean, I had taken care of my mom while she declined with her pancreatic cancer, but the big decisions and power of attorney and all that? That had been Copper.

He'd always known what to do.

I drove myself to Seattle and my little pottery shop off Airport Way in the Georgetown neighborhood.

It sat in an old, squat, brick building just a bit down and across the street from the old Rainier beer brewery and down the block from one of the oldest bars in Seattle – the Jules Maes Saloon.

Georgetown was quickly becoming the second artsiest neighborhood in Seattle. The first always was, and always would be Fremont, but the prices to rent in Fremont were exorbitant and a little shop like me would struggle to survive.

I keyed my way in the front door, raised the blinds to let the natural light in the front windows and with a sigh, went and put my purse and jacket away and to don my clay-and-glazed-stained apron.

It was time to unload the kilns, restock the shelves, and see what pieces I was getting low on to make some more. I was almost certain I would be at the wheel churning out some more potbellied mugs – those always went fast.

My thoughts turned back to Fenris and the baby goats on his farm from the day before and I smiled. He was strange, such a mixed dichotomy of dark and light, gentle yet rough. He'd been so selfless and I didn't feel right, like I'd not properly thanked him.

I thought about his house, and how rustic, yet homey it was. How he and his father really seemed to appreciate the simple things, and I had a sudden idea.

"You're crazy," I muttered to myself but I was smiling, and it felt good to do something good. As soon as I had enough mugs made to go into the kiln for a first firing, I took stock of how much room I had left and set to work on some more dishes.

I liked working the wheel. It allowed my mind to click off and for me to just coast for a while. I didn't have to think. I just had to concentrate on what I was doing so whatever piece I was working on didn't come out malformed. The nice thing about clay, unlike my life, was if it wasn't cooperating or turning out how you wanted it to? You just slapped it down into a lump and could start again.

I wish everything else was so simple.

CHAPTER FOUR

*F*enris...

"Yeah, Pops, what's up?" I pressed my cell to my ear and plugged the other with the middle finger of my other hand.

"Where the fuck you at, boy?" he demanded gruffly through the line.

"Waiting out this rain shower under an overpass, why?"

"Just wanted to let you know, the stray kitty you picked up at the bar last week was back. Left a couple heavy-ass boxes here for you."

"Shit, yeah?" I asked surprised. I hadn't heard from Aspen and I'd be lying if I said I hadn't been massively disappointed by that.

"No, I'm making it up," he said dryly. "How far out are yah?"

"Twenty more minutes if this shit would settle to a dull roar," I answered. I didn't mind riding in the rain but when it came down *this bad*, it wasn't a question of my riding but of citizen's driving. I didn't want to get slammed into by a cage or worse because they couldn't see my ass for the road spray. So, when it hit a certain threshold, I pulled my ass over to wait it out a few minutes so shit could settle down.

"Fine," he grumbled.

"Well, open 'em up if you're that damn curious," I said laughing.

"I can wait," he said and with a harrumph, ended the call on me. I laughed again and tucked my phone away. The rain wasn't exactly letting up, but my curiosity was getting the better of me, so goggles down, I fired my bike back up and cautiously pulled back into the flow of traffic on 18.

When I got home, my dad was out back under the eave of the house, cigar between his teeth and a steaming cup of coffee in his hand, the mug big, brown, and handsome – almost a tankard versus a mug. The clay was thick and sturdy, the layers of coating or whatever artistic and rustic.

"Where'd you get that?" I asked, getting off my bike under the overhang and whipping my goggles off over my head as soon as I could get them off my face. They did the job and I needed them, but I didn't like them.

"One of your boxes," he answered. "All sorts of dishes and things in there. All like this."

"Jesus, that must have cost a fucking fortune!" I said. I knew what the handmade pottery pieces around here went for and it wasn't cheap.

"Full service for eight," he said with a shrug. "I don't think it cost her much but time, Son. I think she made them."

"No shit?"

"Wipe your boots before you go in that house!" he called after me sternly like I was twelve. I stopped in the mudroom, excited to see what was sitting on the table through the back door, but not so excited I was gonna tromp a mess through the place.

I hung my jacket and cut to dry and pulled off my chaps to hang next to the other leather, all of it supple with how waterlogged it was. I pulled off my boots for good measure and went into the kitchen in my sock feet. Sure as shit, here was all this handmade dishware stacked and scattered over the dining table, the cupboards open and our old dishes coming out of the cabinets to make way for 'em.

"Odin's beard," I said in awe, picking one of the heavy pieces up.

"She left that for you." My pops gestured with his coffee mug at a white rectangle on the tabletop. I picked it up, and he leaned his shoulder against the back doorway and took a sip of his ever-present coffee. He'd ditched the cigar out back somewhere. The card read…

Clayrity Studios

Aspen ~~Lawson~~-Craig

The address was in Seattle, on Airport Way – I had to bet Georgetown. There was a number, but I was betting it was a business line. I pulled my phone out of my back pocket where I'd stuck it when I'd hung up my coat and unlocked it.

I dialed her up and waited as it rang through.

"Clayrity Studios, this is Amber, how can I help you?"

"Uh, yeah, is Aspen there?" I asked.

"She's teaching a class right now, is there something I can help you with?"

I cleared my throat and said, "Uh, no, just tell her that Fen… er, Fenris called, would you do that for me?"

I could hear Amber's smile in her voice. "Absolutely! You want to leave a number or does she have it?"

"She should have it, but just in case…" I rattled off my cell.

"Okay." She repeated it back to me.

"That's correct," I said.

"Alright Mr. Fenris, I have this all down and she'll get back to you as soon as possible, okay?"

"Alright, thanks," I said.

"Of course!"

The line went dead and I let my gaze wander over all the fine dishes and shook my head. This was *way too much.*

"First time anyone you brought home from Mitch's like that has done anything like *this*." my dad said coming fully into the kitchen.

"I see you wasted no time," I said with a grin and he grinned back.

"It's good shit, better 'n' what we got."

"True that," I said nodding.

"Right, so get to work, boy."

I laughed a little and helped clear cabinets and hand washed the new dishes before putting them away.

"She's got talent if she made these," my dad observed.

"I don't think it's an 'if,' looks like she runs a whole damn pottery studio."

"Yeah? Nice."

"What'd you think of her?" I asked my dad, and he raised a bushy steel gray eyebrow at me.

"Seems like a lost soul," he said carefully. "Seems like a good girl." He eyed me equally carefully as when he'd spoken. When I didn't say anything, he asked me, "Why, what you thinkin'?"

"Nothing, Pops. I don't know…"

He harrumphed and shook his head, "Your mom was a good girl when I met her and I broke her damn heart." He slid up onto one of the breakfast bar's tall chairs and wrapped his hands around the big mug he'd pilfered from the pile before I could even get a look at all of it.

"You went to prison," I said with a sigh. "Mom knew what she was signing up for when she married you," I reminded him.

"Did she, though?" he asked and stared off into nothingness.

"Do I think she had herself convinced you'd never get pinched for nothing? Yes. Do I think she fell apart when you did?" I remembered. I'd been about seven, my sister nine or ten. It'd been ugly – Mom left scrambling, but a lot of that had been her fault. The club had tried to take care of us, but she'd blamed them as much as she'd blamed my pops, so she wouldn't take their money.

"Shit fell apart," my dad said in a tone that brooked no argument.

"Yeah." I nodded a little sadly. "Yeah, they did."

My dad had served eight years, and my sister had headed off to college right before he'd gotten out. Mom wouldn't let my ass see him at first, but then Lacy had died and she couldn't stop me if she wanted to.

My pops had been the path to revenge, but I'd carried most of it out on my own.

"You want my opinion, or don't you?" he asked, and I shook my head.

"Naw, man, I don't."

He nodded carefully and said with a grunt and a sigh getting up,

"Then you already know what it is and you know I'm right. You just don't wanna hear it."

I hissed out a disgruntled chuckle and carried on washing and rinsing the bowl I had in my hands.

"Either get over here and dry or fuck off," I told him.

"And away I go," he said with a shrug, and he fucked off toward the living room. That's just the way we were. Brothers via the club more than father and son, then again, he hadn't been around to be a father much after he'd been sent up.

I was just finishing up drying and stacking things in the cupboards when my phone rang. I picked it up from where it was blaring Wardruna on the kitchen counter and answered it, even though it was an unknown number. I had a sneaking suspicion I knew who it was.

"Hello?"

"Hi." Her voice was soft and nervous at the same time. She cleared her throat and said, "Amber said you called?"

"Yeah, I'm here washing up these dishes, getting 'em put away. I wanted to say thank you, they're real nice. Definitely way too much, though. You shouldn't have."

"You didn't have to do what you did either," she murmured, and I chuckled.

"You're not the first, baby. You won't be the last, either. That's just to say it's what I do."

"Oh, well, you're a kind man, Fenris... consider it a kindness for a kindness."

"You make these?" I asked abruptly, dying to know.

"Oh, yeah... it didn't exactly come up in conversation, but it's what I do." She laughed a little nervously and said, "It was one of the few things my mom and I could bond over."

"I know *that* feeling," I said and glanced behind me at the open archway into the living room. I couldn't see my dad seated in his chair with the back of it to the other side of the wall that separated the dining area from the living room. I knew he was listening. I would have been listening too.

"Anyway, I hope you enjoy them," she said, and I chuckled.

"Dad had his coffee in one of the cups before I could even ride up. The man never met a coffee mug he liked until yours," I said. "Just nothing out there big enough."

"I could make a bigger one," she said laughing, and I laughed with her.

"No, God, please no," I said.

"Well, alright then. I would have happily taken the challenge."

Seemed to me she had plenty of those lately, I didn't want to add any others so as much as I wanted to get to know Ms. Aspen Lawson, I took my dad's warning to heart and let this long ship pass me by.

"I'm sure you would have, but there's no need. Like I said, this was really too much. I didn't do anything special."

"On the contrary," she said softly. "You did. At least to me. Thanks for reinforcing my faith in humanity."

"Shit, I wouldn't want to do that, now," I joked.

"Why not?" she asked curiously.

"Because then you might *really* get hurt. Just do me a favor," I said. "Stay safe for me."

There was a long pause and finally a reserved, "I'll do that."

"Right, well, call me if you need anything," I said. "I mean it."

"I will. Thank you again, Fenris." She said my name like she was still trying to get used to it.

I smiled and said, "You too, Aspen. Have a good night."

"You too."

I listened to the line go dead and sighed.

I really found myself wanting to get to know this woman, but my dad was right. She just didn't seem the type to be able to handle the life and I couldn't change. It would leave my brother's in a lurch.

I set my phone aside and went back to work on cleaning up the smooth, earthenware dishes.

FOUR OR FIVE DAYS LATER AND I STILL COULDN'T GET ASPEN OUT OF MY mind. It was driving me nuts, and I finally broke.

"Hey, D.T." The big man looked up from his phone, his beer sitting frosty but untouched nearby on the bar.

"What's up?" he asked.

"Take a short ride with me?"

He frowned, looked around and asked, "How short?"

"Georgetown."

"What's in Georgetown?"

"Man, never mind." I shook my head.

"Man, don't be like that! Little Bird is on her way back. I don't want to leave before she gets here," he said.

"Oh. Well, she can ride with us on this one," I said. "It's nothing sketch."

"Why you being all cagey?" he asked with a grin. I shrugged and didn't say anything. I didn't want the rest of the guys to give me a ration of shit, and I didn't want to ride past her shop by myself. If we rode past, the pair of us, then it wouldn't look like I was being a creepy stalker fuck… which yeah, okay, I was sort of being a creepy stalker fuck, what of it?

Dump Truck turned around more fully and fixed me with a look. I cocked my head and gave him a warning glare and his eyebrows went up. He held up his hands in surrender and cocked his head just as Little Bird came in the back door.

"Hey, baby," she called and the smile he had for her was something else.

"That's my line," he said, pulling her into the circle of his arms and laying one on her. She giggled and twined her arms around his neck and not for the first time – I was jealous.

"Wanna take a ride with me and Fen to Georgetown?" he asked her. She drew her head back in confusion.

"What's in Georgetown?" she asked.

"Fen won't tell me," he said, and she glanced in my direction and gave a shrug.

"Not like we have anything else going on tonight, so sure, let's go."

I stood up, my own beer half empty and forgotten on the coffee table in front of the couch I'd been sitting on.

"Alright then, let's go."

We rode down Roxbury, got over the First Ave. S. bridge and took the exit onto Michigan. I followed it all the way to Airport Way and hung a left, Dump Truck and Little Bird keeping pace and following my lead. I slowed down to a cruise and checked out Clayrity as we rode by. The lights were on, but dim. Shelves lined the walls all the way around the space with long tables set up.

I glimpsed Aspen behind the register, a mousy young thing chatting with her as she did the night's paperwork. It was a hell of a candid look and for whatever reason, it just made me want to know the woman *more.*

I pulled up down the block, flipping an illegal U-turn in the middle of the block to back in against the curb in front of the Jules Maes Saloon. Dump Truck followed suit and killed the engine to his bike the same time I did.

"Okay, brother, enough of the cloak and dagger bullshit. Why you so suddenly interested in fuckin' pottery?"

"He's not," Little Bird said, grinning, lifting off her lid. "I'd say it was the blonde, if I had to guess."

I tapped my index finger against the tip of my nose and Little Bird grinned.

"No shit? You? Going to any kind of trouble over a *woman*? This I gotta hear." D.T. pulled his cane from the bracket built onto his bike and heaved himself into a standing position with a wince.

"I need alcohol for this story," I grated, and he gestured with a sweeping hand to lead the way.

We went into Jules Maes. A lot of the local hipster scene and old barflies startled, straightening up when they realized a couple of Sacred Hearts had walked in. The bartender, a white chick in her mid to late twenties who was tatted and pierced to within an inch of her life, her long hair dyed a vibrant green and laying along her back in thick dreadlocks, called out, "Take a seat anywhere, I'll come around to get your order."

"Thank you, kindly," Dump Truck said with a disarming smile. Little Bird wrapped both of her slender arms around one of D.T.'s and I jerked my head at a nearby booth. Dump Truck nodded and gave me the option of putting my back to the wall so I could keep an eye on the door and who was coming in.

"Thanks," I grunted.

"I know you got me," he said. I nodded, and we settled in.

"So, what's the deal?" Little Bird asked, smiling faintly with good humor, kindness radiating from her lovely eyes.

"Took the words right out of my mouth, babe. How'd you and blondie in the pottery shop go about meeting up?" Dump Truck asked, raising his eyebrows high enough they met the swath of red bandana across his forehead, holding back his long hair and keeping it neat under his lid when we'd rode.

"Happened a week or two back," I declared. "She came into Mitch's place with a friend of hers. Friend hooked up with a couple of cowboy posers and left Aspen drunk as fuck and stranded without her phone or a ride."

"That's fucked up," Little Bird uttered, and I smiled. We'd been a bad influence on her in a couple ways – her letting fly with the f-bomb regularly being one of them but then again, the girl had needed to loosen up some. She certainly hadn't been in Kansas anymore once D.T. had picked her ass up from Vegas.

She'd been a good girl. It was kind of why I wanted to talk to them both. See if there was a chance worth taking when it came to Aspen for one, and for two, getting some kind of advice on how or if I should proceed.

"That's just the tip of the iceberg."

I told them everything, pausing only long enough to get our drink order in and once again when the bartender returned to serve it up.

"That's… that's a lot." Little Bird leaned back against the high wooden booth back and gave me one long, slow blink.

"I don't really know what to think," I said. "About the dishes. Like, am I supposed to make the next move or was that like, the end – thanks but I never want to see you again kind of a thing? I just don't know."

"Yah got me," Dump Truck said with a shrug of his massive shoulders.

"I figured if anyone would know, it'd be you with all the romance novels and bullshit you read."

He laughed and gave me the finger from across the table, and I grinned savagely.

"I don't think she knows what she wants." Little Bird said. "I mean, it sure puts my situation into some perspective. I don't even know how she's standing after all of that! First her mom, then her brother, and I know her husband didn't *die* but *yikes!* Talk about the icing on the cake! Her whole life went down in flames one thing right after the other, after the other, with *no time* to process."

Little Bird looked like she had a fractured heartache going and it made me love her just a little more that she could feel so strongly a sense of empathy for someone she didn't even know. She was a rare one, and she and my best friend just *fit* in a way I couldn't begin to describe and as much as I wanted that for myself… I just didn't know if it was meant to be. Not with some of the shit that I'd done.

"She's had no time to process," I agreed and traced a runic pattern with a fingertip in the spilled beer foam from my lager on the warm golden lacquered wood of our table.

"So, give her time," Dump Truck said judiciously.

I gave him a dirty look. I mean, clearly, he was right but how the fuck long? I turned back to Little Bird who gave me an apologetic look and a little shrug.

Neither one of them had the answer I was looking for. I guess that made three of us.

"Mind helping me out sometime?" I asked her and she gave me a raised eyebrow.

"Like how?" she asked.

"I don't know," I said with a shrug. "Like go into the shop and feel things out in a few days or something?"

She smiled and said, "What, like you pay for a paint night for me, Marisol, and Dahlia?" she asked sweetly, and I scowled.

"Why you gotta bring those two into it?" I demanded. I liked 'em both well enough but they were a couple of hard cases.

"Because they're my friends and you're asking *me* for the favor.

You know I'm a lover not a fighter," she said with a wink. "And I like to spread the love."

Dump Truck chuckled.

"You been taking lessons in manipulation from Dahlia?" I asked.

"Chess, not checkers," she said softly and her gaze unfocused as she stared over in the direction of the bar. "And no, these particular lessons were learned a long time ago in my old life."

I nodded, my irritation diminishing.

"Fine," I grated out. "If I don't come up with a better plan, or I don't hear from her first in like a week, I'll pay for your girls' night or whatever."

"Thank you!" she said cheerfully and perked up in her seat. "I've always wanted to do a ceramic paint night with some girlfriends. It's just not something you do all on your own."

I grunted and picked up my beer, taking a pretty big swallow and clearing at least a third of the glass with it. Dump Truck laughed softly at my expense and I shook my head.

Well played, Little Bird, I thought to myself. *Well played.*

CHAPTER FIVE

*A*spen...

"So..." Amber trailed off and gave me an impish look and I rolled my eyes.

"Out with it," I ordered my lone employee. Her grin widened and motorcycles went by outside the shop. She waited for the roar of the engines to dissipate into the distance before she picked up where she left off.

"I totally know it's none of my business," she said, holding up her hands. "And you don't have to tell me if you don't want to, but..." and she made an adorable, skeptical little face and squeaked out, "Fenris?"

I gave a light little laugh that edged on nervous and sighed.

Amber was a bright girl. She'd attended a round of my pottery classes, had a natural talent at it, and so I had hired her when she'd said she was looking for a part-time, after-school job. She was a student at South Seattle Community College and I needed someone to run the counter for walk-ins while I ran the evening paint nights and classes.

She was nineteen, mature for her age, and I found myself surprisingly desperate for someone to confide in, so against what should have been my better judgment…

"I don't really know what to say," I told her. "I went out with Lindsay—" She wrinkled her nose in distaste and I frowned but glossed over it for the time being. "And the next thing I know, it was the next day and I woke up at the bouncer's house."

Amber's dove gray eyes went wide and her mouth dropped open.

"Aspen!" she cried. "That is *totally* not your scene! What the hell?"

"I know, I know!" I cried. "I don't know what happened, I swear. I only had a drink or two, but Lindsay went off with these couple of cowboys and I *know* I had to have been a total drag with everything going on with—"

"Stop!" she cried and held up a hand. "With he-who-shall-not-be-named," she said firmly before I could utter Charles' name. I rolled my eyes but smiled.

"Yes, with everything going on with *him*," I said and sighed. "Anyway, the bouncer thinks they maybe slipped me something to make it easier to take Lindsay or for the three of them to get away from me but it was really bad, I guess. I mean, I don't remember any of it at all."

"Oh, wow… was Lindsay okay?" Amber dropped onto the stool I kept behind the register while I counted the money.

"Oh, yeah," I said following it up with an explosive breath. "She had the time of her life, apparently."

"Yeesh." Amber made a face, and I nodded.

"My sentiments exactly," I said. "I mean, don't get me wrong – I know how awful that just sounded and oh, my God! Not how I meant it to come out, I just mean—"

"How could you leave your vulnerable and emotionally shattered friend to her own devices so you can go off and ride a couple of cowboys?" Amber asked, and she winced adorably as she said it.

I winced too. "Yeah, and I know *exactly* how pathetic that makes me sound but, I mean, I guess I am." That awful bereft feeling swept through me and I held back the flood just barely.

"You're not pathetic!" Amber said sternly. "You're just going through *a lot*. All at once. And it's ridiculous."

I nodded, at a loss for anything else to say and she finally prompted me, "So… Fenris?"

"Right, sorry, he's the bouncer that took me home with him," I said.

Her mouth dropped open. "Is he hot?" she asked. "Because he sounded hot." She fixed me with a look and said, "I bet he's hot."

I blushed and said, "He's definitely… different." It took me a moment to settle on a word that didn't sound judgy, rude, or what-not, but I honestly didn't know *how* to describe the man.

"Okay, dish," she demanded. "What's that supposed to mean?"

"Well, he's a biker," I said and Amber's gray eyes widened and she swept her long auburn French braid over her shoulder and gripped it with both hands.

"Like an *actual* biker?" she asked.

"Like, a Sacred Heart biker."

She froze and her eyes grew impossibly wider still and she asked, "Are you for real?"

"Serious as a heart attack," I affirmed.

"Those guys are really bad news!" she said, and I nodded.

"They don't have the best reputation, it's true."

"Okay, so what else? I mean, what's he look like?"

"Well, he's blond and has blue eyes. He had a beard, long, and he braids it and has these silver cylinder beads in it."

"What, like a Viking?" she asked.

"Pretty much exactly like that. His hair is shaved underneath and long like a mohawk, but he has beads and tiny braids throughout that, too."

"You were rescued at a bar by Ragnar Lodbrok from the TV show *Vikings*?" she asked. I paused to think about it and finally nodded.

"Except better looking than the actor." I made a face. I couldn't believe I'd just confessed that out loud. Amber's face lit up, her nude-glossed lips splitting into a grin as she laughed.

"You like him," she said and I couldn't look at her.

"It doesn't matter," I said simply, my mind drifting back to the moment I'd broken down on this strange man's stairs in the middle of his house wearing nothing but his shirt and how he'd helped me. How he'd gotten me through it. I don't think I could express to anyone the depths of my gratitude for that alone, let alone that I had felt absolutely no judgment from him after the fact.

"Of course, it matters!" she cried. "My grandmother always said, the best way to get over a man is to get under a different one."

"Amber!" I cried, blushing furiously, cheeks hot with… well, I don't know what.

"What?" she cried. "It's true!"

I shook my head and said, "I just don't work like that."

"Maybe," she said sliding off the stool with a pointed look, "you should."

I huffed out an aggravated breath, though I couldn't tell if I was really annoyed with Amber or if I was really annoyed with *myself*. I wished Copper was here, that I could call him and talk to him. My older brother always knew what to say to make me feel better – no matter if I was fighting with Mom, Charles, or anything else was bothering me. He just always seemed to have the answers.

I finished up closing with Amber, hiding behind a mask of 'everything's fine' all the while internally dreading going home to my mom's house which was empty of any and all emotion and just chock-full of useless *stuff*. I was only one person, and I was drowning on every front. I didn't know what to do with everything from the mishmash of mine and my mom's things, to the divorce proceedings with Charles, to lawyers I couldn't afford and my business barely breaking even at the moment and to my brother being gone and my mom being gone and just *all of it*…

I turned out the open sign and watched as Amber got into her car at the curb and sighed.

"Just keep going," I reminded myself out loud. It was all I could do.

I drove back to my mom's house. It didn't really feel like home. I mean, I know I had a roof over my head and that I should be grateful for it, but I still felt like I had lost everything, was barely holding what I *did* have left together, and that the rest of me was just hanging by a thread.

I stepped over the pile of mail that'd been delivered through the front door's slot and set down my briefcase and the box of ceramics I wanted to try and paint on my own time so that I could retrieve the letters and junk fliers to sort through them.

I paused a few pieces of mail down and drew in a deep steadying breath at my soon-to-be-ex-husband's divorce attorney's letterhead.

I opened the envelope, scanning the letter inside and felt the color drain from my face. He was going after half my business… Clayrity.

I shook my head, a jumble of emotions tumbling out of their hiding places like an overloaded closet when the door has finally been opened. I stood there with the shattered pieces all around me, twinkling in the dim light from the overhead light of the kitchen stove which I always kept on, and felt like this was it. That that was the last of it and there was nothing left.

I pulled my phone out of the pocket of my coat and tears welled.

I'd been so successfully isolated by my cheating ex-husband, my mother dead, my brother gone – his wife and I never any kind of close… I literally had no one to even call.

Or did I?

Desperate times called for desperate measures.

I went to my little black book on top of the boxes by the front door and flipped it open. Bringing up the keypad on my phone, I dialed and held my breath as the call connected and started ringing.

"Hello?"

I closed my eyes and took a desperate leap.

CHAPTER SIX

*F*enris...

My phone started buzzing across the table in front of me and I picked it up. It was a number I didn't recognize.

"Hello?"

"Hi." The voice was soft, feminine and held a strained quality to it. I didn't like it, but I was thrilled because I knew instantly who it was.

"Aspen?" I asked, and Dump Truck and Little Bird exchanged a look.

"Yeah, um," her voice cracked, "I think I need help."

I sat up straighter and asked, "You at home?"

"Yeah." She sounded mournful.

"Say no more, I'm on my way."

I ended the call and got up, reaching for my wallet.

"I got it, go," Dump Truck said, and he fixed me with a look that said he absolutely understood. I looked at Little Bird and she gave me a sympathetic nod.

"Thank you, brother."

I went for the door and got on my bike. I was a good forty-five or fifty minutes from her place and remembered exactly how to get there like I'd dropped her off just yesterday instead of a couple of weeks ago.

When I pulled up to the curb in front of her house, the windows were dark, but the front porch light glowed dimly. I pulled off my lid, smoothed a hand over the top of my hair to tame any random frizz and marched up the front walk to her door. I knocked twice and held my breath.

She opened it and looked up at me with a tear-stained face, her makeup in muddy tracks down her cheeks.

"What's wrong?" I asked, and she stared stricken for a few heart-beats as if trying to decide how much to tell me. Her expression crumbled, and she started to cry all over again and said to me, "I just don't think I want to be alive anymore and I'm scared."

"Oh, baby. Fuck," I muttered, and I pulled her toward me. She crashed against me, sobbing heartbrokenly into my chest.

I stepped into her, over the threshold and kicked the door shut behind us and just let her cry.

I had no idea what the fuck had happened, but it said something to me that I, the fuckin' guy she'd literally just met, was the only person she had that she could call at a time like this. I mean, that was something fucking tragic. Wasn't it?

"I'm so sorry! I'm sorry!" she cried between her sobs, and I just clutched her tighter to me.

"It's okay, I got yah. It's alright now. You just let it out." I didn't know what else to say. What else to do. So, I just did what my mom had done for me when I was a kid. What I'd seen her do for my sister a thousand times. I gave her a safe place and permission to cry it out. Then I would ask some questions and figure out what needed doing to fix it, if there was even anything to fix. Sometimes with women, that wasn't what they wanted. Or so my sister had told me, once upon a time.

Sometimes all they wanted was to cry and to vent.

I felt helpless in this situation, but I knew in the front of my head, that I wasn't. I was doing exactly what I needed to be doing right this minute by just being here for her. It was my own thoughts and feelings that were racing, that were whispering I should go out and find a motherfucker and do harm. I wanted to hit something, some-one, anyone. I wanted to rend flesh, and I knew it was an impotent rage that was stirring in the center of my chest. I was just angry for the sake of being angry because she hurt and there wasn't anything I could do to stem the flow on it.

We ended up on the couch and she wept brokenly for what felt like an age and I just did what I could to hold her up.

She seemed so fragile; as thin as glass, and I worried gravely over what she'd said… about not wanting to be alive anymore. She was begging for help, crying out, and I was here, but I was no psychologist. I was a hammer where fine surgical instruments were required. I wasn't cut out for this… but she'd called me and I wasn't about to let her down.

I couldn't save my sister, but maybe, just maybe, I could save Aspen. It was a unique set of circumstances and for me to know what I was up against; I would need to pull back some layers.

"How you doing?" I asked when she'd quieted down and settled.

"I honestly don't know," she whispered back dully.

"That's alright," I said and massaged up and down her arm with my hand.

"I'm really sorry," she whispered brokenly, and it was a strange sort of intimacy created by the dark in her house. The only light on in here appeared to be emanating from somewhere in the kitchen, the rest of the house plunged into a dim, close dark that cradled us both in the palm of its hand.

"Stop apologizing, babe. You have nothing to apologize for. Everybody goes through it. I'm just glad you called me so you don't have to go through it alone."

She sniffled and laid her head on my shoulder, the leather of my jacket and cut creaking in the dark. I was warm in here, bordering on too warm, but I didn't want to move her. Didn't want her to think anything negative about herself or this interaction when I could already tell that was where her head was at. She was apologizing for every damn thing and I was expecting any second that she would apologize for simply *existing*. I wanted to know where she got these ideas from and put a hurt on the motherfucker that'd given them to her.

I seethed and simmered in my chest beneath her head, but I don't think she knew. I aimed to keep it that way. She didn't need any more stress.

"Thank you for coming," she murmured and swallowed hard. I couldn't see her face but I could imagine fresh tears tracking down her ivory cheeks just the same.

"Anytime, and I mean that," I said, giving her a light squeeze. "You want to talk about it?"

"No," she whispered. "You've already put up with so much I—"

"I'm not 'putting up' with anything, Aspen. I'm not that kind of guy. I wouldn't be here if I didn't want to be."

She sucked in a breath and held it for a moment before saying, "I apologize, I didn't mean to offend."

"You didn't. It's late. I promise no funny business, but let's get your face washed and get you into something that's more comfortable than these work clothes. I'm staying here tonight. What you said? It's got me worried."

She held still, contemplating my words for a moment before finally nodding.

"I'm worried too," she said. "And I don't want to be alone."

Jesus, fuck. She sounded so vulnerable.

"You're not alone. You're not going to *be* alone. I'm right here for whatever you need."

"You're too kind, you know that?" she asked.

I barked a laugh and bit down on it when she jumped at the abrupt sound.

"Sorry, just never been accused of that, you know what I'm sayin'?"

"What? Of being kind?" she asked, pushing off of my chest and sitting up on her own.

"Yeah."

"That's a shame," she said, and I could barely make out the glitter of those fantastic green eyes in the dark, back lit as she was by the dim light in the kitchen behind her.

"It just is what it is," I said with a gusty sigh.

"I think I'm all cried out," she said, and I nodded.

"How do you feel?" I asked.

She thought about it for a minute and sighed saying to me, "Uncomfortably numb."

"Yeah, time for bed for you," I said. "Things 'll look better in the morning."

She got up, and I followed her to my feet, shrugging out of my jacket and cut and laying them over the arm of her couch.

"Um, you really don't have to stay," she said. "I mean, if you don't want to."

"I want to," I said evenly. "And I'm not going anywhere tonight after what you said when I came in here."

She hung her head, hugged herself, and said, "I don't think I meant it. Not really."

I sighed and felt my shoulders drop and I shook my head.

"My sister…" I started and stopped a moment, getting choked up like I always did when I talked about Lacy. "She, uh, didn't reach out or ask for help. She came back from college up in Bellingham. Wouldn't say what happened. I found her in the bathtub. I couldn't save her."

She covered her mouth with one hand and stared up at me, eyes wide.

"I'm so sorry, I never would have—"

I made a hissing noise to cut her off and raised a hand.

"Doesn't matter," I said. "I'm not going away. Not tonight. I'd like to think the gods put me in your path for a reason. Maybe this is it."

She piped down, a tension leaving her shoulders as she looked away for a moment then back up at me.

"Okay," she said. "I won't argue."

"Thank you. Lead the way, where's your bathroom?"

She took me through the master bedroom and gestured at the bathroom door in here.

"Grab whatever you're going to sleep in," I told her and switched on the light in the bathroom going for the medicine cabinet and the razors. She had a little basket of washcloths on the back of the john within reach of the shower. I stacked the cloths on the counter and started tossing sharps and pill bottles into the basket.

"You don't have to do that, I'm not going to do anything," she said from the bathroom doorway.

I said, "I thought you weren't going to argue." I looked over my shoulder to where she stood in the doorway, clutching fresh PJs to her chest.

"Fair," she said with a fatigued nod. She looked thoroughly strained around her edges.

"You got three minutes to change and I'm coming in," I told her with a faint smile to try and take the sting out of the statement. She tried a tremulous smile back, but it fell a little flat.

"I'll leave the door cracked," she murmured.

"I won't look," I assured her and took the basket of dangerous items into the bedroom with me and dropped onto the edge of the bed. She swung the door shut until only a sliver of light illuminated the bedroom. I lifted the dust ruffle on the bed and slid the basket under it.

While I was down there, I took off my boots and socks.

"Why did you come?" she asked softly, and I tried to glue my eyes to anywhere but that sliver of light as I heard her clothing rustle as she changed it.

"You called. Didn't sound good. Why wouldn't I come?" I asked with a shrug, getting to my feet and working my belt.

She ran water in the sink in the bathroom and I risked a peek. She was changed into this country nightgown, white, eyelets, something that belonged on an old lady except it looked somehow right on her. It made that innocence and purity of hers shine even brighter. I folded my jeans and put them on top of her dresser before I pulled the faded black TOOL tee I had on with the sleeves ripped out off over my head to fold it up too.

I was lucky I hadn't gone commando this morning, instead opting for some form-fitting black boxer briefs. I sniffed, threw my tail of braids with their beads back over my shoulder to hang to just above the middle of my back and turned around just as she halted in the bathroom doorway, her lovely face freshly scrubbed of all that awful, muddied makeup.

Color creeped up from her chest into her cheeks and I made nothing of it, not wanting to make things worse.

"Did you want me to sleep on the couch?" she stammered, and I frowned at her.

"Fuck no," I said. "This is your house."

She shook her head and said, "It's my mom's house, actually."

I got into the bed on one side and lifted the blankets on what would be her side tonight, arching my eyebrows, silently asking what she was waiting for. She stood for a second, her arms crossed over her chest, hands digging into her bare upper arms, one foot adorably crossed over the other and finally with a little sound of defeat, she snapped out the bathroom light and got into bed beside me. She laid down on her side, facing me and I adjusted myself onto my side to face her.

We stared at each other for a moment in silence, the light from outside tinged blue with the night coming in softly through the bedroom window and illuminating her face gently.

"Your mom's gone, baby," I said the gentlest I could. "That makes it yours now."

"Not really. Um, my mom left it to me and my brother, Copper. When Copper died, everything that was his went to Christen and their son, Silver. Everything is sort of a mess right now. Nothing is settled. He and I agreed we would sell it, divide the proceeds in half but that was before he died and I found out what Charles was doing."

I frowned and reached out a hand, curling it around her free hand where it wasn't curled beneath the pillow like her other one was. I gave it a light squeeze and said, "Talk to me. What's up? I can't help you if I don't know the full story."

"The day after Copper died, I was wrung out. Exhausted. I'd been at the hospital all night, worked all day, and when I got home…" she shrugged. "I don't know. I cooked dinner in a fog and when I finally sat down," she shrugged, "I just fell asleep. Charles was on his phone and leaning against me. I woke up and happened to see his screen."

"Texting another woman?" I guessed.

"A man, actually." She snorted. "He was texting back and I quote, 'Well, I was trying to come over and suck your cock but you didn't answer me in time.'"

"Oh, shit," I said, and she closed her eyes and just looked *tired*.

"It was the day after my brother had just *died*, exactly a month after my *mother* died. I'm surprised I didn't lose it."

"You didn't?"

"Mm-mm. I just demanded to know who he was talking to and told him not to lie to me."

"Let me guess, he lied."

"Oh, of course he did."

"What'd you do then?"

"I packed a bag, told him to leave me be, and that I would have the rest of my belongings out by the end of the week. I came here."

"Atta girl," I said evenly, suppressing my savage pride.

"Doesn't matter," she said. "He's going to take everything from me." She gave a bitter laugh and said, "Never mind that I was carrying us, and he was hiding money from me. Never mind that, come to find out, he actually made *more* than me last year. I don't think I can fight him. All of my savings went to inheritance tax… I can barely afford my attorney for the divorce!"

"Hey, hey, hey!" I tried to head off her getting more wrapped around the axle, untangling my hand from hers and smoothing some of her wild blond curls away from her face.

"One thing, one *day* at a time."

She sealed her lips into a grim line and with a slight whimper nodded, trying valiantly to stave off tears.

"You were right to call me," I said, and I took a deep breath and let it out slow. "Nobody should have to deal with this alone."

A tear escaped and dripped down her nose and she squeezed her eyes shut, gritting her teeth through what had to be an unimaginable pain. I thumbed the moisture away and said, "Come here, no fuckery. Just come here."

She came to me and let me hold her tight while a fresh storm went through her. I sighed and had to wonder *why was she alone?* I mean, where were her kickass gal pals? Or had that wild snatch back at the bar been her only friend? God, I fucking hoped not.

There was more to this. I could feel it. All in good time, though.

She had a friend, now. A friend in me. I just hoped it would be enough.

CHAPTER SEVEN

*A*spen…

"Hm, not yet." His arms tightened around me as I went to creep out of bed and I froze. "We still need to talk," he murmured.

I swallowed hard. "T-talk about what?" I stammered.

"About why you would say what you did last night – about not wanting to be alive anymore." His arms tightened again, almost imperceptibly, and I closed my eyes, cautiously relishing the contact, chastising myself for allowing it to feel so good… *too good*.

I couldn't see his face, my back to his front, spooned firmly by his much larger frame. I was glad for that, burning with shame as I was.

"I don't want to talk about it," I said in the barest of whispers.

"Gotta talk to somebody, and I'm right here," he said, and I closed my eyes.

"I shouldn't have called."

"I'm glad that you did. That I could be here for you."

I was too, for that last part, but somehow in the light of day, I felt marginally stronger.

"Thank you," I said, not really knowing what else to say that was the right thing to say beyond that.

"You're welcome," he said, and I didn't know what to do.

Finally, after a long, somewhat tense silence, I said, "I have to go to work."

"You sure you're good?" he asked.

"No," I said honestly. "But even though he's trying to take it from me, work is one of the few stabilizing things I have left."

He didn't let me go, just froze a little behind me and I could almost *feel* his frown.

"Who's trying to take what, now?" he asked and yep, the scowl I couldn't see, I could definitely hear in his voice.

I sighed.

"My ex-husband," I said softly. "I got papers in the mail; he wants half my business."

Fenris grunted and let me go, his hand sliding from my midsection to rest atop my hip. "I'll handle it," he said firmly. I pushed myself up into a sitting position and looked back at him. He twisted, lying on his back and giving a stretch reminiscent of a large cat. I blinked and tried to keep my eyes off of his tattoos and that physique. His blue eyes searched mine carefully, and I swallowed hard.

"Charles isn't a bad guy," I whispered, and it felt strange to defend my ex-husband. Wrong somehow.

"I beg to differ, baby," Fenris said softly. "He broke your heart and now he's coming after the one thing keeping the pieces going. That makes him a shitty person."

I swallowed hard, tears springing to my eyes. I swept my gaze off of Fenris and fixed it onto something nonsensical at the moment – a block of pattern on the covers that had slipped into our laps.

"He just wants me to talk to him," I said and swallowed hard.

"You don't have to," he said. "And it's the mark of a controlling, shitty human being that he's trying to manipulate you into doing it."

"What if I said I didn't want you to do anything?" I asked softly.

He breathed in slow, in through his nose, nostrils flaring slightly, and out through his mouth.

"Then I won't, but I won't let you despair either. Not like this. Not anymore."

"Why?" I asked softly.

"Why do I care?" he asked.

I nodded and couldn't look at him again.

"I just do," he answered and sighed. "You should get ready for work."

I nodded again and slipped over the edge of the bed and put my feet on the floor. I was tired from the late, emotional night, and my thoughts were racing. I moved about the room gathering things to wear that day and slipped into the bathroom, Fenris watching my every move from the bed.

Damn, looking at him in my bed, comforter piled artfully in his lap, muscular tattooed body on full display… the man was an absolute feast for the eyes.

He hadn't made a move, though. His hands always remaining both steady and respectful. I still ached despite it. A part of me wished for a touch more intimate, but I didn't think he was interested like that and I really needed a friend right now, so I didn't want to push my luck. I mean, besides all that, I shouldn't even consider any type of *relationship* right now, right? I mean, I was in the middle of a divorce!

I stared at myself in the mirror – at the dark circles under my eyes and my complexion just… *off*, almost *sallow* from all the stress.

I let out a huge gusty sigh and said out loud to my reflection, "I need a break. From all of it."

It wasn't likely to materialize, and business wasn't exactly booming. I was barely hanging on and I was feeling so very lost – like I was drowning on dry land and there was absolutely nothing to be done for it.

"All you can do is keep going," I murmured, and I piled on the makeup once I was dressed to hide just how awful I was starting to look. It was taking a lot more concealer under my eyes lately, that was for sure.

When I went out, my bed was empty. I slipped into a pair of flats from over in front of the closet and went out into the rest of the house. I found him, dressed and standing near a small pile of moving boxes, the paperwork that'd come in the mail in his big, tattooed hands, his blue eyes keen as it drifted over the legalese.

There was a keen intelligence in those eyes, etched into the lines and angles of his hard face, his expression dark as he absorbed what was in those papers. Except where it had wrought sorrow from my breast, in Fen it stoked anger. I could see the spark, the blaze igniting behind his eyes and I was surprised to find I wasn't at all frightened, but rather... warmed.

"You got a lawyer?" he asked, and I jumped slightly.

"Yes, but they have a lot of cases and I'm afraid they're hard to reach. I'm feeling a little forgotten lately but I'm sure they're doing their best."

He snorted and said, "I'll make some calls."

"To who?" I asked, frowning slightly.

"Club's lawyer, see if he can recommend someone better."

"Oh, I don't know," I said, shaking my head. "I've already put so much into the lawyer I've got and I'm not sure I can afford—"

"Don't worry about that right now," he said gently, and I bit my lips together.

"What should I worry about then?" I asked, the silence too much to handle.

"Getting to work on time would be a good place to start."

"Oh! Right!"

He smiled at me as I rushed to gather my coat and purse and twisted this way and that taking in the disaster that was my mom's kitchen and living room.

"How long's it been like this?" he asked.

I let out a breath and looked around myself and confessed, "Too long. I mean, everything has been happening all at once – first Mom and then Copper, then my husband all together like that. Then when I said I was leaving, Charles insisted I be the one to leave the house, and I wasn't even a quarter done boxing things for Goodwill here. I just, I don't know... it just all got to be too much," I stammered, realizing I was rambling, my face growing hot.

"Okay, this is easy. We'll take it one box at a time."

"What?" I asked, looking up at him in surprise.

"I'll come by tonight and bring a pizza and some beers. We'll get through some of it. A little at a time."

"I can't ask you to do that," I said, voice trembling.

"You didn't ask, and I'm not either. I'm coming by tonight and I'm going to help you."

I gave him a watered-down smile and said, "A little pushy, aren't you?"

He swung into his jacket with the brightly patched, if dirty, vest on over it and gave me an ironic smile bordering on shy.

"Am I giving off some red flag vibes?" he asked, and I folded my arms across my chest, hugging myself.

"Maybe a little," I said, timidly. I wouldn't look at him, my eyes fixed on the floor. I jumped when his boots appeared followed by his hand. He tipped my chin and I looked at him.

"You don't have anything to be afraid of from me," he said and his tone was so resolute. I mean, I knew he could be lying but my shoulders unknotted anyway.

"That's good to know," I murmured, taking a half step back. He dropped his hand and smiled, the expression holding a hint of sadness.

"You got your things?" he asked softly, and I nodded.

"Alright, let's get you on the road."

We left my mother's house, and I locked the door. I looked out to the street, at my car parked at the curb, his bike parked just behind it and asked, "You're sure?"

"When do you get off work?" he asked.

"Seven."

"See you here at eight?"

"Okay."

"Have a good day at work, Aspen. I'll swing by and check on how you're doing if you're alright with that."

I couldn't look at him, but I nodded. I was so torn. I felt pathetic, but I couldn't deny I needed the help, even if it was just the company while I worked.

"Here at eight, sure," I agreed.

"I'll bring my truck; take anything you don't want to Goodwill."

"That would be helpful," I said gratefully.

"Okay."

He put his hand to my lower back and ushered me down the walk to my car, standing on the curb until I'd pulled away. I kept glancing in my rearview mirror, watching as he climbed onto his bike before I had to turn the corner.

I let out a breath I hadn't realized I'd been holding and with shaking hands, guided my steering wheel and my little car through another turn as I wound my way to the freeway.

It was practically a straight shot up I-5 North to my little shop in the artsy corner of Georgetown, a neighborhood patrolled by the Seattle Police. Seattle as a city was full of these little pockets of neighborhoods with their own identities. Nobody local blinked about saying you were headed to Ballard, Georgetown, or Fremont as if they were little towns and cities all their own and not just a scrap of neighborhood that was a part of some larger whole.

I took the Swift-Albro exit and wound my way down over the freeway to the little intersection interchange that led me onto Airport Way. Parking in the lot behind my storefront, a block down from the old Jules Maes Saloon, I let myself in the back door and into the room that held my shelves of projects waiting to be fired.

I ducked into the little back office to set my things down and to take up my apron, slipping it over my head and tying it around my waist. I checked the messages on Clayrity's phone system, putting them on speaker as I always did as I went about my morning duties of emptying kilns, putting finished, fired projects on their shelves, and unglazed or only first-fired projects on another as I listened and took mental notes.

"Hey Aspen, it's Penny. I just wanted to let you know that your soon-to-be-ex was making inquiries about your financials. He's still listed on your accounts so I had to give him the information. Please, do not tell anyone I told you. I could so get fired. I'll see you on Paint Night and I'll bring you a bottle of that Ice wine I was telling you about. I'm so sorry this is happening to you; I hope you've got a good lawyer. Okay, bye!"

Penny worked for the credit union I belonged to and had all of *Clayrity's* financials routed through.

I closed my eyes and tried to breathe through the threatening tears. I didn't think I was strong enough to do any of this anymore.

I finally sat down on the step ladder I kept back here to reach the higher shelves and let myself have a good cry.

No, it didn't really help.

I looked up and around my little shop and felt it slipping away as despair surged in.

I think I knew deep down I was going to lose *everything* I had ever loved, but I just wasn't willing to let go. Not yet anyway.

Too much, I thought to myself. *It's all just too much…*

CHAPTER EIGHT

*F*enris...

"The fuck you been?" my dad asked as I killed the motor on my bike.

"Out. Why the fuck you care?"

He shook his head and flicked the butt of his joint he'd been toking off of into the grass and said, "Believe it or not, no matter what you do and no matter where you go, you're still my kid and I'm always going to care. No matter how much of a hard-ass you are."

I smirked and bowed my head, laughing slightly, but then the reality of exactly where I'd been crept back in and curb stomped my smile back into a frown.

"Remember the chick I brought home from Mitch's place a few weeks back?"

"Blond, pretty, got hysterical really damn quick?" he asked.

"Yeah, yeah she did," I said slowly and sighed at the memory. "She's got her reasons and I hate to say, they're good ones."

"Coffee?" my old man asked.

"Yeah." I nodded and got up off my bike, body groaning in protest for a lot of reasons – the damp, the chill, a piss poor night's sleep in an unfamiliar bed, mind racing over her words falling from her lips with the weight of utter despair…

"I just don't think I want to be alive anymore and I'm scared."

Scared me, too, for a variety of reasons. None of which I could quite put my finger on. I mean, *why did I care?* She wasn't anyone to me.

"Alright, so what's eating you, boy?" my dad demanded, sliding a full mug of black coffee across the kitchen counter to me. I motioned for the milk and he turned to open the fridge. I waited until he'd handed me the half and half carton and told him the truth.

"I kind of haven't been able to get her off my mind since she was here," I said.

"Seems to me the feeling's mutual." He nodded toward the mug in my hands and I frowned in thought, taking a drink.

"She called me last night, upset. I went to check things out." I shook my head, feeling a little guilty for telling her secrets.

"And?"

"She's suicidal," I answered simply. "Doesn't have anyone to lean on. She's been through more shit than I can talk about in the last couple of months, man." I shook my head and stared into my coffee, finally deciding I'd might as well go for broke. "Her mom died of a long illness, a month later – like a month *to the day,* her brother dies in an accident and the very next day after that she catches her husband cheating on her with other dudes. Now he's turned into a real wank-puffin and is trying to take half her business that she built from the ground up all by herself. She's done. Just run out of gas, and I can't say I blame her."

"Sounds like the husband's a problem," my dad said sucking his teeth and leaning on his hands against the counter across from me.

"She asked me not to do anything," I said.

"You gonna listen?" he countered with a raised eyebrow and I gave him a look.

"For now, I'm going to try a different tactic first."

"Yeah? What's that?"

"Gonna get a shower, head down to the club, and see if Mav can't put me in touch with the club's lawyers."

"They're criminal law, Son, not divorce attorneys."

"I know that Pops, but lawyers are their own weird little community. Bet they know somebody who is."

"Got a point there."

"Borrowing the truck tonight," I said.

"Oh, you are now?" He looked amused.

"Yup."

"Fine, you go get my honey."

"Shit, fuck. I forgot about that," I said.

"Oh, I know you did."

"Fine," I grated. "I'll get my shower, get your honey, bring it back here, *then* go to the club."

"Then you can borrow my truck," he said.

"Rat bastard," I muttered, getting up.

"What's that make you?" he asked as I was leaving, making for the stairs up to my room and the bathroom.

"Makes me a rodent of unusual size," I said flexing and took the stairs to a track of my dad's laughter.

It'd been my sister's favorite movie when we were kids – *The Princess Bride*.

I stayed under the hot shower's spray for a while and thought furiously, questioning myself, trying to decide if that was why I was doing the things I was doing where Aspen was concerned.

Did she remind me of my sister?

No, not really. I mean, maybe in some ways but definitely not looks or anything. That'd be creepy as fuck and incestuous and that was *not* my bag.

What was my bag were those green eyes of hers; luminous, like pale green kunzite crystal set in her round face. Her pale cheeks dusted with her blushing, those Hollywood lips of hers so full and beautiful, I couldn't help but imagine all the ways I would like to defile them.

I closed my eyes and fisted my cock, imagining what it would look like, her on her knees, pressing the head of my dick to that pouting bottom lip of hers, begging for entry. Her hot, wet, little pink tongue flashing out to taste the tip.

I groaned, letting my imagination run away from me, stroking my cock with my hand as it throbbed with desire.

Did I think I would ever get the opportunity to receive a blowjob from Miss Aspen Lawson? No, not really, but a guy could dream.

I took my time, let my imagination run wild, and finished to a rather unsatisfactory conclusion. That conclusion being there wouldn't be anything like the real thing but I was also pretty keenly aware that I was cruising toward the friend zone.

While the notion was disappointing, I was okay with that. I wanted to be her friend and see her heal. I guess I'd been taking people apart for so long, I wanted to know what it felt like to put one back together.

Huh.

That piece of self-analysis and introspection went way deeper than I thought it would.

I shut off the water and sighed out. I had pretty much all day to kill before meeting up with Aspen. The errand I had to run for my dad wouldn't take much time, just a run out to the Bee Queen farm in Puyallup for the couple of five-gallon buckets of wildflower honey they had set aside for me and my pops. We were supposed to get our homebrew on this weekend.

We were a couple of Viking types for sure – very into our heritage, cooking meat over fire, homebrewing mead, taking an axe to a few motherfuckers that deserved it.

I stopped drying myself as memories flooded in that were best left locked in their vault. I really didn't want to think about some of the shit I'd done. While I didn't regret doing it for the bastards that I'd killed, I *did* regret some things. Sleeping at night was entirely too easy after some of the shit I'd gotten away with.

Still, nothing I'd done was going to bring my sister back. I'd turned myself into one grade-A fucking monster and though it wasn't for nothing in the face of her loss, it sure felt like it.

Disconcerted by my introspections, I gritted my teeth, got my ass fixed up and dressed and took myself back downstairs.

"Honey," my dad reminded me, and I scowled at him.

"I ain't old like you," I said, lifting his truck keys off their hook and putting mine up. "I ain't got memory problems."

"Har, har, fuck you, boy! You're gonna be me sooner rather than later."

"Odin's beard I hope I'm fuckin' not," I said.

"Need money?" he asked without looking up from where he was unloading the dishwasher.

"I got it," I said.

"Good, then get you gone."

"Love you, too, you old bastard."

"Yeah, yeah, love you, Son, but fuck you."

I laughed as I went out through the mud room and out the back door. We were always up each other's ass. We didn't even know why. It drove my mom nuts when she was around and had the occasion to see it.

I stuck the key in the ignition of the truck and pulled down on the gearshift to get it into drive.

Maybe I should call Mom and get her advice on this one… then again, maybe not. I didn't know when it came to Mom what was going to be a good day versus a bad one. She missed Lacy the hardest of all of us and she absolutely fucking *hated* that I'd joined the club and had taken the road less traveled like I'd done.

I'd disappointed her, but I couldn't say I shared her disappointment. Did I have regrets? Sure, sometimes, like now… I was a monster, and there were no regrets about that. Never really had been, until now. Now, I had only one regret. That I hadn't let myself stay human enough to know exactly what to do to help Aspen through her situation that didn't involve blood and violence.

I hadn't had a lot of practice being human, being *normal* by citizen standards, but then again, I'd never had the occasion to be those things.

I took 18 to 167 and headed south, swinging around onto 410 when I got there to get on out to the honey farm.

I picked up three buckets and headed back to the goat farm, dropping them off with my pops who hauled them out to our homebrew shed on his own, telling me to fuck off when I asked if he needed a hand.

"You need your truck?" I called after him.

"No, now I said fuck off with you!"

I shook my head. "Crazy old bastard," I muttered and decided fuck it. It was getting on toward noon and if I rode, I would only have to ride back and pick up the truck before heading to Aspen's place and I didn't feel much like taking the extra steps.

I headed for the club's old Ironhorse Boneyard and to cross the whole lawyer thing off my list. Did I think hooking her up with a better lawyer was the way to go? Meh, only partially. What she needed was someone to whoop her ex's ass, but she wasn't there. I didn't know if she was ever the type to get there, either, and that was honestly okay. She didn't need to be there. She wasn't one of us, and I honestly kind of liked that, I guess.

Not sure why it made a difference, it just did. Not that big of one, but it was there.

"What is your fuckin' *deal*, bro?" I asked myself softly as I steered the truck back onto Highway 18.

I didn't have the answer to that one.

I pulled into the end of the Eagle's lot next to the boneyard and shut off the truck something like forty minutes later. I sat for a second, gathered my cut off the seat next to me and keyring looped around my index finger, gave them a casual spin and caught them in my palm, holding tight, the metal nubs of the key cuts digging into my palm. I got out, shut the door behind me, and shrugged into my cut as I stepped over the curb and walked through the patch of grass to the gravel of the drive.

Rat City was a bad place to be, but the locals knew it could get a whole lot worse if they fucked with our shit, so I didn't have to lock the truck's door.

"What're you doin' here?" Dump Truck grunted as I passed by the yard's open gate and started past his open garage bay door.

"Seein' if Mav was around," I said, changing tract and stopping by the dude that honestly passed for my closest friend.

"He's around, how'd things go last night?"

I let out a pent-up breath and a bit of a nervous laugh. "It's kind of a shitshow."

"Oh, yeah?" He looked up at me, squinting at the light coming in through the bay door. It wasn't too bright out, overcast as it was, but it was a fuckton brighter than in here.

"She was still a hot mess when I got there, looked me right in the eyes and told me she didn't want to be alive anymore."

Dump Truck looked up sharply at that and scowled, rolling back on his stool and giving me a hard look.

"What'd you do?" he asked.

"Stayed with her, made sure she was solid this morning, made plans with her for tonight and let her go to work."

"What brought that on? Do you know?"

I nodded. "That's what I want to talk to Mav about."

"We going to dish out a lesson in how to treat a lady?" he asked, and I took a deep breath, blew out my cheeks and shook my head.

"She asked me not to."

He leaned back and eyed me critically. "And you're gonna listen?"

"For now," I said.

"Then what's Mav got to do with anything?" he asked, dark brows knitting together.

"Was hoping that he could put me in touch with the club's lawyers. See if they knew a good divorce one for Aspen. Hers, apparently, isn't doing a whole lot."

"You really like this girl," he stated, and he wasn't asking so I didn't answer. Beside that, I didn't think there was any denying it at this point. I knew myself – enough to know that I hadn't and wouldn't do this for just anyone.

He stared at me until I finally had to relent, roll my eyes, and nod some kind of affirmation.

"So, you seen Mav?" I asked and Dump Truck, still looking at me as if he were mystified, jerked his head toward the dividing wall and the counter beyond.

I followed the gesture with my gaze and noted Little Bird on the phone with a customer and the office door behind her which usually stood open, shut tight.

"Thanks, bro."

"No problem, let me know how things turn out."

"I surely will," I promised.

I went to see what the boss man had to say, see if he maybe had any insight.

CHAPTER NINE

spen...

I missed Fenris when he came to the shop to check on me, but Amber sure hadn't. I'd stepped out to grab myself something to eat and to bring Amber something to drink from the nearby Starbucks on Michigan Street, and boy when I got back, she looked like she was fit to burst with her excitement.

She quickly walked over to me, her blue eyes sparkling under her fringe of auburn bangs and practically squealed with excitement. I had *no idea* what was going on until she opened her mouth and said, "You weren't kidding when you said your biker was *hot*! Does he have any friends my age?"

"Oh, Lord!" I cried, and laughed slightly. "I guess I missed him?"

"Only just," she said. "Couldn't have been even two minutes. He left you a note." She held out a folded piece of paper to me that was off one of our scratch pads. I traded her the drink she'd ordered for it and opened it, eagerly.

Hey, sorry I missed you. I got some things to tell you. I'll see you at your place at eight, pizza and beers riding shotgun. Try to have a good rest of your day. – Fen.

I nodded and creased the note along it's already folded line and tucked it in my purse.

"I'm going to grab this bite in the office," I said and Amber grinned at me around her green straw.

"Have fun," she said, and I smiled.

"You're insufferable," I said.

"I'm also closing tonight so you can leave early if you want," she called over her shoulder. I turned back before slipping through the curtain to the storeroom and kiln room and gave her a curious look.

"See what a good employee I am?" she asked.

"What happened between you and Ian?" I asked and arched a brow.

"He cheated, I dumped him." She shrugged. "Good riddance to bad rubbish."

I smiled in spite of the seriousness of what she'd said. Her parting shot such a funny and old-fashioned thing for her to say at her age.

"Indeed," I said. "I'm sorry he did that to you."

She rolled her eyes. "We're teenagers, it's expected. It's nothing," she declared and the all too familiar lines of worry pinched her equally too young face as she looked at me.

I glanced away and said, "I'll take the phone if it rings."

"'Kay," she said, and I slipped through the office door, which was honestly more of a closet with a desk and a lone filing cabinet. I sat down to snarf the salad and afternoon iced coffee I'd bought for my late lunch and let my eyes roam invoices and schedules, calendars and a myriad of other business-related things, though none of it seemed to really stick. I had nothing for an attention span anymore and the memory of a goldfish.

I slogged through the rest of my day and finally, *finally*, I could let myself go home. Fenris was already parked and waiting in front of my house when I got there. He looked up from his phone as I pulled past his truck and into my usual spot in front of my mom's house.

The way the houses in the majority of Tacoma were built, the driveways weren't on the street. Rather, they were *behind* the house –

alleyways leading through to each person's parking in what was either the side of their house or their backyard.

My mom's car was still out back, and I still didn't feel right parking mine there. I mean, I never did. I was a visitor, a guest. I still didn't feel like I belonged here. I *didn't* belong here.

I guess… I guess, I didn't really belong anywhere anymore.

An abrupt knock on my driver's side window made me jump and shriek. Shaking, I looked up at Fenris who wore an expression of compassion mixed with empathy. I shut off the ignition, and he reached for my door handle and tried it. My car was locked. It automatically locked when I started driving. I unlatched the door from the inside and the locks popped on all of my doors and my back hatch.

"Hi," he said gently, a saran-wrapped take-and-bake pizza balanced on one arm. I stared up at him and blinked stupidly, tired from the long day and echoed the greeting back at him, "Hi."

"You okay?" he asked, and I started to nod and then decided I just didn't have the energy to lie about it and shook my head.

"No," I said, taking in a slow deep breath.

"What can I do to help?" he asked gently, and I swallowed the threatening tears.

"You're already doing it just by being here," I said truthfully. I didn't want to be alone.

"Got anything you need to bring in?" he asked.

"Just my purse and briefcase," I said, twisting in my seat to grab them from the passenger side.

"Gimme the briefcase, I'll carry it for you."

"It's okay, I've got it." I appreciated the fact that he didn't argue with me, that he simply lifted a shoulder slightly in a shrug and instead held my car door open for me, shielding me in a way from the open road as I stepped out onto the asphalt, shouldering both my purse and my briefcase with my laptop, etc.

"You're early," I murmured, and he smiled, closing my door behind me as I chirped the alarm.

"If you're early you're on time, if you're on time, you're late," he declared, and I smiled slightly and nodded.

"I'm the same way."

I led the way up the walk to my mother's front door and unlocked it, stepping in and clearing out of his way so he could come through.

"Hungry?" he asked.

"Starving, actually," I replied, and he didn't miss a beat, just went into the kitchen and looking at the oven for a moment, turned the appropriate dial.

Meanwhile, I set down my things on one end of the couch and sighed, once again overwhelmed by the sheer number of boxes and the absolute disarray everything was in. I had no idea how I was supposed to whittle through all of it even with his help. I wasn't even sure what he was supposed to *do* by way of help. I mean, this was really all on me.

"You okay?" he asked as I surveyed the room and I shook my head.

"I don't know how I'm supposed to do it all," I answered.

He came around and picked up a box, handing it to me. I took it and blinked up at him a little shocky. I think and he gave me a sardonic little half-smile, so gentle there was no sting to it when he said, "One box at a time, starting with this one. You got a roll of trash bags right there. You don't want it, fill one up and I'll take it out to the truck. You finish going through this box? I'll bring you another. Steady as she goes."

I nodded and went over to the recliner and sank into it, the box in my lap, letting out a shaky breath as he unrolled a trash bag off of the roll and opened it up.

One box at a time, starting with this one, I thought to myself.

I opened the top, took a deep breath and woodenly started to sort. Meanwhile, Fenris moved around the living room and kitchen quietly, putting the pizza in the oven, starting a timer, answering texts and surfing the internet on his phone, just being a presence while I worked.

When I had sorted through the first box and set it aside with just a few items I wanted to keep inside of it, the trash bag holding the rest, he brought me another.

"Oh…" I murmured when I opened it up to my wedding album on the top.

"Wanna set it aside and burn it later?" he asked, and I wrinkled my brow.

"I-I mean, I don't know the answer to that," I said overwhelmed. "You don't think it's childish? I mean, what if I want those memories later?"

"Why?" he asked.

"Why would I want them?"

"Yeah. I mean, look how it ended."

"I mean, I definitely know how it ended, but it wasn't *all* bad."

"The look on your face says otherwise, baby," he said so softly, so sympathetically, I looked up sharply.

I met his blue eyes, and he smiled at me, the gesture forced and the tightness around his eyes belying his anger. Not at me, but *for* me. I couldn't ever remember a time that happened. That anyone got so righteously angry on my behalf. It was a little strange but a relief at the same time, you know?

That expression of his lent more to strengthening my resolve to get through this than I had to date.

I looked down at my wedding album, at my happy, smiling, unassuming face and back up to Fenris and held it out to him.

"I guess we need to start a burn pile."

His smile was a proud one that made me melt just a bit and he said, "Atta girl!"

He started a burn pile and went to get the pizza out of the oven.

We sat and ate off paper towels, talking over some things that shifted from boxes to trash, boxes to other boxes to keep, and boxes to a neat little pile by the door to burn.

I mean, I could always change my mind later, but for now… it was cathartic in a sense. You know?

When a trash bag filled, or we ran across a box that needed to be completely tossed, he didn't wait. There was no preamble. As soon as I declared it was junk, he took it out the front door and tossed it into the back of his truck.

Within the hour, it was feeling much less claustrophobic in my mother's house and it really was like I could start to breathe in an emotional sense once again.

Fenris set another box into my lap and we were laughing a little, talking. The laughter died on my lips with a wave of nostalgia as I pulled the lid off the banker's box to reveal a nest of tangled fair ribbons.

"Oh." I lifted a blue ribbon off the top with shaking fingers.

"What's that?" he asked, the tears already leaking out of the corners of my eyes.

I sniffed and said, "The first time I took a blue ribbon at the Puyallup Fair for one of my pottery pieces."

I picked up the picture buried under the nest of ribbons of me flanked by Charles and Copper. My mom had been behind the camera.

"Memory good, bad, or indifferent?" he asked cautiously.

"I don't know anymore," I whispered and something inside of me broke all over again.

He came over, took the box from my lap and the ribbon from my one hand and set it aside, pulling me into a hug as I clutched the photograph to my chest. The realization hit me that nothing would ever be the same again. The comfort of that time – knowing I was loved and supported and knowing that Copper, my mother, and my husband were proud of me. Now my family was gone and my husband? Well, that was all a lie, wasn't it?

"Shh, I got you," he whispered, his hand cupping the back of my head, fingers threaded through my hair as he held me tight, and pressed me into his shoulder, sheltering and letting me cry it out.

I was so sick of crying. So sick of hurting. So sick and tired of it all…

"Okay, time to change tact, you need a break," he said and gently let me go.

"Pack a bag."

"What?" I asked, voice warbling.

"Whatever you need for work for the next couple of days and some clothes for the weekend. Come on, let's go. Lock it up and let's get you out of here."

"I don't understand…"

"We're leaving. Just put it down. We're walking out of here and getting a few days between you and the pain and we'll come back to it. This isn't working for you."

"I can't just leave," I protested weakly. "Where would I go?"

He looked at me judiciously and asked me point blank, "Do you think you can trust me?"

I made eye contact and there was something in his eyes, something I couldn't explain with words but the *feeling*…

"Yes, of course," I said breathlessly.

"Pack a bag, at least four days, through the weekend. You need a break from this place. I'm gonna need you to follow me."

"Okay," I said nodding carefully.

"I'm going to take this trash out, these empty boxes. You gonna need those, am I right?" He indicated my briefcase and my purse.

"Yes."

"Okay, I'll put them in your car."

"Thank you?" I said, and he smiled.

"You're welcome. Go on now, pack up."

I got up slowly and mechanically, and went into the bedroom to start pulling things from my mother's dresser drawers.

It was the only thing I had managed to do in the house that was easy… throw all of her clothes into trash bags that resided in the living room and put all of my things away… and I hated it.

I think Fenris was right. I needed a break, someplace other than here to collect myself. Maybe find myself.

I didn't even know who I was anymore. I certainly had no idea who I was supposed to be now.

I needed a new foundation.

CHAPTER TEN

*F*enris...

I shot a text to my dad that I was going to have company for a few nights and got to work tossing the trash bags of what felt like clothes that were meant for Goodwill into the back of his truck up near the cab. The trash I kept in the middle of the bed and toward the tailgate? The burn pile. I wanted to offload that shit first and spirit it away in the corner of the barn until I was ready for it. My pagan ass had a multitude of reasons for wanting to burn some of it.

Mostly to purify Aspen of some of the negativity that was hanging around her like a pall in the air. Sometimes it was so thick, it was no wonder she was drowning in her own tears.

She needed a breath of fresh air, to shake some of it off, and I aimed to get her back on track... or hell, maybe on a new set of tracks altogether.

Whatever was best for her, and I meant that. She was a beautiful soul, inside and out. I could see it in her green eyes plain as day. She was so pure it almost burned to look at her.

Do enough evil shit like I had, you knew pure goodness when you saw it and Aspen was pure goodness, desperate to heal. I was just as desperate to see her heal. Some of that echoes from Lacy, but I sure didn't look at Aspen like she was my sister. No, she smelled too good, *felt* too good tucked into my arms.

Now was *definitely* not the time to make any moves, though.

I found her keys, forlorn up against her briefcase on the couch, and used them to unlock her car so I could stow her purse and work stuff in the back. When I went back into the house, I cleaned up from our dinner and took out the kitchen trash so it wouldn't stink since she would be gone.

I went to the door of her room and watched her pack for a moment. She looked lost – in thought, in her feelings, directionless and tired, the weight of the world on her shoulders.

"How you doing in here?" I asked, and she jumped, letting out a cry and pressing a hand to her chest.

"Shit, sorry." I couldn't help the chuckle.

"It's alright, just make some noise or something? For as big as you are, you're so dang quiet!"

"Practice makes perfect," I said with a shrug. Doesn't help to let whatever your quarry might be know that you're coming. It kind of negates the whole point of hunting. She didn't need to know all of that, though.

"I, uh, I don't know about this. I have to work and—"

"You'll get to work on time, I promise," I said. "You need the break, babe."

"I do," she confessed, and she looked so damned *sad*. I wondered what it was going to take to see this woman smile again, and I mean *really* smile. I had to give that some serious thought.

"Nothing wrong with taking help when it's offered." I said gently.

"What?" She jumped slightly and turned her gaze up and over to me from where she ran a top or something between her hands over an open, leather duffel bag. "Oh, no, it's not that." She bowed her head and shook it.

"What is it, then?"

"I don't know, I'm just tired, I guess. Not thinking straight."

"Okay, what else do you need?" I asked.

"Um, shampoo and conditioner, soap and the like from the bathroom."

"Cool, I got it."

"Oh, no, that's okay! I can—"

"Too late," I said and went into the bathroom. There was a lot of shit in there. I called back out, "Which stuff is yours? Just tell me."

She did, and I threw it all together in the sink so I could put it in the grocery bag I saw out front.

It was ramshackle and rude as hell treating her shit that way, but I wanted to get her someplace organized where she had a hope of finding some time away from the memories, to build some scar tissue up over her grief and recent emotional wounds.

Her hurt was palpable, throbbing, throwing off heat that I could almost feel from the next room as I grabbed a bag for her toiletries. I loaded them up and turned as she zipped her bag closed and turned to look at me.

"I don't know about this," she murmured.

"I promise, I'm just trying to help," I said, and she sank down to sit on the edge of the bed.

"I know."

I sat down next to her and waited out whatever thought process she had going on. Finally, with a large sigh she committed and said, "Okay. I'm ready; let's go."

"You sure?" I double-checked because she didn't really seem like it.

"No," she whispered reluctantly.

"Okay, what's going on in there?" I smoothed some of her loose hair back from her face to get a better look at her.

"I feel like I'm asking way too much of you."

"You aren't asking for anything, babe. I'm sort of over here insisting."

"I don't know what to think anymore," she whispered, and I hugged her to my side, her head naturally finding my shoulder.

"That's the whole point of this field trip – to get you out of this house full of old ghosts and memories and someplace different, neutral, so you can begin to sort out what's in your head."

She nodded and stood up slowly and I gathered her bags.

She followed me in her Prius up I-5 and across Highway 18 to the Auburn-Black Diamond Road exit, then a sharp pair of turns up Green Valley Road and the city feel was left behind fairly swiftly.

We pulled up outside my house and I got out of the truck. The goats were bedded down for the most part, but there was still an excited bleat or two out in the dark. I immediately went to Aspen's door and opened it up for her and she got out of the car.

"Thank you," she murmured.

"No problem. Pop your hatch."

She did from her key fob and I retrieved her gear. My pops was already at the kitchen door, a rectangle of light spilling over the gravel.

"C'mon and get in here, girl. It's damp and cold out here."

Aspen rushed ahead, and he stood sideways, letting her slide past him.

"I'm sorry if we've kept you up," she said.

"Nah, I've always been a night owl. Y'all eat?"

"Yeah," I answered. "Go on upstairs, let's get you settled," I said. She nodded and went for the stairs.

"All good?" my dad asked.

I gave him a nod and twisted to get through the door and around the counters with my cargo without banging into anything.

"Night then," he called after me when I went right for the stairs myself.

"Night," I grunted back.

She was waiting at the top of the stairs and I gestured with a handful of bags to my room. She nodded and went into it and I followed just to set things down and get her settled.

"I can stay on the couch for now," I told her.

"You don't really have to do that," she said. "I'm okay if you're okay. I mean, um…" she was blushing hardcore, and it was fucking cute.

I smiled, nodding, but still asked, "You sure?"

"Yeah."

"Okay, here's your bag." I handed her the bag she packed, and I set her briefcase and purse aside. I held out her toiletries in the grocery sack and said, "You know where the bathroom is. Take your time getting ready. Okay?"

"Okay, thank you," she said, and she ducked out into the hallway and across the hall. I went across to the dresser and lit all the candles on top so I could switch out the overhead light. I hated artificial light and went with flame whenever possible.

Candles lit, I went over to the window and raised it up to get some airflow.

I changed for bed, and by that I mean, I just stripped down to my boxer briefs and got between the sheets under the furs and waited for her to come back, leaving enough room for her to get into bed, my nerves jangling with a low-key excitement of having her cuddled against me again.

I liked the feel of her in my arms. It was different. *She* was different. There was just something about a good girl, I guess. She had drama around her, but it wasn't the melodrama of club girls. It wasn't stupid head games and a bunch of bull fuckery.

Still, I was used to breaking heads not mending hearts, and I worried just about constantly if I was doing things right, especially given my level of attraction to her. I lay there, fingers laced behind my head, on my back, staring at the patterns of firelight on my ceiling and I sighed. I reached over and paired my phone to the Bluetooth speakers in the room, and made sure it was plugged in.

I had a sleep playlist full of lower key, slower, Wardruna tracks I liked on repeat and a stretch of tracks that were just like fifteen minutes of rain falling. I kept the volume low so it was calm, chill, trance inducing. I hoped it worked for her, because without it, I would be lucky if I could get my mind to shut the fuck up long enough to let me get to sleep.

I had started to drift already when she came back in. I jumped slightly as she set her bag down against the chest of drawers inside the door and she straightened looking a little guilty.

"Sorry, didn't mean to startle you."

"It's cool, you didn't. Just c'mere so we can sleep."

"Yeah, um, is there someplace I can plug this in?" she asked and held up her phone.

"What kind?" I asked.

We got her sorted, and she sat down on the edge of the bed with a slow sigh.

"C'mere, if you like," I said and held my arms open. She nodded and cuddled into my side, resting her head on my shoulder and breathing out slowly.

"Music going to bother you?" I asked quietly, running my hand up and down her arm, kneading it rhythmically to banish some of the tension she held in her body.

"No, its… nice. I don't know what they're saying, though."

"It's Norse." I chuckled slightly.

"Oh."

I closed my eyes, and we listened to the rhythmic beat, slow like a heartbeat, the overlay of lilting voices, primal, rich and nuanced, evoking images of rich earth and green growing things, of livestock and farm life, of cold still waters, straights and fjords.

I pressed a kiss to Aspen's forehead and my lips curved as she melted into my side further – tension draining from her, her body soft and yielding against the hard planes and angles of mine.

"Thank you," she whispered, and I let out a slow breath.

"You got nothing to thank me for," I told her. "This is nice for me, too."

The confession was an easy one to make and cost me nothing.

"Is it safe to leave the candles burning like that?" she asked.

"Do it all the time," I said. They were the church kind, in the tall, thick glass.

"It's cozy."

"Yeah."

We lay in the warm golden glow, silent, wrapped in comfort, and I couldn't remember a time when my soul felt so much peace.

That part was unexpected… but I liked it.

CHAPTER ELEVEN

*A*spen...

"What time will you be home? My pops is planning on grilling up some meat for the three of us."

Home...

I wished that it was, wistfully thinking back on the night before – falling asleep in Fenris' arms, feeling absurdly protected and safe even though I wasn't in any sort of danger. It was like he had held me together and the candlelight and soft drumming and rhythmic vocals of whatever we listened to soothed the soul, lulling me into a deep and dreamless sleep.

I can't say how absolutely invaluable the dreamless part of that was to me. It was priceless.

So priceless that when the morning had arrived and my alarm had gone off, I hadn't wanted to get up and for a completely different reason than the weight of my sorrow holding me down.

I hadn't wanted to get up because I was so... *content*. I don't think I was ready to go as far as *happy* yet, but it was close. Closer than I had been in a long time. The feeling returned with hearing his deep and velvety tone over the telephone's line.

"Aspen?"

"Sorry!" I said quickly. "Lost in thought for a moment, there. Um, it's Paint Night here and I won't be off until something like ten... I thought I had said something. If that's too late to come back, I can always go back to Tacoma tonight."

He chuckled, and I looked out over my little shop. I was just about to set the long tables for tonight's Paint Night. I would *much* rather spend the evening with Fenris in the countryside, but I also had a divorce to pay for and a myriad of other bills that would be due next month just as they had been this month.

"No, don't do that. Just come this way when you're done and we can reheat it."

"Don't wait to eat on my account, please."

"Don't you worry about that. By the time you make it back, I'll probably be hungry again."

I smiled at the smile in his voice.

"Okay," I agreed.

"See you around ten-thirty, eleven o'clock?"

"Absolutely, I look forward to it," I said.

"Good."

I ended the call and with a gusty sigh started the process of setting up for tonight's Paint Night. Some were better than others, and tonight was looking to be decent with twenty ladies or so signed up via the website.

It was a harrowing few hours when the ladies finally arrived, but I loved the paint nights and classes. It made me happy sharing the joy of shaping the earth into beautiful things with other people. Typically, my clientele ranged from the extremely creative to the people who thought they weren't good at anything with a creative bent. I loved to prove the latter wrong when I could, but sometimes shaping clay just really *wasn't* their thing. Still, I definitely encouraged them to find for themselves what was up their alley. Everyone deserved to find some kind of joy in life.

Tonight's Paint Night was good, a lot of laughter and more than a few inappropriately wonderful jokes. I had a good time, despite myself and my desire to be back in the country. The little goat farm was utterly peaceful and charming and the quiet stillness… I was quickly becoming addicted, I think.

I was looking forward to spending time on it in the daylight. I think Fenris was right, I needed a break. Just some time to get away from it all, to catch my breath, to feel my feelings and to allow my broken spirit to mend just that little bit so that when I did turn to face the monumental tasks in front of me, my grief and the loss I felt wasn't quite so monstrous and I had enough of me restored to give to the tasks at hand.

I did a cursory cleanup around the shop, surveyed it all, and decided that it would be alright if I left the rest until morning when I opened. I was tired, and I wanted to go back to Fenris' farm, have a bite, and sleep.

I seriously wanted nothing more than to sleep lately. I honestly thought I could sleep for a thousand days and nights and it *still* wouldn't feel like enough.

God, I was depressed, but could you blame me?

"I hope this wears off soon. I don't know how long I can honestly live like this," I said to no one in particular. I was alone… but I didn't feel lonely anymore. At least, not nearly as much.

Fenris was such an unexpected gift in that regard.

The drive back to that little slice of farmland and countryside between Auburn and Black Diamond felt excruciatingly long. It felt like the only thing keeping me awake was the glow from the navigational display on my phone, and the mechanical woman's voice from *Google Maps*. I turned my little car as instructed automatically and was relieved when the rush of pavement turned to the crunch of gravel beneath my tires.

The turn onto the gravel drive took me through a short tunnel of trees. The foliage, a natural privacy screen around the property, made it feel a little like a hidden oasis of peace during the day. At night, like this, it was foreboding, bordering on menacing.

The warm glow of firelight ahead was a beacon in the dark. My headlights swept over Fenris holding his hands out to the flames, his father, Vyking, standing nearby at the fireside, a large one of my mugs of what I assumed was coffee in one hand, the other stuffed in the pocket of his jeans.

I pulled up and put my car in park, meeting Fenris' eyes as he came around the fifty-five-gallon steel drum that the flames licked out of.

"Hi," he called out gently as I stood up. I smiled over the roof of my car at him.

"Hi," I echoed.

"You look beat."

"I am," I said honestly.

"Busy night?"

"Oh, about twenty or so, so yeah; busy, but good."

He smiled. "And y'all just sit around, drink wine, and paint?" he asked.

"And talk, and laugh," I said with a light chuckle.

"That's nuts," he said with a rueful look and a shake of his head. I shut my car door and the dome light went out, plunging his features into darkness, back lit as he was by the fire.

My breath plumed the damp night air, and I shivered with a stuttering involuntary breath at the sharp autumn chill as I went around the front of my car to join him.

He hugged me almost immediately and I laughed a bit, nervously, but I hugged him back, the leather of his jacket and vest slick and chilly beneath my fingers and my cheek as he gave me a squeeze.

"Hungry?" he asked, turning to walk beside me, arm around my shoulders.

"Yeah, starving actually."

"Food's in the kitchen, warming in the oven," Vyking declared.

"You guys always have fires out here like this?" I asked as Fenris and I stopped by the cheery blaze. I held out my hands and soaked up the warmth it had to offer.

"Meh, seemed a shame to waste the coals from the barbecue," Vyking declared. "Perfectly good to get a fire going out here." He kicked the side of the drum with his thick-soled boot.

"You wanna head inside or hang out here for a bit?" Fenris asked.

"Uh, I'm good with either," I said sighing.

"How hungry are you?" he asked.

I chuckled lightly. "Famished."

"Go on in, then," Vyking said on a yawn. "I don't need you to keep me company."

I nodded and Fen went for the door leading through the mud room and into the back of the kitchen.

"I'll probably go right to bed after," I said.

"Oh, well, g'night then," Vyking said and it was ambivalent – neither disappointed nor pleased.

"Thank you for fixing me dinner and keeping it warm," I said.

"Don't mention it," he said affably.

"Goodnight," I murmured.

"Night, honey."

Fenris waited, holding the door open for me and I scooted across the final expanse of the gravel drive to the house and ducked through the door, not wishing to let the cold damp from outside into the house.

Fen followed me in and shut the door tightly behind me.

"Have a seat, I'll get your food."

I hung my purse over the back of one of the high bar chairs pushed up to the counter and shrugged out of my overcoat and scarf.

"Woo, it's cold out there," I mentioned and he gave me a crooked smile, meeting my eyes with his almost feral blue ones.

God, there was something irredeemably sexy about that look.

He took a plate down and got into the oven, loading things from various foil packets onto it for me.

"This'll warm you up in no time," he said as he worked. "What it doesn't manage, I'll finish upstairs."

I blinked, my eyes going wide as I stared at him, a blush creeping into my cheeks.

He laughed at himself, and closed his eyes, shaking his head back and forth as he slid the plate of food at me.

"That came out really bad, didn't it?" he asked.

I didn't speak. I didn't exactly know what to say. I was twisted up in knots inside with wanting to say 'yes' but not knowing precisely what I was saying yes *to*. I mean, did it sound bad? Yes. Did it also sound really, really *good*? Also, yes.

Should I be thinking that way after all that'd been said and done?

I didn't know… I mean, I really didn't know. I wasn't even *divorced* yet.

Does that really matter? Your marriage is over. Charles checked out a hell of a long time ago. Why should you adhere to antiquated standards? Because you're a woman? I think not.

"Beer?" Fenris asked, looking at me almost strangely.

"Depends, what kind have you got?"

He opened the fridge, leaned in and said, "Looks like a red, an IPA, and a couple of ciders. What's your poison?"

I completely missed the question. He straightened up slightly and looked back at me over his shoulder and I snapped out of it, barely. I'd been unabashedly staring at his ass which looked really damn good in it's sheath of lighter denim.

"I'm sorry, repeat the choices?" I squeaked.

His slow smile made my heart stutter and skip.

"Red, IPA, or Hard Cider?" he asked.

"Cider please," I murmured, my breath stolen by the warmth in his steady, unwavering gaze.

He nodded once and turned back to the fridge, retrieving a brown glass bottle with a blue label. He used the bottom of a lighter to leverage the lid off and held it out to me, the light glinting off of the heavy silver rings on his fingers.

"Thanks." I took the offered bottle and took several healthy swallows. His smile grew.

"Glad to see you're doing better," he murmured, and I felt the heat of my blush resurge and kiss my cheeks with flame.

"Are we flirting?" I asked.

Fenris shrugged the chains at one shoulder looping under his arm rattling against the stiff leather of his jacket.

"I don't know about you, but I am. Need me to knock it off?"

"No!" I said quickly, then chased it just as quickly with, "I mean, I don't know." I scowled at myself and the mixed signals I was giving.

Fenris chuckled and said, "Not that I was doing it too hard to begin with, but I'll slow it way down."

"I mean, why would you want to?" I asked and squeezed my eyes shut and covered my face, hiding my mortification. "Christ, that sounded way worse out loud than it did in my head. I didn't mean it like that. I just meant—" I stopped and lowered my hands and looked at him, face vermillion with shame. "I guess I did mean it like that," I said miserably. "No reflection on you. You've been so wonderful to me."

He put his hands on the countertop and leaned on them, looking down, not looking at me. He rolled his lips together in careful consideration of what he was going to say next. I shrank in on myself, my appetite suddenly fleeing in the face of my discomfort.

I felt like I was in some kind of trouble.

Fenris looked up at me and sighed.

"Why wouldn't I want to get involved with you?" he asked.

"I can list a lot more reasons why you shouldn't than why you should," I answered quietly, fixing my gaze to my plate, clutching my hands in my lap.

He dragged in a deep breath slowly and let it out in a gusty sigh.

"You're beautiful," he said. "You're sweet, you're kind, and I know it probably sounds tacky given that you are going what you're going through, but you're sexy as hell without even trying."

I felt my mouth drop open in disbelief.

He searched my face, concern in his bright blue eyes and it was his turn to look resigned.

"I can wait," he said. "It's whatever you want; whatever you need right now. And if you gotta friend zone me, I'll live with it because I may be an asshole, but I'm not a rapey fucker and never will be. Whatever you decide – it's cool, and I mean that."

I felt my jaw work, but no sound came out at first, as I didn't quite know what to say. Finally, what came out was, "Thank you," but it didn't seem like enough – not nearly enough in the face of the wellspring of gratitude pouring out of me.

He fixed my gaze with his and nodded after a moment, satisfied with whatever he saw in mine.

"No problem," he murmured.

"I mean, I don't think I could friend zone you," I said, and my blush was back. He smiled slightly, a watered-down echo of the sexy one-sided grin of earlier.

"Just take your time," he said. "I mean that. I'm good. It's about you, not me."

"You are entirely too understanding," I said, taking another healthy swig of cider before I picked up a rib, sticky with barbecue sauce, off of my plate.

"Not as much as you'd think," he said with a laugh. "Not typically, anyway. There's just something about you." He shrugged as I took a bite, my gaze fixed on his over my mouthful of food.

I had no idea what I had just put in my mouth. The meat didn't taste like beef or pork. Fenris laughed slightly at the strange look on my face as I tried to identify what I was slowly chewing.

"It's goat. If you hate it, I completely understand. It can be a bit… I don't know, musky."

"No, it's fine, I just wasn't expecting it. It's good, I promise."

"You're sure? 'Cause if you hate it, I can totally make you a sandwich or something. Fix you something else."

I smiled and shook my head and said, "It's *fine*, I promise. I'm no shrinking violet when it comes to unusual meats. I've had my fair share of venison and other game. We're on a goat farm, goat isn't that unusual."

He smiled appreciatively and said, "Still had to tell you what it was."

I laughed slightly and said, "Shut up!" which made him chuckled harder.

"Good to know you're a natural blonde."

I made an indignant noise. "So are you!"

"True, true," he said, nodding before turning to reach into the fridge for a beer.

I admired the view a little more covertly. The food was helping. I think my sugar was a little low or something. It'd been a while since I'd last eaten. The disconnected fogginess I hadn't even realized was there in the beginning was dissipating from my head but my tiredness remained; stubbornly I might add.

"Okay, in all fairness, I'm really tired and lunch was a long time ago," I said with a rueful smile as I polished off the first rib and picked up the half an ear of corn from the edge of my plate.

"Finish up and take yourself upstairs and get ready for bed while I tidy up down here and I'll come tuck you in."

I felt my expression soften and a smile grace my lips.

"That sounds really awesome," I confessed.

"Good deal." He nodded.

I finished my meal and it really was good. We chatted while I finished up my cider, lips faintly burning from the slightly spicy barbecue sauce that'd been in a sticky slather on the meat.

Finally, when I was yawning just about every other sentence, Fenris shooed me away from the kitchen bar.

"Off you fuck," he said kindly. "Go get ready for bed. I'll come up in a minute."

"Okay," I murmured gratefully as I drifted toward the stairs.

I fetched down a clean towel from the closet in the hall and thought about how it had only been around a month or so ago that I'd woken up in this strange place unexpectedly and how off-putting it had been. A wry smile twisted my lips as I thought to myself, *my how some things change.*

I grabbed my nightgown, went into the bathroom, brushed my teeth, clipped up my hair so it wouldn't get wet, and took a quick shower to wash off the day.

I scrubbed my face twice to get the worst of my makeup off and knew I would still have to finish up with micellar water on a cotton pad around my eyes. My mascara and eyeliner could sometimes be stubborn.

Fenris knocked on the bathroom door as I stood dressed in my nightgown in front of the mirror and finished off my nightly beauty routine with a little toner.

I opened the door and he leaned against the frame. His height should have been imposing but it wasn't. I mean, not anymore.

"Whatcha doin'?" he asked.

"Just taking the rest of my makeup off and using a little toner on my skin."

He smiled a bit, almost shyly and said, "I suppose if I told you that you don't need all that, you'd scoff at me."

"Right now," I said, straightening and gathering up my used cotton pads from my makeup kit, "absolutely. I don't usually wear a full face, but the stress has waged some war on my complexion and I've needed all the extra help I can get."

"I wasn't lying when I said you were beautiful, downstairs," he said, and I looked up at him.

"I'm happy you think so," I said softly.

"Yeah?"

"Yeah."

A strained silence stretched between us, full of promise and desire. His eyes gravitating from mine to my lips as he clearly considered kissing me and I swear to God, that simple flick of his gaze just mere inches lower caused a hitch in my breath. I held it, rendered absolutely inert as I wished he would go for it.

I simply wasn't brave enough to make the first move which sounds silly! I know! I just… I just couldn't, though.

How soon was too soon? That ever-present inner voice, full of speculation ceased quickly by the one filled with derision. *Too soon and what will people think?*

What would people think, indeed? There was a certain unfairness to that considering the circumstances. It wasn't as though Charles had died… he'd just left me. Cheated on me, used me as cover from the word go, a lie… I was just a lie. All of it was a *lie.*

"Let's get you tucked in. You look like you could use another good night's sleep," Fenris declared quietly.

He wasn't wrong.

"Okay," I murmured and took his hand. He gave mine a little squeeze and led me across the hall, guiding me in front of him through the door.

The bed had been turned down for me and I felt the tightness of anxiety in my chest loosen some.

For all of his rough exterior, his frightening countenance, he was so very sweet to me.

"Up you go," he whispered and I got up into his comfortable bed.

"You're not coming?" I asked.

"Nah, I have some shit to do out in the barn. We got a couple goats about to give birth, but I'll be in at some point."

"Okay."

"You want some music?"

"Yeah, if you don't mind, please?"

"You got it."

He tucked me in close and went to the candle-covered dresser and switched on a couple of the flameless, yet realistic LED kind. I smiled and he turned on a speaker, tapping buttons on the top a few times to get the soothing rhythmic melodies going.

He came back to me and leaned down, brushing his lips against mine. It was so unexpected; I froze, and it was over before I even had time to register what'd just happened.

Damn it.

"Was that okay?" he asked, voice strained.

"No," I whispered. "It was too short. Come back down here."

He smiled and it held a wicked edge to it, but he obliged me. Bending at the waist, supporting himself on the bed with a hand pressed into the pillow by my head, he bent to cover my mouth with his.

His lips were soft, his beard lightly tickling my face as he brushed his lips against mine. I closed my eyes and captured his face between my hands, kissing him back this time, pressing both my lips to his bottom one.

He kissed me back, and it evolved until my lips naturally parted to let him in.

He groaned slightly against my mouth and flicked his tongue past my lips and teeth to stroke it against mine. He tasted masculine – hops from the beer he'd drunk lingering and mixing with the taste that was so intoxicating and purely *him.*

I whimpered slightly, wanting so badly for him to come to bed, but he pulled back carefully and let his eyes drift over my freshly scrubbed face.

"Get some rest," he urged. "I'll be in to snuggle you as soon as I can."

I smiled and nodded. He straightened and boy, it was the hardest thing ever to let him go.

CHAPTER TWELVE

Fenris...

I was having trouble deciding which was hardest. My dick or leaving her in my bed to get some sleep without me.

I wanted to ravish her. Wanted to mark her with my scent, hold her under the shelter of my body and make her scream her pleasure into the candlelit dark, but I had shit to do.

When I finally did get to go in to her, she was fast asleep, the lines of worry and the weight of her circumstances erased from her face, the tension that rode her neck and shoulders a thing of the past.

I loved that she unconsciously pulled herself into my side, cuddling close when I came to bed and I couldn't remember falling asleep so quickly. A night without visions of the things that I'd done...

The next morning, she was gone when I woke, light streaming in the bedroom window between the cracked curtains.

Fuck.

I got up, took a hot shower, beat off to the imagined image of those green eyes surrounded by her tousled blonde hair looking up at me, my cock pressed between her pussy lips as she begged me to fill her and just as soon as I came, I started on my second orgasm when my cock didn't lose even one iota of its turgidity.

As soon as I was out and dressed, I picked up my phone to text her.

Me: What time you gonna be home?

It was like she was waiting to hear from me, because her reply was immediate.

Her: 7?

Me: LOL u askin'?

Her: LOL, no, could be a little before, could be a little after.

Me: Is it your Friday yet?

Her: No, tomorrow.

Me: K

Her: Why?

Me: Dunno yet. I'll figure it out and let you know.

Her: Ok?

I shot back a smartassed emoji and went downstairs. We'd had a couple of babies the night before. Well, three actually. A single kid and a pair of twins, but one of the twins didn't make it.

My dad came in the back door just as I poured myself some coffee.

"How are they?" I asked.

"Good, no complaints. Both are up and eating off their moms, so I think we're good."

"Right on."

He eyed me and it held the feel of criticalness.

"Say whatever you're gonna say, Pops."

"Aspen," he said. "You plannin' on keepin' her?"

"She's not a stray cat, Dad."

"No shit, that's what I'm worried about, Boy."

I chuckled mirthlessly. "Just takin' it one day at a time, if you don't mind."

"Seal the deal yet?" he asked.

"Oh, what the fuck?" I demanded and he gave me a shallow and knowing grin.

"She's a keeper, then. Good to know. Better than your last girl-friend – that's for sure." I scowled at him.

"Shit, anything's better than that ho."

He chuckled and changed the subject. "Wanna get that mead started tonight?"

I nodded. "Yeah, we can do that."

"What time's she gettin' here?"

"Doesn't matter," I told him. "I can do it; and to answer your question, sometime around seven."

"Oh, good to know – and it's your night to cook."

I shook my head and sighed, my phone vibrating in my jacket pocket. I answered it.

"Yeah?"

"Hey, it's Mav."

"Sup?" I asked.

"Need you to take care of something, real quick."

"What's that?"

"Tell you when you get here."

Shit, okay, it was that kind of a thing.

"On my way." I sighed, ending the call before telling my dad, "I'll be back."

My dad raised an eyebrow. "When?"

"When whatever needs doin' gets done," I answered and he waved me off. Club business. He knew.

"Don't get caught," was his parting shot.

"You jinx me, we fightin'," I told him and he just laughed at me.

I rode out to the club and found Mav at the bar, a steaming cup of coffee at his elbow as he talked on the phone, a pair of aviators on his face despite the dim interior of the barroom.

"What's shakin'?" I asked.

He held up a hand, finished his call, and then looked at me.

"Dumb fuck broke into the boneyard last night."

"Shit, cops get him?"

"Nope."

"Got any leads?"

"Yup." He slid a piece of paper down the bar to me and I looked it over.

"How bad's the damage?"

"Just got off the phone with the claims adjuster; they're on their way to asses."

"What you want to have happen here, P.?"

"Dump Truck is going with you. I'm pissed, so I'll let him be the judge."

"Anything we looking to recover?"

"About two thousand in cash, that's it."

"Get what we can, he'll owe us the rest?"

"With interest."

I nodded. I knew the interest rate was going to be steep but we didn't want to say more in front of the cell phones. I shot a text to Aspen that I would be working in the fields for most of the day and I'd be away from my phone - didn't want it damaged or anything.

As soon as Dump Truck came through the back door, we left the electronics on the big table in the chapel and headed out.

The kid was something like twenty-two or twenty-three and living with his brother in a house off 23rd SW, so not far from the boneyard which was on 15th SW. He was heavy into drugs – meth or heroine, and had to be some kind of a serious bonehead to fuck with our shit.

Well, it couldn't be helped. He was about to reap what he sowed here in a big way. Best-case scenario, he would come out the other side of this shit with enough of a fear of the gods put into him, he would get his ass straight. That was about as far as I went with the bleeding-heart schtick, though.

"Go around back," Dump Truck grated and I tossed him some chin in a nod of acknowledgement.

I waited in the overgrown backyard. There was a dog chain back here but no fuckin' dog, which was concerning.

The chain-link fence that ran around the backyard's perimeter was a short one – three feet or so and just enough to hem a dog in. I cursed silently when I heard the dog barking its fucking head off when DT pounded on the front door.

Someone inside shouted at the mutt to shut it, and I got ready. As predicted, the back door burst open and dude came flying over the back step. I heard Dump Truck shout but I had a hold of the dude and slammed him down into the patch of dirt at the base of the back stoop.

It was our guy. He ain't changed from the printed-out image from the security systems at the boneyard. I heaved a fist, and let it crash into his face. Blood spurted and he grunted, both hands going around my one wrist where it was buried in the front of his shirt.

"You fucked up," I declared. "You got once chance to fix it."

"Man, what the fuck? I didn't do nothin'!"

"There you go fuckin' up all over again by lying to me," I said and dragged him over to one of those old-school fixed head rotary clotheslines, the base of which had some cinder blocks on either side of the aluminum pole.

"Fen!" I heard Dump Truck call from in the house.

"Yeah, I got him! You okay?"

"Fuckin' dog bit me. I got him locked in one of the bedrooms."

"Man, don't hurt my brother's dog! Cujo ain't do nothin'!"

"Cujo." Dump Truck spit off the back stoop. "Cute."

"You hurt bad?" I asked.

"Jacket took the most of it, I'll be alright."

"Where's the money?" I demanded without any more preamble.

"Man, I don't know what you're talking about!"

"Put your arm on that block there," I ordered.

He was already hyperventilating. I didn't care. I was in that place that was divorced from all emotion. He, of course, didn't comply.

"I said put your arm out. You can either do that or I'll put your mouth against this brick and stomp the back of your head so hard it'll not only knock the teeth outta your lying mouth, it'll break your fuckin' jaw."

He put his arm out.

"Where's our fuckin' money?"

"I smoked it!"

I stomped on his fucking arm and heard it snap. He screamed, long and entirely too fucking loud. I looked up and around.

"You got a week to come up with the fuckin' money and get it to us," I told him.

"Break the other one," Dump Truck said and sniffed.

I dragged him around so he could set his other arm up for me and he twisted and damn near broke free.

"Motherfucker, you asked for it!" I grounded out. I got ahold of his other fuckin' arm and pressed it against my knee. I broke it like fucking kindling. He screamed, wailed, and cried like a little bitch and I had no fucks to give.

"That'll teach you to keep your fuckin' hands to yourself, huh?" Dump Truck demanded.

We left him sobbing on the ground behind us.

"Get us our fuckin' money that you stole. Interest is accruing, and don't think to tell a fuckin' soul about what went down here," Dump Truck said.

"I don't give a shit who I hurt," I said to drive the point home. Even if it was a lie, he didn't need to know that.

The club had a creed, no matter how much a man fucked up and got in deep with a Sacred Heart, his wife, girlfriend, or whatever and his kids were off-limits. That is kids that were still minor children. If his kid was eighteen, a man, and somehow involved, all bets were off. The kid wasn't involved in whatever bull fuckery that earned our pissed off, we let them alone.

Who said there was no honor among brigands, eh?

Dump Truck and I hustled up the block and got on our bikes, riding away and taking some hard turns down streets to avoid the approaching sirens. The pigs were expected. That dude hollered like a fuckin' baby.

Back at the clubhouse, we retrieved our phones.

"So, how're things going with the blonde?"

I looked up from my phone screen.

"Alright, I guess."

My buddy arched a dark eyebrow at me, his coal-black eyes raking me over.

"She's been staying at my place with me the last couple of nights."

Dump Truck failed to keep his look neutral and I frowned at what I unexpectedly saw – pride and like he was impressed.

"What do you think?" he asked.

"I like her," I said carefully, then added, "And I'd rather not talk about it."

DT put up his hands, as though to say he was hands-off the subject.

"The fact you *don't* want to talk about it tells me this one's serious, brother. Good for you, man."

I nodded but wouldn't look at him.

"I don't like that look," he said plaintively. "What'd you just think about?"

Honestly, as serious as I was about Aspen, as much as I liked her, I was worried that I wasn't good for her. She'd already been through so much fuckin' pain. I didn't want to end up the cause of more.

"Talk to me," DT said, like he was trying to sooth an angry dog. He wasn't terribly far off the mark. I wasn't the best at processing feelings without lashing out or having anger enter into the equation – usually at myself for not being, I don't know, *normal*. As fuckin' boring as that was, you pretty much always wanted what you couldn't have and there was no way living this life I would ever have normal... but what if that was what Aspen wanted?

A normal life.

She was so damn low-key, I kind of figured it was her default.

Dump Truck swung the door to the chapel closed and I sighed.

"Talk to me, bro," he repeated and he crossed his arms over his chest.

"I'm a fuckin' monster on a bad day, and an oddity – a freak – on a good one," I said coming clean.

He gave me a crooked grin.

"And?"

"And what if that's not what she wants?" I asked. "What if it's not what she needs right now?"

"You *really* like this woman."

I nodded. "I don't know what it is, but yeah. She sort of soothes the beast, you know what I mean?"

"Special kind of woman to sooth the rage and pain," he agreed. "My Little Bird is like that for me."

"She's also a kind of project for you," I said without thinking, but Dump Truck was an analytical short. He didn't get pissed or snap off, that was my *modus operandi*, no he thought about what I said and finally nodded.

"I can see what you're saying there. You're not wrong. I like putting broken things back together just as much as I enjoy breaking 'em."

I nodded, relieved. "That's exactly what I meant, Dude."

"Not your usual thing, though. Is it?"

I shook my head. "Nah, not really."

"Scared you're gonna do more harm than good?" he asked.

I nodded.

"Good," he said judiciously.

"The fuck?" I asked.

"You stop bein' scared about that kind of shit, that's the minute you do somethin' stupid to fuck it up," he said. "So, hang onto that. Let it be a net positive in that regard. In the meantime, enjoy, my brother. There's nothing better than a beautiful woman in your bed and by your side making you better."

He clapped me on the shoulder and opened up the door to the chapel to let us out.

"I don't know. I'm still finding that last part out," I said, thoughts consumed by Aspen and just how much I wanted to do *with* her, not just *to* her.

CHAPTER THIRTEEN

*A*spen...

When I pulled down the farm's long driveway, there was another car up ahead that I hadn't seen before. It was a black and white Jeep of some kind, heavily modified for off-road capability, the top soft and awkward, not typically 'Jeep' in that it didn't cover the back seat area – which didn't have seats in it. It gave the beastly looking vehicle the appearance of being a Jeep/pickup hybrid and made me wistfully lonesome for my brother. Copper loved off-roading. It was something he was super excited about sharing with his son, Silver – yes, I know, I'd argued with my brother and sister-in-law slightly over that one, too... but that was Copper. Always joking, always smiling, and he was seriously hoping that when the time came, he would have a grandson named 'Gold' or 'Golden.'

Such a big dork.

While the memory made me sad, it also made me smile and that smile that ghosted my lips was *everything*. It was the first time I think I'd managed since, well, *everything*, to smile instead of immediately crying. I think this timeout, or break, or whatever it was from my mom's place where I was sorting through so many photos and old things was good, *needed*. That despite there being no use for them, going through them was good. I mean, they somehow held senti-mental value for my mother who had been just two steps shy of being a hoarder, I swear to God, and going through them was sort of this long but necessary goodbye.

I sighed as I rolled to a stop and put my car in park, careful to leave enough room for the Jeep to back up and go around the main pasture and around and back out. Fenris had plans to gravel the rest of the track around that pasture but hadn't gotten to it yet.

My little Prius couldn't do the mud, but the Jeep looked like it would definitely have no problem.

I looked over at the overhang off the back of the house and the men gathered beneath it. It was Fen and Vyking, but the third man and likely owner of the Jeep, I didn't know.

He wasn't nearly as tall as Fen or Vyking, but he was still taller than me. He had his arms crossed over his chest, which was covered in a black tee, the spill of his beard fiery and impressive as well as nearly to his belt line.

He was bald, his light eyes smiling and kind as he turned his head in my direction when I got out of my car.

"Hey, Aspen. Like you to meet my buddy Jon Oppegaard."

"Hi!" I called out over the roof of my car.

"Hey, how's it going?" he called back, and his tone was friendly. He was the kind of guy who was instantly likeable – clearly laid back and genuinely nice.

"Good! How about yourself?" I asked as I crunched across the drive.

"Aspen makes heavy earthenware plates and mugs and shit. I like 'em," Vyking said, taking a drink out of one of my coffee mugs I'd gifted Fenris.

"I'm glad," I told Vyking.

"You made that?" Jon asked, jerking a thumb at the mug in Vyking's hand.

"I did! I run a shop called Clayrity in Georgetown off Airport Way."

"Oh, cool. Another mead guy, Brandon has a shop out that way on Airport called Mr. B's Meadery. He's a good guy, does a real nice Ginger Cardamom mead I hear, which is all him. I hate ginger."

"Oh, nice," I said, faltering a bit. I had no idea what he was talking about.

Fenris, as ever, came to the rescue.

"Jon's the owner of Oppegaard Mead out there in Tukwila. He came buy to check on a batch we were making, to determine if it was infected."

"Infected?" I made a face.

"It's all good," Jon said affably. "Sounds worse than it is. Just means your equipment maybe wasn't properly sanitized and you got some bacteria growth going on that you maybe didn't want in there. Mead is a lot more forgiving than wine or beer, but it's still subject to similar issues in the brewing process."

"So, was it?" I asked, as Fenris tucked me under his arm and into his side.

"Looks like it," Vyking grumbled.

"So, what's the cure?" I asked.

"Start over," Jon said with a shrug.

"Geesh, that doesn't sound fun."

"It's not too bad, it was just one carboy, the rest seem to be alright," Fen said.

"Onward and upward," Vyking agreed. "Let's get this new batch going."

"Want a hand with that?" Jon asked.

"Love one," Fen said. "You give my pops a hand and I'll get some dinner going. Pretty sure my lady's hungry."

I felt a warm, tingling rush at Fen's words and smiled again, blushing at the thought. *His lady* had a nice ring to it, even more so with the reverence with which he said it.

"Come on, you can gimme a hand in the kitchen if you don't mind," he said, jostling me lightly. I looked up and nodded.

"Love to," I murmured.

Just inside the back door of the house, well away from prying eyes, he pulled me against his body and lowered his mouth to mine. I closed my eyes and kissed him back, and wow, he was a skillful kisser. With a touch of his lips, a stroke of his tongue against mine, I felt knotted muscles loosen right along with my inhibitions.

I groaned into his mouth and he pulled away gently, a mischievous smile on his lips.

"Yeah," he said with conviction. "I'll be doing more of that tonight, if you'll let me."

"Let you?" I asked, chest heaving with my breathlessness. "Pretty sure I'm going to beg you."

He laughed and said, "Good to know. Think you can fix up a salad while I get the grill lit?"

"Sure."

"Knives there, cutting board here." He pulled the built-in one out from where it was hidden under the lip of the counter. "Bowl up there." He indicated, and I nodded.

"Okay."

We worked together mostly in silence, and it was comfortable – moving around one another and trading little touches when we could.

It didn't seem to matter how damp or how cold it was outside, no matter the weather, Fenris and Vyking were fanatics about cooking with fire. I didn't think the oven got much use. I made the salad while Fenris seasoned some thick steaks for the grill.

"Wish we had corn," I said, and he opened up the fridge and brought out a bag of ears.

"Your wish is my command, my lady."

"Awesome, where's the foil?" I asked. He brought a roll down from the top of the fridge as I tore into the corn, shucking it with the practice of a thousand summertime barbecues. I was impressed that he had it. It was getting close to the end of its season as we headed into deepest fall. In fact, it was already dark outside.

"I'll be back in a minute for those," he said, letting the meat rest as he went outside to fire up the grill.

I fell into the peacefulness that being domestic always brought me, fixing the corn up with butter and a touch of salt to each packet and peeking in the oven.

I was right. It looked barely used. There were some pans in it, a couple of cookie sheets, a roasting pan, and a cast-iron Dutch oven by the looks of it. I pulled all of it out and heard something rattle in the Dutch oven and lifted its giant lid.

"Ah ha," I voiced triumphantly, and lifted out the two muffin tins.

By the time Fenris came back in, I had the oven preheating and was whisking mayonnaise into my thin roll batter.

"*Mayonnaise?*" Fenris demanded with a look of disgust on his face that instantly had me howling with laughter.

"Shut up, you'll like these, I promise."

"What the fuck are they supposed to be?" he demanded suspiciously as I dropped a heavy-handed spoonful of batter into each muffin tin.

"Dinner rolls," I said, rolling my eyes. "They have a sort of biscuit texture and flavor but come out in a muffin-like shape."

"I'll take your word for it," he said, hefting the cookie sheet I'd stacked the foil-wrapped corn on, and the other cookie sheet lined with parchment he'd set the steaks to rest on. He raised an eyebrow at me suspiciously as he backed out the door, nudging it open with his shapely butt to exit out through the mudroom.

Long story short, the dinner rolls were well received, the conversation with the three men lively, and as evening wore on into night, we sat comfortably at the picnic table under the extended roof overhang from the back of the house.

Vyking and Fen had hung lanterns at even intervals from the underside of the roof's edge and the light from them was warm and just enough along with the lantern at the center of the table. It seemed if they could get away with skipping the use of electricity, they would. I couldn't decide if it was a cost-saving measure, or what, but I liked it whatever the case may be. It was simpler somehow, certainly more rustic, and just made things peaceful.

"What about you, Aspen?"

"What?" I looked up from my plate where I'd been chasing my last bite of salad across its surface.

Jon chuckled. "We were talking about travel. If you could go anyplace in the world, where would you go?"

"Oh, I don't know," I said. I blew out a big breath. "With every-thing going on, travel has honestly been the last thing on my mind."

"Oh yeah? What's going on?" he asked, catching whatever look Fenris beside me cast him too late. I put my hand on Fenris' arm and he looked down at me. I shook my head slightly, indicating that he didn't need to protect me from having to talk about my life – shitty though it may be for the time being.

I gave Jon the CliffsNotes and he gave a low whistle.

"Yeah, you got a lot on your plate. All that aside, I know exactly what you're going through with your business. I had something similar happen to me when it came to the meadery and getting it going."

"Really?" I asked.

"Man, I didn't know that," Fen said.

"Me either," Vyking declared.

"Oh, yeah. It's a long story, and it's getting late, otherwise I'd get into it for y'all. I promise, though. Rain check. It's a wild ride from start to finish."

"Love to hear it, brother. Can't be as crazy as your trip to the old country," Vyking said.

"Oh, that's *part of it*," Jon said.

"Shit, you're gonna have to come back real soon, then." Fenris got to his feet and stepped out over the bench of the table to get out.

"After a meal like that, what's for dinner tomorrow night, man?"

The guys had a laugh and I smiled and giggled along with them as I started to gather plates and utensils to bring everything inside.

"Leave it," Vyking grunted. "You and the boy cooked; I clean. Fair is fair."

"Let me give you a hand bringing this inside," Jon said affably. "Then I'll get out of here."

"Thank you," I murmured.

"Hope things get better for you," he said, and I smiled.

"Thank you. I hope so, too."

"Come on, let's get you to bed. It's past your bedtime," Fen said gently and put an arm around me.

"K. Goodnight, Jon, goodnight, Vyking."

"Night, girly," Vyking declared and I went with Fen inside.

"Go brush your teeth, I'll turn down the bed," Fen said at the top of the stairs.

I rolled my eyes slightly and said, "Yes, Dad."

"Oh, you'll call me daddy, alright," he said with a wink, and I burst out laughing.

"No," I said with certainty. "Not my thing."

He grinned at me and I stepped into the bathroom and shut the door.

I scrubbed my face, brushed my teeth, and stood in front of the mirror and stared at my reflection.

I had blond hair in crazy unruly curls around a too-round face. I liked my eyes, a vivid green, the outside ring of my iris ringed in jade smoke, but other than that, I felt I was wholly unremarkable to look at. Plain. Boring.

I sighed.

I didn't know what Fenris saw in me, but it was nice. Nice to have someone to listen to me. Nice that someone cared. Nice that he was so genuine about things. Simple about them. So matter of fact.

There was something… different about Fenris.

He has absolutely no fucks to give, I told myself. *That's what it is.*

The realization wasn't exactly a stunner, but it *was* the truth. He didn't sweat the small stuff. He didn't care about the divorce, or the fact that I was basically financially ruined at this point. He didn't seem to care either way if I kept my shop or lost it, just in how it affected me and my happiness, and I didn't understand it. I didn't understand it at all…

Why do you care about me? *Boring, unimaginative, little me… the quiet girl, the unobtrusive girl.*

How was it this man saw me when it felt like practically *no one else* did?

Two rapid knocks fell at the bathroom door and I jumped.

"Aspen? You good in there?" he asked and I realized I didn't know how long I'd been standing here, staring at myself in the mirror.

"Yeah!" I called out. "Just a second!"

I opened the door after an intrepid and at once, cleansing breath.

"Hey, pretty girl," he breathed as I looked up into those so-blue eyes of his.

"Hey, yourself," I murmured.

"I'm going to take a minute to brush my own teeth and I'll be in with you, that alright?"

"Yes, of course!" I said with a laugh. "Don't be ridiculous."

"Okay," he said with a laugh of his own and a bob of his head. He stood aside so I could exit the bathroom and he could take my place.

"Two seconds," he said with a wink and I smiled and nodded.

I let out a breath I hadn't known I'd been holding when the bathroom door shut.

Shit. We were about to be alone, sharing a bed, and with all the kissing lately…

Are you seriously going to get cold feet and chicken out now? I asked myself harshly as I changed into my nightgown, suddenly feeling like it was more frumpy and less country chic. Like it was something my grandma would wear and not something someone my age should be wearing, never mind how comfortable it was.

I jumped and shrieked slightly when his hand fell on my shoulder in a light touch. I had all of the things I'd worn that day gathered in my arms, about to dump them into a trash bag I'd brought for my dirty clothes. Instead, they went everywhere. I whirled to make sure nothing went on to or over any of the lit candles, but no, we were good except for the frantic beating of my heart.

He grasped me lightly by the shoulders and turned me to face him, his hands warm, strong, and rough with callouses against my skin.

"It's all good," he said softly, his voice deep and soothing. "I got you."

It was a strange sort of thing to say when he'd been the one to startle me so, but at the same time, it was the *right* thing to say

I looked up at him and he drew me in, putting his arms around me and holding me tight. I closed my eyes and laid my head on his chest and just soaked it in – the warmth, the security, the way he just felt so good against me, and I against him.

He held me like that for countless seconds that probably dragged on to minutes and only shifted once I let out a sigh of contentment, my shoulders and back muscles easing when I hadn't even realized I'd held them tense.

He was so warm and alive beneath my hands as I wrapped my arms around his trim waist and I was keenly aware of how little was between us by way of clothing – just my nightgown and panties, his black boxer briefs…

He smelled so *good*. Like the outdoors – all clean air, damp earth, and rich wood. Like the mountains smelled when you stood at the edge of the river or falls. I closed my eyes and breathed him in, letting him hold me, and for one brief moment, I left it all behind and just lived fully in the moment.

"You feel so damn good in my arms," he breathed against the top of my head and I looked up at him, feeling almost, I don't know, drunk? I couldn't really describe the feeling, the languid sort of *relief* that made muscles that had been tensed forever relax and my mind which had seemed to race nonstop finally be *quiet*.

"It feels really good to be here, with you, like this," I whispered nervously.

He lifted an arm, his hand brushing my hair away, his thumb grazing my cheek in a light and sweet caress.

"Everything at your pace, honey," he murmured and I looked up and blinked rapidly as I processed what he said. I mean, as the meaning behind his hushed words finally sank in. I mean, really sank in… *he wanted me. Badly.*

"I mean, how soon is too soon?" I whispered quietly and shuddered. He smiled a little sadly at me.

"Worried about what people will think, you getting with another man so soon after getting divorced?" he asked.

I swallowed hard and nodded since I couldn't find my voice quite yet. When I did, I said, "I'm not even divorced yet, not really. I mean, I only just filed and—"

He placed a fingertip against my lips and hushed me.

"There's an old saying out there," he murmured, drawing me close again and I couldn't even remember taking a step back from him. I felt a little awful about that. I mean, I wanted him too, desperately, and under no circumstances did I want him to think I didn't.

"What's that? The old saying?" I asked.

He tipped my chin, ducking his head, bringing his lips a hair's breadth from my own. I closed my eyes as the warmth of his breath fanned across my lips and sent a tingling rush to all the right places.

"Best way to get over a man is to get under a different one," he murmured, and I sucked in a quick, sharp breath as his lips made contact with mine.

The absolute *rush* that came from the contact was indescribable. I don't know what it was that curled through my body, licking the nerve endings every which way with pleasure. Flame like, fairy like, flitting through my body, butterflies taking flight in my stomach as I was drawn to his warmth like a moth to flame, my hands making contact with his waist, pulling myself in close and closer still until I was fetched up right against him while he ravaged my mouth with his.

Adrenaline surged through me as his arms closed around me, one hand threading through my blond locks, cradling the back of my head as his tongue swept into my mouth and stroked against mine. I moaned, and he devoured the sound like it was candy, a rich chocolate upon our tongues.

He moaned back like I was the most decadent thing he had ever tasted and *God*, I wanted more.

I wanted him to hold me close and never let go. I wanted him to touch me, kiss me, *fuck me*, and I didn't at all know where that came from. All I knew was that I wanted it, I wanted him, and I didn't know the first thing about how to express any of it because I was *paralyzed* by my insecurities.

He broke the kiss, as though he sensed the two wolves raging inside of me, light and dark, the indecision maddening, the desire, at times, overpowering the back-and-forth bringing me to a low, roiling boil inside that I thought sure would be the death of me. The needle pegged in the red as the pressure built.

"Arms up," he ordered gruffly, but gently, and I put my arms up in perfect supplication as he lifted my nightgown off over my head.

"Good girl," he whispered, dropping it to the floor and pulling me close, rewarding me with another deep kiss.

I put my arms around him, the air of the room cool against my skin, his warmth so inviting, his arms going back around me, his opposite hand cradling my head, the other around my back as my breasts crushed flat against his chest and oh my, *that* was a sensation. My nipples teased by the crisp smattering of hair across his chest.

The hand not occupied with supporting my head found my ass and a handful of it. He kneaded the one cheek, fingers slipping up, under the leg of my panties to bypass the fabric and help himself to more of the feel of my skin. The sensation of his rough fingertips against such an intimate area unused to being touched made my eyes roll back in my head and I absolutely know how pathetic that sounds, but it had been so very long since I had been touched like this. Since I had been attractive to anyone, since anyone had wanted to take their time with me, relish me, as Fenris was doing now.

His hand slid along my ass and down the outside of my thigh and I twined my arms around his neck and lifted my leg, over his hip, around his leg, the material of his boxer briefs almost a satiny feel against my inner thigh.

My pussy ached to be filled, throbbing with desire. I couldn't get close enough to him and I had to imagine he felt the same with the intensity with which he kissed me.

He turned, pivoting us so that my back was to the bed and he broke our fervent kissing and smiled faintly at me, lips red and blue eyes kind.

"You're really good at that," he said breathlessly, and I felt myself blush at the high praise. I mean, I don't think I was anywhere near as experienced as him in that particular arena. Despite being married for as long as I had been, there wasn't a whole lot of sex going on.

Of course, hindsight being twenty-twenty, I thought, but I didn't get to think for long. Fenris brought his lips to the side of my neck, and all coherent thoughts fled before the shimmer of magic it sent through me, swept over me in a rush of violent tingling that made me weak in the knees.

"Lie back," he practically growled against my throat and the deep, guttural sound of it made me tremor. The man was a walking orgasm waiting to happen, and I was happy to throw myself on his mercy. Either way, I was certain I would not be disappointed.

I laid back and he shucked himself out of his boxer briefs in one super sexy, fluid motion and the monster he freed was more than a little intimidating. He gave me a slow, sexy, and almost *shy* little grin, biting his bottom lip as my gaze roved over him hungrily and I watched him warily, almost.

Don't get me wrong, I was *very* into the idea of being physical with him, even despite the fact his size was so intimidating, but that had always been the case. Fenris was a big man, it stood to reason all of him would be, ahem, in proportion.

"Hips up," he ordered and I pressed my head and shoulders into the fur-covered bed and raised my hips up off of it obediently. He whisked my panties away just as efficiently as he had divested himself of his boxer shorts then kneeled down by the side of the bed.

He wrapped strong arms around my legs and pulled me bodily to the edge, the display of strength both startling and erotic, as I let out a slight yelp in surprise.

"By the gods, I've wanted to do this from the moment I first laid eyes on you," he murmured, voice low and thrumming with the desire of a man who saw a personal victory in his grasp, and I wasn't at all surprised to find that I wanted to be the one to hand him that victory.

He fixed his gaze upon mine, and whatever he saw in my eyes sealed the deal because with a grunt of satisfaction and a chuckle, he lowered his mouth to my pussy, and gaze still fixed on mine with the intensity of a predator that'd captured its prey, he tasted me for the first time.

CHAPTER FOURTEEN

Fenris...

She tasted like fresh autumn rains and the thin mountain air – crisp, and cool – but in taste only. She was hot to the touch, her pussy slick with arousal and perfuming the air with the delicate scent of her sex. It was so sensual, so organic and raw, and the only thing better was her reaction.

Her keen green eyes met mine without hesitation as she watched me both curiously and with trepidation. When my tongue parted her pussy lips and I teased her clit with the tip? That was enough for her to relax any tension or resistance her body held.

Her head dropped back and her hands tangled in the furs by her hips. I grasped her between my hands, delving them beneath her bottom to cradle her while I lapped at her pussy, feasting on her panting breaths, her little moans, and loving every twitch and writhing pleasure I dragged out of her.

I slid a finger in her and gave an "Mm" in appreciation. She was *tight* and I could only imagine if she felt this way around my middle finger, how she was going to feel around my cock.

She was dripping wet for me, her arousal turning me on even further as I felt around the roof of her pussy for that slightly rougher patch, knowing that yeah, I'd found *exactly* the right spot when she sucked in a sharp breath and her hips bucked. I lavished her clit with attention from my tongue and teased her from the inside simultaneously while her pussy put a stranglehold on my finger. I couldn't wait for that same sensation around my dick, but it wasn't about me right now, tonight… it was about shaking Aspen's tree and seeing if I could loosen her up a little.

"Oh, my God!" she cried and sucked in a sharp breath. I fought to finish the job and not to smile just yet, not until I had her fucking coming all over my face. It didn't take long, she cried out, stuffed the heel of her hand to quiet herself and practically convulsed on my bed, her pussy rhythmically gripping my finger, as I played things out, teasing her clit with my tongue, sucking in a deep breath of my own as her thighs clapped shut around my ears.

I didn't let up until she begged me to stop and let me go. I stood slowly, sucking her essence off my fingers and looking down at the beautiful, shattered mess of her lying in my bed. I wondered if she wanted anymore or if I'd finished her with the one orgasm. She looked up at me, green eyes heavy lidded with satiation, her perfect tits rising and falling with her panting breaths and I loved that I could unmake her so thoroughly.

"You want this?" I asked, gripping my cock and stroking it lazily.

She nodded, unable to speak, and I smiled, feeling cocky.

"You sure?" I asked and she nodded again and reached for me. I went to her, crawling over the top of her, settling between her thighs. She pulled my mouth to hers, kissing me thoroughly, and I was thoroughly impressed. Some women didn't dig making out after I'd just gone down on them. Aspen really didn't care.

"You want me to fuck you?" I growled in her ear and her words slowed my ass way the hell down.

"I want you to *love* me," she whispered back, and her voice was so brittle, so vulnerable, I pulled back to look her in the eyes.

There was something there in the glittering green depths of her eyes, the window down into her very soul… a profound weakness, a deep and abiding hurt, her self-esteem in a deeply crumbling and eroded ruin. A pain I couldn't even begin to speak of.

She was a maiden who held her hand out to me, for the injured, wild animal inside me that'd had its foot in a trap for I don't know how long. That hand promised an end to the hurt, promised to sooth the rage and pain I'd held inside for so long… too long.

"I can't help but love you, baby," I whispered and kissed her gently, taking my time to work my way inside her carefully, letting her body adjust to mine.

She whimpered slightly, and I stilled and asked softly, "Too much?"

She shook her head and answered back, "Not enough."

Her arms went around my neck and I braced my forearms to the bed so I wouldn't crush her as I glided through her wetness and barely kept control of myself when I fit myself all the way inside of her. I drew back slowly and surged forward carefully, striking a slower, gentler rhythm than I normally would have for my own satisfaction.

This wasn't something that was meant to be rushed. No, Aspen was a woman meant to be savored.

I rolled my hips slowly, deeply and she wrapped herself around me as best she could. It was work keeping up this pace, but worth it with every gasp I brought from her lips, swollen with my kiss; and likewise, with every one of her breathy exclamations of pleasure, I felt a small jolt of my own fulfillment.

Nothing left me feeling like more of a man than having my hands slicked with the blood of my enemy or turning a woman boneless beneath me with rapture and bliss.

With how unhappy Aspen had been, and with good reason, without a doubt the fact that she writhed like some goddess of sex and power beneath me right now made me feel on top of the world.

She was sinuous, all gracious curves and perfect grace. Her skin satin and silk, her pussy warm velvet where it gripped my cock as I slid myself with some effort in and out of her body, pressing for that spot. I delved my arm beneath her, raising her hips off the bed, driving into her rock steady, searching for her G-spot, determined to absolutely wreck her, to blow her fucking mind, to make her come so hard she left the earth behind.

She belonged among the stars. The crescent moon her throne, my beauty, my queen, and I would worship her until the end of all time if she would let me.

I'd never in my entire existence, up until now, felt this way about anybody. I couldn't tell you why I felt this way about her. There was just something about her – beautifully broken on the inside, an echo of my own hurts. So brave, that she could mend, could heal from all of the shit she'd been through. She made me believe again. That if she could do it, so the fuck could I.

"Oh, God, Fen!" she cried and clung to me as I stroked just right. She held onto me, gripped me, worked me into a fervor that wouldn't be contained.

"That's it, baby," I urged. "Tell me when you're gonna come."

"Close, I'm so close." Her voice was breathy, beautiful, ethereal, the barest of breezes through the tall pines, and I loved it. I loved the sounds she made. I loved the feel of her. I loved how she arched, and how, as I brought her close and closer to that final shining plunge, she forgot to breathe altogether. I loved how her eyes closed, her head fell back, her mouth worked but no sound came out, how she cried, straining to get the words out, "Oh, God, I'm coming!" before she clenched around me so tightly, I couldn't move an inch further inside her or withdraw.

I grunted as she dragged me into the maelstrom with her, even though I would have gone willingly, stayed by her side, cradled her beneath my body to protect her and give her the love that she so craved and that I craved, too.

I kissed her as we both drifted lazily in satisfaction, my cock softening inside her, glued together with our mutual passion for one another. I stroked her hair back from those hallowed green eyes and met her gaze with my own. I fell into her eyes; so far down.

She took my breath away, too.

An hour later, she lay sleeping against me, her head on my shoulder, her arm across my chest as I stared at the flickering candlelight on my ceiling and traced lazy, mindless patterns against her soft skin wherever I could reach it with the tip of my middle finger.

I felt satiated and guilty.

As though I had somehow stolen her innocence by making love to her.

If she only knew what kind of man I was, I don't think she would have given of herself so freely.

The thought kept me awake, late into the night, her rhythmic breathing the thing to finally lull me into an uneasy slumber, plagued by the ghost of memory.

CHAPTER FIFTEEN

*A*spen...

I woke, Fenris was still sleeping. I was languorous and knew I had work but it was Saturday and Amber's full day. I wanted nothing more than to stay with him, so I allowed myself this one concession to my workaholic personality and sent Amber a text message. I asked if she felt confident holding down the fort on her own for today, and barely as soon as I sent it, my phone vibrated in my hand with the return message of yes, absolutely, it was about time I took a day off.

I smiled, ditched my phone on the bedside table, and cuddled up to Fenris, holding to him tightly. I fell back asleep, likely in desperate need of the rest, and when I woke, he was looking at me, his so-blue eyes roving my face and his lips curled into a surprising smile in the midst of his blond beard.

"You're still here," he said, and I smiled back.

"I am," I agreed.

"What time is it?" he asked.

"Doesn't matter," I murmured. "I took the day off."

"Three-day weekend?" he asked, and I nodded. He broke into a grin and turned on me, gathering me close and pressing his mouth to mine.

I laughed, delighted, against his mouth and he rolled me onto my back, settling between my thighs.

"Mm, maybe later?" I winced slightly.

"I hurt you?" he asked, pushing up off of me.

"Oh, no! Not at all, um, I just am feeling, well… less than fresh down there. I feel like I should take a shower or something before we go at it again."

He looked bemused at me.

"The best sex is messy," he said.

"Oh, I agree, but I really don't like the idea of going again when I feel this sticky and gross. I mean…" I stopped as his expression grew more amused. "It doesn't matter what I say, it's all going to come out bad or wrong or whatever, isn't it?" I asked.

He laughed a little and nodded, saying, "Uh, yeah, pretty much, but I get what you're saying and it's alright with me."

"You promise?" I asked skeptically.

"I promise," he said and leaned down for another kiss to prove his point.

"You want a bath or a shower?" he asked me, and I looked up at him and cocked my head slightly.

"Whichever you can share with me," I answered.

"Shower it is. Don't move. I'll come back when it's ready."

"What?"

"Don't question me, woman! Not when I'm trying to spoil you a little."

I laughed and cuddled back into the warm bed listening to him grab towels out of the closet and get the shower started.

A nostalgia mixed with an unhealthy dose of sadness swept over and through me as I thought *this was what it was supposed to be like* in regard to my marriage. We were supposed to take care of each other, respect each other, and love one another. It was with a grim hindsight that I realized none of those things had been reciprocated by my ex. I had let him charm me, but the moment we had gotten married, that was it… he didn't need to try anymore, and he didn't.

It was never real. None of it had ever been real… I was simply his cover. I was simply a means to an end and that end was keeping him in the life he was accustomed to, getting him through college and well on his way and once that was accomplished? He quit and had just been going through the motions.

And to think, I had thought it'd been me – that I wasn't good enough, that I didn't anticipate his needs, or work hard enough to meet them, or that there was something *wrong* with me.

It wasn't me, though. It was Charles… and it hurt on top of everything else but I was honestly just so emotionally *exhausted*, I couldn't seem to muster up any anger. I just felt spent, drained; and I know how pathetic in some ways that made me but it was true.

Fenris was changing all of that, and I know that probably wasn't exactly healthy either. My self-worth shouldn't be dependent upon any man, but I wasn't entirely sure it was like that with Fen. It was just nice to have someone interested in me, and if Fenris were this interested in me as I was right now, stripped absolutely bare, soul floating, tattered, wafting in the wind and barely clinging to what was left of me…

Well, I couldn't wait for him to see what I could be like when I wasn't so wrecked, when I didn't feel so raw and bleeding, which I had to say, I was feeling much better after last night. So much more, I don't know… present? Solid? Here?

He returned to me in a few short minutes, bending at the waist to kiss me, pulling the covers away from my body. He helped himself to a handful of my chest, kneading my breast, massaging the ampleness of it and pinching the nipple between forefinger and thumb.

I moaned deeply into his mouth and he chuckled back into mine – the sound rich, the vibration decadent, the entire exchange sinfully delicious, like a slice of chocolate torte for dessert when you know you *really* shouldn't.

"Come on, let's get on with the day," he said. "Feel like I should maybe give you a little break."

He spanked my pussy lightly, sending a shock and a thrill through me and I let him pull me up and onto my feet, curling my bare toes into the fur rug at his bedside.

"Do you have to?" I squeaked and he laughed, head thrown back; a full-throated sound. I smiled, and he winked at me and led me across the hall to the bathroom which was steamy and inviting.

We made out in the shower like a pair of teens, his hands slick with my bodywash running all over me, washing me clean and turning me on. Likewise, I did the same for him, the sweet scent of my soap mingling with the earthy tones of his – not quite clashing, but definitely not very compatible. Mine smelled like a bright champagne, girly with a grapefruit finish. His smelled like rich earth, the forest after a rain, the loam on the ground turned up and fragrant with notes of cedar and musk.

I ran my hands over his muscular body, inked with tattoos of ancient knotwork and animals, over innumerable scars, slick and flat, tan of the relatively new and pale, pale white with age. Seams along ribs, gash marks and what I assumed had to be knife marks. Knicks and the like along his hands, rough with work and tears along his forearms.

"What are these?" I asked softly, finding my courage *to* ask.

"Fights, some," he said with a sniff. "Others, accidents. Some from farm work."

"This one?" I asked, running a fingertip along a tan line along his ribs, dotted to either side with punctures from stitches.

"Fight at one of our rallies over the summer," he said. "Good fun."

I hugged him close and looked up into his bright blue eyes.

"Your idea of fun and my idea of fun are two very different things, then," I said with a faint smile.

"I live for the thrill," he said, pinching his nose and wiping the streaming water from it and his beard.

"I just want peace," I said quietly, the first misgivings beginning to stir.

He reached out and caressed my face, and I closed my eyes, turning into the touch.

"Then no worries," he said. "I'll protect you, do everything I can so your peace isn't disturbed. I'm happy to take the heat." He grinned as he said the last and winked at me, and I laughed slightly.

"I'm not sure that's how it works," I said.

"No?" he asked.

"No," I said, drawing nearer and tipping my face up to his.

He brought his mouth to mine and murmured, "Well, I'll figure it out."

"Compromise, you mean?"

"Happy to, for you," he whispered, and we kissed.

"Seems like I would be asking a lot," I murmured when the kiss reached its natural conclusion.

He stroked my cheek, the barest whisper of a touch with his thumb and said, "I don't give anything I'm not willing to give up," he said. "I'm also not getting any younger, and if I'm going to keep up with this place, I'm going to need to slow down at some point."

That I could buy into and I did, wrapping my arms around him and resting my forehead in the center of his chest. He held onto me, loosely, just letting me rest against him and soak up what I needed from him while the steam gently wafted around us.

When I shook myself as though waking from a dream, he smiled down at me and shut off the water.

"So, what do you want to show me today?" he asked.

"Show you?" I asked, taken a bit aback.

"Your life. You took the day off, it's all you, baby."

"And tomorrow?" I asked, and he gave me a wicked grin.

"Tomorrow, you learn about me."

"Sounds exciting," I said smiling.

"Should be," he agreed. "Take a ride with me."

"Are you asking or are you telling me that's what we're going to do?" I asked playfully.

The smile he gave me as he wrapped me in a towel and rubbed me down briskly through the material was playful, but his eyes were serious.

"It'll be on very rare occasions that I tell you to do anything, usually regarding the club or club stuff. When it comes to that, no arguments. At least not until I get home, or it's just you and me," he said and his tone was serious.

"Okay," I agreed.

"I mean it, Aspen," he said, tipping my chin, making certain to capture my eyes with his. "It's the only way I see this working."

The seriousness in his eyes took my breath away. I didn't say anything, I didn't know what *to* say.

"I made my peace with what kind of man I am years ago," he said, and the sadness in his eyes told me to the contrary, he hadn't. He'd just perhaps convinced himself that he had. I doubted that Fenris didn't do anything without his own reasons, however.

This was a part of him that was complex, confusing, and one that would require patience.

"You do a lot of reckless and dangerous things for the club?" I asked softly.

He shook his head. "No more than the next brother," he said.

"That didn't answer my question," I said softly.

"Sometimes that's the best answer I can give you."

I stepped out of the tub and held the towel around me, handing him his with the other. He took it and dried off and it was a treat to simply be allowed to watch.

"You do a lot of illegal things for the club?" I asked softly.

"There's a difference between legality and what's morally right," he said pointedly, and I thought about that for a minute.

"You're right," I said after a while, nodding. "There is."

"All I can do is promise to keep you out of it," he said. "Hence, why, if there's a time I tell you to do something, I'm going to need you to do it. To keep you out of it. To keep you safe from any blow-back from your world."

"My world?" I asked softly.

"For now, still, yeah," he agreed.

"Are they really all that different?" I murmured softly and looked up at him.

"On the surface, it doesn't always seem like it," he said. "Underneath, we couldn't be more different, if you know what I mean."

I shook my head. "I think you lost me, because I don't quite follow, no."

He smiled and hooked the back of my head with one big hand, dragging my forehead to his lips and kissing it soundly, pausing to soak in the gesture as much as I, myself, relished it. My muscles going loose beneath it as I soaked in his love and care – a pathetic, starving thing for love and affection that Fenris was proving to be ultimately patient with on that front.

Then again, perhaps he was just as starved in a way, as desperate to give it as I was to soak it in.

It didn't seem like something to discuss, just something to enjoy while we each had the ability to enjoy it from one another.

"Thank you," I whispered when he finally let me go.

"For what?" he asked softly.

"Everything," I said simply. "For taking me in, taking me away from all that mess for a while and giving me a chance to breathe. For all of the care, for the amazing sex—" He laughed abruptly, and I smiled. "And most of all for all the orgasms," I said laughing myself.

He hooked an arm around me and pulled me in to hold me tight, whispering in my ear, "The best is yet to come."

I shivered with delight.

"I like the sound of that," I whispered.

"Good."

Alas, there was no rest for the wicked in my case. Amber called and said we were dangerously low on the colonial mugs that I made, which wouldn't have been a terribly big deal except for the fact that they were the subject of the upcoming Thursday night Paint Night and I had twenty-three signups. I made my apologies to Fenris and he shook his head.

"Head on into your shop," he said. *"I'll get some shit done around here and ride on over when I'm through. The day's not completely shot. It's nothing to worry your pretty little head about."*

I smiled at the memory as my hands crafted the bodies of the mugs on my pottery wheel in the back.

It took some doing, but I was good at these ones. The time-consuming part came with attaching the handles, to be honest, making sure the edges wouldn't fire up sharp and that they didn't have any burs or spurs.

I smiled when I heard Fenris' bass growl out in the front of the shop, asking after me. Amber seemed a bit tongue-tied.

"Back here, baby!" I called out, my smile growing when he batted aside the curtain to my little workspace back here.

"Tight quarters," he said, looking at all of the looming shelves and the pocket of kilns. It was warm back here, the kilns firing, and I had the back door propped for some fresh air.

"Hi," I said and tipped my face up for a kiss, keeping my hands rooted on the lump of spinning clay and silt-water on my wheel. "Watch yourself, I'm a mess," I declared.

He laughed and said, "You look happier than… and don't take this the wrong way—"

"A pig in mud?" I asked, finishing his thought and smiling pleased. "You're not wrong. Getting my hands dirty is one of the best parts of this job."

He found a seat nearby and with great effort, I trained my eyes back down to the clay on my wheel as I began to shape it.

Fen made an incredulous noise and said, "That's crazy."

"What?" I asked, smiling with charmed pride.

"You make it look so easy," he said, and my smile grew.

"Ah, just practice. Lots and lots of practice."

"How many more of these have you got to go?" he asked.

"Oh, let me see." I glanced up at the worktable and asked, "How many are up there?"

"Uh," he stood up from the folding metal chair in the corner and counted, "fourteen."

"I probably have a few hours left. I'd like to get up to twenty, then I need to roll out some flats and make and attach handles to each one. That's the labor intensive and time-consuming part.

"Then what do you do?" he asked.

"Load up those shelves there and wait for the kilns to be available to fire them into bisque."

"Then what?"

I smiled to myself. "Then put some out front and have the rest ready for the paint night this week. They get glazed and then fired again and there you have it, a finished mug."

"Neat," he grunted and asked with a sniff, "You got a broom back here?"

"Uh, yeah, why?"

"Mind if I work on a little somethin' somethin' of my own?"

"No, not at all. Go right ahead."

"Cool."

He pulled out a whittling knife, clipped to his jeans pocket and brought out a Crown Royal bag from his inside jacket pocket. He slipped out a chunk of stick and began peeling off the bark with his knife while I looked on curiously and let the mug's body, I was working on, warp.

"Oh, shoot!" I turned my attention back to my work.

Fenris chuckled and looked up and over at me, blue eyes sparkling.

"I got it," I muttered and fixed my inattentive mistake.

"What are you making over there?" I asked a time later.

"Oh, just carving up some rune sticks for a buddy of mine," he said. "It's a trade."

"Oh?" I asked. "What are you trading for?"

"Some arrow repairs," he answered. "It's a fair trade."

"Good deal," I said. "You do that a lot?"

"What? Trade?"

"Yeah."

"Yeah, I do. It's a lost art. One of the oldest forms of commerce, I dig it. Especially when I get a good deal."

"Nice," I murmured, and smiled at my work. I loved that. It sounded so simple, even though I was sure there were hidden complexities to it.

"There are a lot of folks around here involved in the SCA and the local renaissance fairs. I do a lot of bartering with 'em – mead, goat meat, some handcrafted shit like these runes. It keeps the old ways alive."

"What do you get in return?" I asked, mostly to make conversation, partially because I was curious.

"Bows, hand forged knives better than you can get in any store nowadays, sometimes help around the farm, that sort of thing."

We chatted amicably while I worked at my wheel and fell into a comfortable silence as I rose to make and attach handles to the heavy clay, pot bellied tankard type mugs that I called part of my colonial line.

"So, what do you do with all this?" he asked and glanced up as I made the score marks in one of the mugs where I would attach the handle with some slip.

"Some I fire to make into hard bisque like those ones," I pointed indicating a shelf full of hard, white, fired clay vessels, "so that patrons can glaze their own."

"Yeah? What about the rest?"

"The rest I leave like this, unfinished, so that they can be carved and underglazes can be used."

"Carving sounds cool, underglaze sounds just like what you would think it would be."

"Yeah." I smiled faintly. "Some of them underglaze decals get used."

"What, like sheets?" he asked.

"Precisely," I said with a bigger smile.

"Sounds easy, which means it's probably hard as fuck to do," he said, and I laughed.

"Easier than you'd think. Hard in that you really do have to get placement just right on the first try. A lot like getting the stencil placed for a tattoo."

He looked up. "You don't have any tattoos. How would you know that?" he asked.

"My brother, Copper," I said. "He took me with him once, lost a bet and I got to pick his next tattoo."

"Oh, man. I hope you picked something awful."

I giggled. "I did!" The memory made me laugh so hard I cried. When I finally got ahold of myself, I said. "It was so awful, but it wasn't very big. It was a pair of cherries, but instead of stems, it had a cock nestled between them, half flaccid and dripping cum."

"Holy shit, I've seen those flash art pieces and just – *why?*"

"He was being a dick, that's why! I didn't expect him to go through with it. I mean, it was utterly ridiculous, but he did, right here." I tapped the outside of my ankle over my jeans. "I told him he could cover it up, but he wouldn't hear of it. He kept it, and any time anyone would ask him, he would say his sister picked it and he was so *proud* of it." I shook my head. "This little half-mast dick with its little cherry balls."

Fenris laughed, and laughed with me, then wiping a tear from his eye said, "Well, you're never picking one of my tats if that's what I'm going to end up with."

It spurred another peal of laughter out of me and I shook my head.

"I wouldn't do that to you unless you really deserved it. Copper was something else," I said with a heavy sigh. "We went back and forth, you know?"

"Yeah," he said quietly, evenly. "It was the same between me and my sister, Lacy."

I looked up and our eyes met, a silent understanding of each other's pain passing between us and that one look spoke such *volumes* to me and was probably the most singular expression of *you are not alone* that I had ever seen or felt.

"Thanks," I whispered softly, and he must have felt it too, because he didn't question me at all. He simply ducked his head in a nod, and we went back to our respective creative endeavors.

It was nice – peaceful, sweet, soothing to the soul which was just what I needed right then.

"Got any big ideas on what you want to do tonight?" he asked.

"Mm-mm, no. I figured we would just go with the flow," I said with a gusty sigh.

"You feel up to people?" he asked me, and I appreciated that he did.

"Maybe tomorrow. I mean, I didn't know what you had planned for tomorrow, if it involved anyone else."

"Actually, now that you mention it," he said. "Yeah, my boy Dump Truck and his girl Little Bird were going to join us on our Sunday ride."

I perked up a bit at the thought of meeting some of his friends and club.

"Yeah?"

"Yeah, I mean is that cool with you?"

"Yes! Absolutely! I just get tired after all day of something like this and I don't know if I would make good company for other people."

"That's fair," he said with a nod. "I get the same way after a long day of farm chores sometimes. Other times, I just want to get out with some *people* after all day with the goats."

"Oh, believe me, I get that," I said with a laugh. As cute as they may be, they were *a lot* of work.

"So, a quiet night in?" he asked after a bit. "Maybe watch a movie?"

"That sounds absolutely lovely," I declared.

He grinned at me. "Good deal."

CHAPTER SIXTEEN

Fenris...

I called up Mav just to make sure I wasn't needed for anything tonight. He put me off and told me to relax and take care of my lady friend and I thought that damn, word traveled fast. Of course, with Little Bird, Marisol, and Dahlia as thick as thieves, that didn't really surprise me much. All roads led back to Mav when it came to Marisol and Dahlia.

I sighed and looked up, taking another hit off the joint in my hand as I waited for Aspen to come out the back door. I was going to ride, she was going to drive, but I still didn't much feel like leaving without her.

Today felt good. Like she was hitting the apex of the curve on her grief. That any second, she would come around the bend and follow it out onto the open road of her new beginning. I had yet to brooch the topic of a new lawyer. I had no desire to kick her back into the pit of despair that she'd only begun to crawl her way out of.

She was doing good. Doing much better, much quicker, than I expected. I was glad I'd been right about taking a break from that place, but I knew it couldn't be forever, that she'd have to go back soon and face the ghosts of memory, and tackle the piles of stuff and the thoughts and whatnot that came with them.

I got the impression that Aspen's childhood had somehow set her up for failure when it came to her douche lord ex-husband. I cracked knuckles and sighed. There would be no putting a hurt on the asshole. Aspen just wasn't that way and I was far from wanting to corrupt her so thoroughly as to bend her that direction. Violence was my gig, the thing I had to reckon with. The demon that raged inside my skull and gods be praised; the thing that was finally fucking *quiet* when I was around this woman.

She had me know peace, a feat that was not easily managed when it came to me, but one she managed to make look like it was as effortless as breathing. Like when she molded the earth between her hands into such beautiful things.

I closed my eyes and pictured her slick fingers, pressing against the mound of shapeless clay as it spun on her wheel – giving it form, giving it life, turning it into something useful and beautiful.

I felt like she was doing the same to me, shaping me into a better person by just her mere presence and it was nice. It felt good, and I liked it.

Like I had meaning again aside from the usual: being a blunt weapon of force.

"Fenris, what's wrong?" she called from the back door, shutting it tightly and turning back to it with her keys, locking it up.

"Nothing!" I called back, and I went to take another hit off my joint only to discover it'd gone out. I tucked it behind my ear instead as she practically skipped down the back steps to come to me.

"Oooh." She pulled back and wrinkled her nose.

"Not a fan of the ganja?" I asked.

"Not the smell, I don't care about it otherwise."

"Oh yeah? You use?"

"Edibles sometimes," she said with a shrug. "Helps when my back is all tight."

"Good to know," I said with a bit of a smile. "I'd like to get you buzzed and fuck you slow."

She blushed and murmured, "I think I'd be down to try that."

"Not outside your comfort zone?" I asked while studying her face.

Yeah, it was, but I could see it before she said it. "It is, but the more I think about it, the more I could come around."

I chuckled and kissed her temple. "I got a better adventure in store for you tomorrow that doesn't involve mind-altering substances."

"Oh yeah?" she quirked an eyebrow. "Where we going?"

"That's for me to know and for you to find out." I gave her gorgeous ass a little swat and sent her in the direction of her Prius.

"Meet you back at my place," I said. "I'm right behind you."

"Okay," she agreed softly.

We went back to my place, my pops coming back to the house from the barn calling out to me as I shut off the bike. "Hey, what you two got planned for tonight?"

"Quiet one in," I called back, and he nodded.

"Good deal, you got the place to yourself," he said.

"Aw yeah? How's that?"

"Headed out to the cabin with Mitch for some fishin' at the lake."

"Alright, good deal." I nodded.

"How you doin', Aspen?" he called out to my girl, and I felt my eyebrows go up. He never gave a fuck about any of the women I'd brought around before.

"I'm good, Vyking. How about you?"

"Doin' alright."

They chatted, and I stood kind of gobsmacked, lookin' at my dad like he'd grown some kind of second head. Aspen shouldered her purse and her briefcase and came around her car. She and my pops went back and forth amicably for a moment and I watched the exchange, curious.

My old man was a mystery sometimes, and this was one of them. Like, *hadn't he just been the one warning my ass off of her? What the fuck?*

I held out my hand to my woman at a natural break in the conversation and she came to me, slipping her hand into mine.

"Well, have fun at the cabin," she said with a laugh.

"Not as much as you two are plannin' to do," my dad said with a lecherous wink which sent Aspen into a slightly uncomfortable giggle, her face flushing pink.

"Why you always gotta be a creepy asshole?" I muttered, and my dad laughed.

"Just remember, boy, you're a chip off the ol' block."

I rolled my eyes and shot back, "I think I got enough of Mom in me to balance me out." His face fell into a bit of a glower.

"You sure about that?" he asked as I led Aspen through the back door in front of me.

"Maybe not as much as I'd like," I conceded. That'd been a low fuckin' blow even for me, but he'd made my girl uncomfortable, even if he didn't mean shit by it. I think I'd given him a sharp enough reminder to stay in his own fuckin' lane. We made eye contact, and he gave me a nod.

We were cool, he knew and could accept what I was puttin' down, picking it up just fuckin' fine.

"Sorry about him," I said as I shut the door behind us. "Sometimes he gets too familiar, too quick."

"Oh, it's fine," Aspen declared.

"No, it wasn't, and it won't happen again," I promised.

"You don't need to talk to him about it or anything," she said soothingly, and I grinned at her.

"You're cute," I told her. "I just did. My dad and I have a long history of fuckin' with each other. Doesn't mean he gets to mess with you, not until you're ready. The thing to know is you gotta dish it right back. You can't let him roll you. He'll lose respect, quick."

She nodded and considered me a moment then said, "Your family has some strange ways."

I chuckled. "Ain't nothing to do with family. My dad was in prison for a lot of mine and my sister's childhood. We're more club brothers than father and son in a lot of ways."

"Oh, that's right, I'm sorry," she murmured.

"Nothing to apologize for, baby. Just explains a few things, yeah?"

She smiled and nodded then said, "Let me put this upstairs and then, I guess it's all down to what are we watching?"

"What are you hungry for?" I asked, and she twisted her lips back and forth in indecision. "What *don't* you like?" I asked finally.

"Not a big fan of green peppers," she said honestly, but I could tell she was drawing a blank otherwise.

"I'll order a pizza, no green peppers. Mushrooms and olives okay?"

"Yeah, those are good."

"Okay, go do your thing and meet me back down here," I said, divesting myself of my jacket and cut, hanging them by the back door.

"Okay," she said with a smile and went upstairs.

I pulled my phone out of my pants pocket and pulled up the food delivery app, placing my usual order just no green peppers.

We ate, we talked, shared some laughs and I realized that Aspen was incredibly easy to talk to. Not only that, we enjoyed enough of the same things that the conversation never really strayed into territory that made either of us uncomfortable.

I too, realized, that she was *incredibly* laid back – like on a deep level – none of this surface fake ass shit that women liked to pretend to be. *Oh, I'm so laid back!* Until you realized that no, no they weren't. Of course, Aspen didn't really feel the need to talk herself up in that regard. She just *was*, and it made her even more beautiful to me.

"What do you want to watch?" I asked her and I genuinely didn't know what to expect her to say.

"You pick first," she said. "I'm horribly indecisive and if you leave it to me, we're going to spend all night trying to find something to do."

"Oh, I'm going to have no trouble at all finding something to do when it comes to you," I said with a wink.

She blushed and laughed and threw a balled-up napkin at me, hitting me in the arm.

I laughed with her, but I had something in mind. Something I'd seen probably a thousand times, enjoyed, but it would let me focus on the woman I intended to have in my arms for the whole show.

"You ever read any Michael Crichton?" I asked.

"What, like *Jurassic Park*?" she asked, taking a bite of her pizza.

"Well, yeah, that's what he's most known for but I mean like *Timeline*, or *The 13th Warrior*."

"Mm-mm," she hummed as she chewed, shaking her head.

"Have you ever seen *The 13th Warrior*?" I asked.

"Mm." She nodded, swallowed, and said, "A long time ago. Isn't that the one with Antonio Banderas?"

"The one and the same," I answered. "It was based on the book *The Eaters of the Dead* by Michael Crichton, but in actuality, the first three chapters of that book are based on the actual Arab dude's journal. Like he was real, and actually alive and traveled with these Viking dudes."

"And the rest?" she asked, genuinely interested.

"Loosely based on *Beowulf*," I answered.

"It's been so long since I've seen it," she said. "I don't really remember it. I think it sounds great, though."

"Yeah?"

"Yeah!"

"Awesome, go on upstairs and find some comfortable clothes. I'll clean up down here, get things cued up on the big screen, and then do the same and we'll settle in for the night. Sound good?"

"Sounds great," she agreed.

"Go team," I joked, and she laughed and got up.

She went upstairs, I cleaned up, and found the DVD among the racks against the one living room wall and got things ready. She was brushing her teeth in her adorable country nightgown when I went up to change myself.

"All good?" I asked, and she smiled shyly around her toothbrush and nodded.

I would keep her here forever if I could. It was nice having a woman here. Someone to come home to. Someone to hold and to wake up in the middle of the night with, her cuddled into my side, holding me.

I was going to miss this when she went back to Tacoma.

I was hoping that we could keep something going. That she would want that with me.

I went into my bedroom and changed into a pair of flannel

pajama bottoms and a thermal shirt. It was getting colder at night, the autumn rains rolling in. The chill and the damp rolling in could sometimes permeate the house and I didn't want to turn on the heat, not yet. I wanted Aspen close and cozy, so I split the difference and pulled a warm, microfiber blanket, down from the top of my closet.

"Here, take this down for me," I murmured and passed it to her in the hallway. "I'll be down in a minute."

"Okay." she smiled and hugged the blanket to her and disappeared down the stairs.

I rushed through brushing my own teeth and with a sigh, looked at myself in the mirror above the bathroom sink.

Not for the first time I asked myself, *was this fair to her? Getting involved like this?* I wouldn't typically describe myself as a particularly insecure man, but she brought it out in me somehow. Like, I genuinely worried about disappointing her. About letting her down. About doing to her what my dad did to my mom.

I mean, he knew… but he hadn't been there to actually *see it*. I had – the weeping, the longing, the loneliness and waiting. The guilt when she couldn't do it. When she couldn't go on that way, and finally the anger and bitter resentment for my pops having put her through it.

I could handle a lot of shit, but I don't know if I would be able to handle my woman looking at me the way my mom looked at my dad on the last visit she ever took me and Lacy on to see him when he'd been locked up.

How she'd sent us to stand in the corner to talk to him alone. How his expression had iced over and how he'd looked at our mother with a calculated and almost murderous stare when she told him she was moving on without him, and not only that, how she was taking us kids along for that particular ride.

My dad had lost his whole family that day and that shit had been *fucked*. I don't know if I was willing to repeat history. You know?

So, don't get caught, a deriding voice from within said.

If only it were that easy.

I mean, Aspen had already caught me, thoroughly entangling me in her web, and I couldn't for one second say I was sorry for myself on that score.

It just remained to be seen if I would be sorry for her.

I pushed off the counter and left the bathroom, switching out the light. With a determined sigh at not being caught out over my inner dilemma, I went down to the waiting woman in my living room, to hold her, to love her like she asked, and to cement the good memories in place before it all went to hell and the good times were a thing of the past.

It wasn't exactly pessimism. It was how the life went. You seized the good times while you had them because the bad times were always on your tail.

CHAPTER SEVENTEEN

Aspen...

I smiled up at Fenris as he came around the corner from the stairwell. He smiled back at me and I edged down the couch to make room for him, the blanket clutched to me.

"Let me get this going. You alright with lying down so I can spoon you?" he asked.

"That actually sounds really great," I murmured.

It took us a minute to get situated, but once we were? Pure and epic bliss. I can't tell you how much I loved being cuddled by Fenris. How safe, warm, and appreciated I felt. How utterly and thoroughly I felt spoiled by his affections.

"This is nice," I murmured, burrowed back into the warmth of his body, the warmth of mine reflected back at me from the cozy blanket over the top of us.

"Have to agree, babe. I have to agree," he said and pressed a kiss to where my neck sloped into my shoulder. I sighed in contentment and he started the movie.

God, we were like a pair of teenagers. The movie played, but it was really just background noise when the light touching began – a soundtrack to my whimpering moans and desire for more as that light touching turned to heavy petting.

Fen gathered the skirt of my nightgown, rucking it up with one fist, pulling it away from my pussy before cupping it with his big hand, grinding fingertips against my clit as he used his other hand to tip my chin and claim my mouth with his.

I was stretched taut, arched back, as he played with my pussy and stroked his tongue against mine. I gripped a fistful of his pajama pant in one hand, the other forgotten and useless as I gave myself over completely to his touch.

He moaned appreciatively into my mouth and I groaned into his sweet surrender. I didn't care. He could do whatever he wanted to me; I would submit happily to whatever he wanted me to do so long as he kept on making me feel this way.

He broke our kiss and sucked in a breath between his teeth as I ground my ass back against his erection.

"Oh, baby girl," he moaned coarsely. "You keep doing that and I'm going to take you right on this couch."

"Mmm." I moaned the imagery decadent, and with a slow sexy smile made my move.

"Not if I take you first," I said, and he chuckled darkly and sat up as I got up. I gripped his waistband in both hands and he lifted his hips so I could free his waiting cock. A low thrum of excitement coursed through me and I already knew that I was more than wet enough to take him. He had that effect on me.

I rucked my nightgown up and mounted him, a knee to either side of his hips and he helped me, pushing his cock down so it jutted at the right angle between us.

His aim was perfect. The head of his cock sinking into my pussy like he was meant to fucking be there and I can't tell you how much I *loved* that.

"Oh, fuck, Aspen," he moaned, voice deep with wonder and that oh-so-sexy growl of his. "Just like that, baby." He slapped my ass, the mark stinging and sweet. "Ride me, baby girl. Ride me and fucking touch yourself while you do it. I want to watch you."

I would do anything for him, and what he asked of me was definitely no hardship. I held my nightgown out of my way with one hand and pressed fingertips from my other against my clit, rubbing delicious circles as I rose and fell along his shaft. God, I was so wet, he was so hard, and we were so perfect for one another.

He fit me as though it were meant to be, as if we were two halves of the same whole, and I never wanted anyone or anything different again with how good he felt.

I kissed him, holding his face between my hands as I rocked my hips and ground myself against him and oh, God, the delicious sensations that came from that! It was a wonderful, beautiful, sharing and I didn't fight him when he whisked my nightgown off over the top of my head and tossed it aside. He did the same with his long-sleeved shirt that clung to his upper body showcasing just a hint of his fantastic physique. God, when that physique was revealed to my eyes, covered in his beautiful tattoos, I felt my pussy throb of its own accord in delight.

This man was so wonderful, so gorgeous to my eyes, I almost couldn't stand it. He was that kind of man most women would stop mid-sentence and stare at from across the room. He had that bad boy appeal that drove most women nuts and had them seriously fantasizing inside three minutes, and here I was with him inside me, and I swear, he looked at me almost the same way.

I kissed him, not knowing or wanting to take anything for granted, but finding myself wishing anyway that this could and would last.

"Lean back, baby. I've got you." I did as I was told, trusting him, and he did indeed, have me. His broad hands at my lower back arms at my hips, held me up as I arched back, and he adjusted his sitting position.

Oh, my God.

I'd never felt anything like it as he moved inside of me, his cock hitting that spot that sent shivers out from my center, the tingling energy building in such a way, I almost swore I could come from it and it alone.

I'd never been able to do that before. I always had to get my clit involved to orgasm, but in Fenris' grasp, I was absolutely willing to believe anything was possible and it was as though he were a man possessed, determined to prove anything were possible.

He drove himself up inside me with these short little strokes, agitating that secret place inside of me that sent stardust through my veins and took me to such unearthly heights. Higher and higher we climbed, and I gasped in rhythmic splendor at the sensations he wrought throughout my body.

All the while he loved me like this, he whispered encouraging things, telling me I was beautiful, how good I felt, how sexy I was, all of these things that were almost impossible to believe, I mean, *me?* Surely, all of those things couldn't be true about *me.* Yet with every thrust, every grunt, through every groan of pleasure he took in me? He edged me not only closer to my own orgasm, but closer and closer still toward *believing,* which was almost more pleasurable and wonderful than I could take.

"Oh, God, oh, God, Fenris, I'm going to come!" I cried and his hold tightened on me even as I tightened *around him* just that last little bit. It took only one or two final jerking little thrusts to run himself over my G-spot and I came completely undone. The feral sound of my pleasure climbed from my throat and spilled out of my mouth in a veritable wolf's howl of pleasure directed toward the ceiling, as he cried out himself and lost all semblance of rhythm, plunging into the warm bathwater abyss of afterglow sensation with me.

We came back to one another almost too quickly, both panting, both shattered and still on the mend. It felt like Kintsugi to me. The artform out of Japan of mending broken things with gold at the seams. A beautiful way of recognizing the history of the object in question. I smiled down at Fenris and kissed him softly with gratitude – for mending me so beautifully, and for becoming a part of my history; that no matter what happened from here on out would always remain a treasured memory.

I felt a deep awakening of emotion in that moment, frightening in its intensity. As he looked into my eyes, I saw it reflected in his, but also something deep and unspoken on his side – something akin to fear.

"What is it? What's wrong?" I asked softly, turning his face back to mine gently with my hands when he looked away.

"Nothing," he lied and tried a smile, but it slipped away along with mine.

"You know, I think I knew," I confessed, and it was hard to say out loud.

"Knew what?" he asked, clear blue eyes clouding with concern even as he softened inside of me.

"That Charles was lying. I think I knew for a long time. A lot longer than I even want to admit to myself," I said. Fenris' arms tightened around me and I leaned back over them slightly to keep his face in view. "The vibe you're putting off right now is the same," I said, sorrow swirling in my breast. "You're lying to me," I murmured. "And I can't tell you how much that hurts."

"Oh, shit. Babe, no. It's not like that… It's not like that at all."

"Then please, talk to me… what's wrong?" I asked gently.

He sighed, heavily, and said without looking at me, "This is nice. Probably the nicest thing I've ever had, but I can't help but worry that I'm not the right kind of man for you."

"Why?" I asked, stricken. Of all the things to come out of his mouth, I somehow hadn't expected that at all. I mean, Fenris was so… *confident.* Why on earth would he ever think something like that?

"There are some things I can't tell you, that I'll never be able to tell you, you have to understand that."

I felt my shoulders drop in something akin to defeat. *Secrets.* I felt like I'd had my fill of secrets as of late… but something deep inside me, despite the instant misgivings, told me to hear him out.

"Explain," I urged, and he reached down to the floor and pulled the blanket up around my shoulders, tucking it around me to keep my warm as the struggle of what to say crossed his gorgeous features.

"It's the life," he said finally. "We live by our own set of rules," he said.

"Like what?" I asked softly.

"In a lot of ways, it's simpler than what you live by as a citizen," he said. "In other ways, it's a lot more complicated."

"Give me an example," I murmured, caressing the side of his face, temple to chin, down the side of his neck, along his collarbone, over the swell of his shoulder, down his arm. I couldn't help but smile gently as he closed his eyes and at the wave of gooseflesh that erupted in the wake of my touch.

I don't think I'd ever affected someone so thoroughly before, and I really kind of liked it. I liked it a lot.

"For example, violence is sort of a way of life for us. We don't hide from it. We don't shrink from it. A motherfucker needs his ass kicked; we kick it."

"Okay, hypothetically, why would a motherfucker need his ass kicked?" I asked and Fenris chuckled, touching the bottom of my chin with a crooked forefinger, pulling down on my bottom lip gently with his thumb at my language.

"Kiss me with that dirty mouth," he said and his voice was warm with a low, seductive heat.

I kissed him gently, chastely, but leaned back up out of reach and arched an eyebrow expectantly.

"A lot of reasons. Disrespecting me, one of my brothers, my property."

"What, like touching your bike or something?" I asked.

He nodded. "Or you," he said and I blinked, an abrupt laugh sneaking out of my throat before I could stop it, but on second thought...

"I'm not your *property*, I'm a *woman*."

He smiled and nodded, giving me a little swat on the ass beneath the blanket.

"My woman, for all intents and purposes at the moment," he said.

I softened a bit at that, a fission of anxiety trilling down my spine at his words. I mean, it sounded *really* nice, but it also sounded *way too soon*. I mean, wasn't it?

"What?" he asked cautiously at the expression that flitted across my face.

Honest to a fault, I told him exactly what I was thinking. "You're sure it's not too soon?" I asked softly.

He smiled and said, "There's another good example. That's you thinking like a citizen all the way. I don't give a *fuck* what anybody else thinks, baby. You're a treasure. Beautiful, gracious, smart, and kind. One touch from you soothes the rage and pain…" His hand slid along the side of my neck, fingers wrapping around the back, fingertips pressing and kneading at the spot at the base of my skull where all my tension, nervousness, and fear tended to hide.

I closed my eyes as he worked some of those things out of me with gentle fingertips and basked in the warmth of his startling compliment.

"What do you and the club do?" I asked softly.

"A bunch of random shit, mostly legal. Some of it should be legal." He lifted one shoulder in a shrug. "A bunch of it I can't and won't tell you."

"I don't like the idea of secrets," I whispered.

"It's not about keeping secrets from you, baby. It's about keeping you safe."

"Safe from what?" I asked, and put my hands lightly to his chest, pushing back just enough to let him know he had *better* answer that one.

He breathed in deep, in through his nose and out through his mouth in a great sigh.

"Arrest, mostly."

"You aren't into anything serious like illegal drugs, are you?" I demanded.

"Define illegal drugs," he said carefully.

"Meth, coke, heroine?" I listed the worst offenders off.

He shook his head. "No, none of that shit."

"Illegal guns?" I asked.

"Nope, none of those either," he said, and he met my gaze, dead serious. "Most of what you would consider an illegal drug is shit we hold for personal use, and I'm talking shit like Molly, none of it in quantities that could get any of us busted for selling."

"You do it?" I asked, worried.

He shook his head. "Nah, worst I do is weed to mellow out, and they legalized that shit so…"

I nodded carefully. "You hurt people, though," I whispered.

"Only if they really fucking deserve it, but I'm not going to lie to you. Yeah."

"That's really scary," I confessed.

"Why?" he asked, cocking his head, scanning my face, genuinely trying to understand.

"What if you get mad at me?" I asked quietly and couldn't look at him. He chased some of my hair behind my ear and turned me to face him, to look him in the eyes.

"Never going to happen. I'll go outside and break shit. Butcher some goats, maybe yell, maybe scream, but I will *never* lay a hand on you. If I did, my brothers would beat my fucking ass and rightfully so."

"They would?" I asked confused. "Why?"

"Part of the club's creed, the rules. No women, no children."

"Meaning?"

"Meaning we aren't animals. We're men, and we'll act like men, no matter what anybody says or thinks of us. We know what we're about. We don't hit women; we don't beat our children. Our vocab is a little different from the citizenry of the world," he explained.

"*'Property'* isn't just the land we own, or the house that sits on it. It's the things we would die for, the things we would kill for. Our bike is our property because it represents our freedom. Our colors, likewise, set us apart and represent our love, life, and loyalty to and for the club. Our women, our children, are likewise our property. We would kill for you; I would die for you. Not a second thought about it."

I stared at him and he stared back, letting his words fill the silence that stretched between us.

"It sounds sort of… romantic," I murmured and he smiled.

"Nothing real romantic about it since we're being honest."

I asked again, "Explain," and bit my bottom lip.

"Society has their own ideas about us," he answered. "Some of us, like my dad, got arrested. At any given moment, we could go away, do long stretches of time. That's not easy on our women or kids. Believe me, I lived it."

"Then why do you do it?" I asked.

"C'mere," he whispered, and I went to him. He put his arms around me and rubbed up and down my back through the blanket, cuddling me close. He sighed, hard, and said, "My dad went up on attempted murder charges," he answered.

"Oh, what happened?" I asked.

"He was at a bar with a couple of other brothers. The Sacred Hearts, we have a reputation," he murmured.

"I know," I whispered, and he chuckled.

"You don't know the half of it," he said mirthlessly, "Not discounting you, not trying to be a holier-than-thou asshole about it, it's just the truth. No matter what you've heard, the reality is likely ten times worse."

"Okay," I said cuddling close. "That's scary."

"Yeah, well, there are always some dumb motherfuckers trying to test their mettle with us, and that's what happened with my dad, Herbo, and Deacon that night. Some dumb motherfuckers full of too much piss and vinegar decided to try the Sacred Hearts on for size."

"Okay," I murmured.

"So, the fight goes down, my dad lost his shit, stabs one of these assholes who just won't quit with a broken beer bottle. The cops, of course, as always, take the side of the citizens and the prosecutors office, always with a hard-on for us, upped the ante on my dad from 'assault with a deadly' to 'attempted murder.' My pops rolled the dice on trial and rolled a one, got sent up for the max."

"Rolled a one?" I asked confused.

Fenris laughed. "Yeah, don't play D&D do you?" he asked.

"Dungeons and Dragons?" I asked.

"Yeah."

"No. I think Copper did, but I didn't really get into it. He and his friends were very 'girls aren't allowed' and I was usually busy making things with my mom."

"Ah, well, your brother and his friends were full of shit," he said. "D&D is for anyone who wants to play it, and one of the main things you do is roll a twenty-sided dice to figure out through some basic math how you did at any given action. To roll a one is to not only fail, but to *spectacularly* fail."

"Ah," I said, thoughts churning. I had a lot to think about.

A lot.

Fenris fell silent, and we just held each other, cuddling, comforting. Finally, he broke the silence and asked, "What are you thinking?"

"I don't know," I said honestly. "I mean, I don't really know if I can handle all of this, but I don't want to just give up, either. I don't want to just walk away." I pushed off of him so I could look him in the eyes. "I care about you too much, too deeply, to just walk away now."

"Not going to lie to you, ever," he said. "There will be times I just straight up won't tell you things, but I'll never lie to you, baby."

"Thank you," I whispered, not knowing what else to say.

"That being said, I care about you, too. I've never felt like this about any other woman before, ever."

"Ever?" I asked, breath stilling in my chest at the sincerity in his eyes.

"Ever," he said firmly.

"So, what are you saying?" I asked softly.

"I guess I'm saying it has the potential for it to hurt a lot less if you walked away now," he said, and the words, they stuck in his throat. He swallowed hard to get past the lump that had formed there at the thought of me walking away now.

I swallowed past the lump of fear in mine and took a deep breath, his clear emotion for me galvanizing my bravery.

"I'm not going to do that," I said, despite my fears.

"Yeah? Can I ask why not?"

"Yeah, and it's because for everything you think can go wrong, what happens if everything goes *right?*" I asked, my inner optimist shining through.

"Things rarely go one hundred percent according to plan, baby," he said.

"I would settle for sixty-forty," I murmured smiling, bringing my lips to his. He kissed me back and pulled back reluctantly.

"Can we maybe shoot for seventy-thirty? Or even seventy-five/twenty-five."

"Eighty-twenty?" I asked, and he chuckled. I felt him getting hard between us again.

"I like those odds better," he whispered. "You sure you want to take this ride?"

"You talking *this* ride?" I asked grinding my hips. "Or an actual relationship?" I asked.

"The latter," he answered in a low husky growl.

"We'll see," I whispered. "But I'm leaning toward 'definitely yes.'"

"I like those odds even better," he said and wrapped his arms around me tight and *stood up*.

I shrieked with laughter and surprise and he turned us both, laying me on the couch, rotating his hips and delving deep. My giggle turned into a moan.

"Hang on tight, baby. Don't ever let go," he whispered and his words had weight and meaning, deep beyond their surface meaning.

So deeply, I fell in love with this man, and his strange and many varied layers.

CHAPTER EIGHTEEN

Fenris…

"Hey, man. It's good to see you." I clasped hands with my brother and we pulled each other in, knocking shoulders.

"How're things going?" he asked, and I lifted one shoulder in a shrug.

"We'll see," I said. "She's citizen and I'm not sure this life would be good for her."

"We all have to start somewhere," Little Bird said with a brittle smile. Her indoctrination into the life had been a trial by fire, for sure.

"She's a good woman," I said with a half-smile.

Dump Truck asked, "Well, where is she?"

"She's comin'," I answered and looked back toward the house. "We gotta get her some gear."

"Oh, fun! Shopping!" Little Bird cried.

"After breakfast," Dump Truck said, and I grinned.

"Black Diamond Bakery?" I asked.

"Shit yeah," Dump Truck answered.

It was a beautiful day for a ride, skies high, clear, and blue. Leaves on the trees changing. Pavement was wet, but things were drying out. It was crisp, but not too bad. Perfect Pacific Northwest fall weather. Might not even need a jacket by the afternoon.

"There she is," Dump Truck grunted, and I turned around. There she was, alright. I smiled faintly. She did her best as I'd asked, but she was so not roadworthy in the safest sense of the word. Sneakers; not good, jeans which were fine, a thick sweater which would keep her warm but still not the best when it came to a slide, and a hooded L.L. Bean raincoat over that.

"Need to get her some fuckin' gear," Dump Truck grated in disapproval and I chuckled.

"I don't disagree, you fuckin' safety Nazi, but breakfast first, yeah?"

"Renton?" he asked.

"Do some research on what's closest when we sit down to breakfast," I said.

"Hi," Aspen said shyly when she reached us.

"Hey, baby." I took her under my arm and made introductions. "This is Dump Truck and this is his lady, Little Bird."

"Hi." Little Bird smiled and raised her hand curling her fingers in a wave.

"Nice to meet you, Aspen."

Aspen smiled up at DT and at Little Bird and asked laughing, "Is everyone in the club as tall as you two?" she asked. "Like is there some kind of a rule, you must be this tall to ride this ride?"

We all laughed. "Naw, we're the biggest," Dump Truck said.

"And the best," Little Bird said with a soft smile that made Aspen's grow.

"Alright, you ready to get this show on the road?" DT asked.

"Absolutely," Aspen said with a smile, but I caught the tightness around her eyes. She was a little trepid about her first ride and I was just plain excited to have her on the back of my bike. I'd already given her the rundown, asked if she'd ever ridden before to which she'd answered when she was a teen, on the back of her brother's old Honda.

This wasn't going to be that, but I was going to let her find that out all on her own once we got going.

I helped her into the lid I'd brought out for her. It was a little big, so I definitely put it on the list of gear we would get her today. Proper fit was important.

I was excited for a couple of reasons. One, as much as I loved riding with Dump Truck and Little Bird, I'd always sort of felt like a third wheel on the occasions we took a Sunday ride or whatever. This time, I was glad to have a lady of my own pressed to my back. The fact that lady was Aspen, was all the better.

I'd warned her about the rough parts of my world, but everybody's world had those. All of them different, some of them higher stakes than others but all of them equally high in the eyes of the people who lived them.

Just like with the bad, there was a lot of good. And one of the good things was the feeling of the ride. The wind rushing over and through you, the freedom and the feeling like flying. The excitement, the rush, the times you were a man on top of the world.

I wanted so badly for Aspen to feel all of those things and to know it wasn't always violence, grit, and mayhem. Just everything had its price.

She got onto the back of my bike, behind me, and I started it up, engine rumbling, Dump Truck's roaring to life just behind mine in a sweet, bass, rumble. We nodded at each other, me and DT, indicating our ready, and the girls tightening their holds on us, we let out the clutch and carefully wheeled around to leave, maneuvering carefully over the loose gravel and not for the first time I thought to myself, *I really had to finish paving this drive around the fuckin' farm.*

My pops and I made more progress every summer, but if I was gonna have precious cargo behind me, I needed to step up my game around here.

We rode up through the hills around Auburn along the Auburn-Black Diamond road. It was a bit dodgy going around wet, fallen leaves in certain spots, but not too bad. I was way more anxious than I ought to be with Aspen behind me without her being properly geared up, but we would fix that as soon as possible. Dump Truck was right, though. We needed to eat first, and we wanted to show the girls a good time.

We pulled up outside the Black Diamond Bakery and Café pretty much at the start of the Sunday rush. Church people coming in droves in their Sunday best, mingling with families from the surrounding area, that just like us, were looking for a decent breakfast and to get out of the house on a nice fall day.

We went up and put our name in with the hostess, little kids staring up at us in unabashed awe and the girls giggling at their expressions. Their giggles ceasing when parents snatched their little darlings away, scolding them for staring around death glares shot in our direction.

Aspen looked a little wilted around the edges and I massaged her shoulders. She was sweet. Sweet as the doughnuts and cakes in the bakery's glass cases, that we went over and looked at next while we waited to be called for our table.

"I've never been here before," Aspen said, looking over the fresh baked breads on the shelves behind the bakery counter.

"They've got good stuff," Little Bird said. "I like their Crystal Mountain bread."

"Tell you what," DT said. "Let's get some of that, and a few other things, then when we're done eatin,' we can wander down the other end to the Smokehouse and get some meats and things. Make some sandwiches and shit for lunch later."

"Sounds good, my brother." I nodded, and we put in an order for a few things.

"You got any of that Coal Candy?" I asked and the bakery lady looked dejected.

"No, the guy at the Firehouse that made it retired, and we haven't been able to source it anywhere else."

"Damn," I muttered. "That was some good shit."

The bakery lady smiled and nodded. "I really miss it, too."

Aspen asked, "What's that?"

"Oh, Black Diamond used to be a mining town," I explained. "Coal."

"Black Diamond, coal, makes sense," she said nodding.

"Right, so they used to have this shit called 'Coal Candy' here, and it was just black rocks of sugar that tasted like black licorice.

Used to love that shit. Before my dad got sent up, he used to bring me up here, and we'd leave suckin' on that stuff. Mom used to hate it." I laughed. "Turned our mouths all black and made us look all ghoulish."

Aspen smiled, and I loved having someone to tell this shit too. My mom fuckin' hated those trips for a lot of reasons. The coal candy was just one more thing to spread her dislike to. She would go to work on the weekends, and my dad would put both me *and* my sister on the back of his bike to come up here when we were small enough but old enough to hang on. She thought it was dangerous, and it was, but fuck it. It was a different time, you know?

"Um, Dump Truck? Table of four?" the hostess called and me and my brother grinned at each other at the note of confusion in her voice.

"Yeah, that's us," DT grated and limped her way; Little Bird trailing behind him. I put Aspen in front of me and brought up the rear as we threaded through tables towering above the craven citizens around us that shrank in their seats or in some cases, studiously avoided looking in our direction as though if they didn't acknowledge us, we wouldn't actually exist.

That shit put a smile on my face, not gonna lie. These idiots didn't have the first clue about what it meant to really live. They never would, and that was no skin off my testicles.

We took our seats, DT and I both seeing to our women's comfort before our own, making sure their jackets were hung on the backs of their chairs, their purses accounted for, and that ever-present annoying shoving their chairs into the backs of their knees because it was the right thing to do. I asked Aspen, "You want I should get your chair for you, or you in the future? I always feel bad knocking the shit out the backs of a lady's knees."

She laughed and smiled at me, her green eyes luminous. "I actually don't mind. I even like it," she said. "Call me old-fashioned that way."

"Never," I said with a grin. "It makes you feel good, I'll keep doing it."

She blushed at the double entendre which made my smile grow.

Little Bird looked back and forth between us at the exchange, her smile infectious and causing DT to smile himself.

We took our time overlooking the menus, ordered our drinks and perused them some more, each of us folding them closed and setting them aside as we made our decisions.

Aspen was the first to break the silence asking, "So, what's the plan for the rest of the day?"

"Gotta get you geared up, little lady," Dump Truck declared, stretching out his bad leg. "Don't ever want you to earn your broken wings, but if it should go down that you do? You need to be in all the gear all the time to give you the best chance of getting 'em and not just getting dead in the process."

"I'm sorry? Broken wings?" she asked, brow wrinkling in confusion.

He pulled up his cut and pointed at the patch on it with a pair of wings, feathers coming off 'em, wrapped around a black and orange sign that read *broken wings*.

"Oh! So, the little patches all mean different things?" she asked, as if it had just occurred to her.

Little Bird laughed lightly and said, "I thought the same thing. It's like a whole other language like the Egyptians and their cartouches."

"*Fascinating,*" Aspen said, staring at our cuts with new eyes.

"So, what do the broken wings mean? That you've been in an accident?"

"Yup, and survived," I answered.

"How I got my road name, too. I got hit by a fucking dump truck."

"*Holy shit,* and you *survived that?*" Aspen's mouth dropped open in shock.

"Barely," DT answered, shifting in his seat. "Fucked my ass up but good. Permanent damage to my leg, some permanent hardware in a few places," he sniffed and cleared his throat, "but I'm here."

Little Bird reached for his hand that rested on the table and clutched it. He looked over at her like she was his world, and she was. He smiled at her.

"Good thing, too. Could have missed out on the best thing to ever happen to me."

"Aww." Aspen smiled. "You two are seriously like relationship goals," she said.

I reached over beneath the table and massaged the top of her thigh through her jeans, intending, if she gave me the chance, to prove that we could meet and smash every goal she ever held in her heart for being one half of a mated pair.

"So, what do the other patches mean?" she asked.

"That's a question for later, baby. We can't be giving away all our secrets now," I said, and she smiled at me and nodded.

"You know, Mace gets out next week?" Dump Truck said, steering the conversation to safety.

"Yes, he does. We riding out to pick his ass up?" I asked.

"We certainly are," he said.

"Are the girls invited on this trip?" Little Bird asked.

"You know it. It's gonna be one hell of a party that night."

"What day is it?" Aspen asked.

"Gets out on Tuesday," I answered. "You'll be working, but I'd love to have you come up to the club for the party once we get in."

"You're sure?" she asked smiling.

"More than," I said.

"Gets pretty wild, fair warning," Dump Truck said.

"Yeah?" Aspen asked, the misgivings flitting across her fair face.

I gave her leg another squeeze, reassuring like, under the table and told her, "A lot of booze, a lot of laughs, and even a lot of pussy – but just a good time. That's all, baby."

She laughed a bit, a mix of incredulous and nervous and I winked at her. That settled her into a smile, and I knew she had questions. She could ask me all the questions she wanted when we were alone and I would do my level best to answer them.

"Can I ask what sent your friend to prison?" she asked softly.

"I like the way you phrased that," Dump Truck said.

"Why?" she asked.

"Non-judgmental," Little Bird answered her. "Usually, when

someone has spent time in jail or prison it's automatically assumed, they deserved it."

"Exactly," Dump Truck said. "Look like one of us, it's automatically assumed we're all criminals, too." He took a sip of his coffee. "I don't have a record."

"Me either," I declared. Not that I'd never done anything wrong by citizen standards, mind you. I'd just never been fuckin' caught.

I flashed on holding the de-fleshed skull of one of my sister's rapists between my hands, slick with blood as I yanked his fuckin' teeth out with the needle nose pliers, the smell of the gore, like wet copper stuffing my damn nose.

I shook my head a little more forcefully than the denial required to clear the image from my mind and kick it back down the dark hole of memory where it'd crawled out of.

"So, what happened?" Aspen asked. "In your friend's case."

"Assault Two," Dump Truck answered. "Some fuckin' asshole in a cage nearly ran him off the road. Mace got a little hyped up on his adrenaline, got pissed off – rightfully so – and took off after him. Ripped him out of his car at a stoplight and beat the brakes off of him with a set of brass knuckles."

"Jesus!" Aspen cried.

"Guy could have killed him," I said unhappily.

"Nearly did," Dump Truck said. "Can't let that type of shit stand."

"Anyway, Mace plead out, got sent up for three years, has only been locked up for half of it. Would have been out sooner but there was a prison yard fight. Ended up getting caught up in it trying to defend a homeboy of his so they tacked on six months," I told her.

She nodded carefully and was clearly trying to process it all.

The topic changed again, thanks to Little Bird, and I could kiss my best friend's girl for saving the day and from distracting Aspen from thinking about the bad things for too long. I'd meant for today to be about showing her the good things and I felt like I was fucking that up.

I mean, reality dictated that at some point, Aspen's indoctrination into the life would become a bit of a baptism by fire. That was sort of always the way these kinds of things went.

I just needed to make sure she was as prepared as possible for it but seeing was believing and there was really only so much I could do on that front. I would be lying if I said I wasn't worried. Still, only time would fuckin' tell. All I could do was keep this longship on an even keel and hope that the gods smiled upon me.

CHAPTER NINETEEN

*A*spen...

To ride with Fenris was nothing short of amazing. The faster we went around swoops and curves the more I could believe the wind washing over and around us carried the burned broken bits of my soul to a better place. The ashes of my marriage stripped away leaving new growth in their place. Raw still, sure, but new and alive and soaking up the light from the sky leaving me feeling refreshed, and my spirit renewed.

I couldn't believe I'd forgotten how *freeing* this was.

I breathed cleanly, the crisp fall day rejuvenating in its own way as we wound our way to the freeways and to the guys' favorite Harley-Davidson dealership.

Dump Truck and Little Bird went in ahead of us and Fenris stopped me at the door.

"Hey," he said, tipping my chin lightly with his crooked finger in that way that made my heart beat faster and the butterflies take flight in my stomach.

"Yeah?" I asked.

"I don't want you thinking that I expect you to pay for any of this," he said.

"I-um, I hadn't thought about it, actually. I thought we were just here looking?" *Shit*, I really *hadn't* thought about it. My head was so full of information from the breakfast conversation that I was still trying to parse through that I hadn't put one thought toward what we were doing here.

"No, babe. I want you to ride in safety, so we're going in there, we're going to get you the best gear money can buy, and I don't want to hear shit else about it. I mean it. This is on me."

I stared up at him, not in disbelief, because I could *see* he was very much so serious. More, I guess, stunned? Surprised? I mean, we were moving awfully fast, but then again, wasn't that how they lived? Didn't they just get through telling me as much?

"Talk to me," he said in that gentle, hushed way that made me feel so ludicrously safe.

"I guess I'm just overwhelmed," I whispered. "You've been so generous and I... I just don't know what to think. There's some real cognitive dissonance and—"

Little Bird came to the door and reached out, capturing my hand with both of hers and dramatically tugged on me with an exaggerated, "Ugh! Come on!" effectively cutting me off from what I was trying to convey.

I laughed, and Fenris nodded at her. He met my eyes with his and that one look conveyed that we would definitely talk later, but also said with his smile and those beautiful blue eyes of his – right now, life was supposed to be fun.

"Anything she likes, whatever she needs," he called to Little Bird who smiled at him serenely and called back, "Roger that!"

"Are they always this intense?" I asked quietly, and she grinned at me.

"Yes, and I know it's a lot to wrap your mind around – the casual violence and all of that, but I promise you there's nothing 'casual' about it to them. Their perceptions vary wildly from the citizen norm."

"I just don't get that," I murmured. "The 'us vs. them' mentality."

Little Bird sighed and took us over to the shoe section, sitting down with me on the bench there.

"I didn't either, at first," she said. "Then I realized that it all boiled down to they're heartily sick of the bullshit, and it's *all* bullshit."

"I still don't get it," I said with a little laugh and she smiled at me, her deep brown eyes warm and her general demeanor sweet. She was effervescent, and a breath of fresh air. A delightful personality from what I had seen so far.

She heaved a sigh and blew out her cheeks.

"Sometimes it's tough to put into words," she said. "Let's put it this way, you remember what we were talking about when it came to Mace?"

"Yes, of course," I said. "We were only just talking about it."

"Right, so this man intentionally tried to run Mace off the road, right?"

"Right, I remember," I said.

"Now imagine Mace did everything you're supposed to do in a scenario like that. Imagine, he pulled over, called the police, and gave him all this guy's information. What do you think would have happened?"

"I don't know," I said. "I suppose it would be naïve of me that anything would."

"Kind of, yeah," she said with a bit of a wince. "It's okay, though. I was there once, too."

"It's a good question, though. What *would* the police do?" I wondered aloud.

"Taken a report and filed it under 'who gives a shit,'" an acerbic woman's voice declared. Little Bird looked up sharply past me and her eyes lit up.

"Dahlia! What are you doing here?"

"Meh, went out for hangover food with Tic-Tac," the woman said, putting her sunglasses up on top of her head and dropped down on the bench on my other side. "We ended up here at the toy store." She rolled her eyes. "I should make him buy me something."

Little Bird laughed and made introductions, "Dahlia, this is Aspen. Aspen, this is Dahlia."

Dahlia was pretty in that pinup girl style sort of way, her black hair up in a red bandana Rosie the Riveter style. She held out a hand with long red nails and I took it. She gave it a sharp shake and asked, "This the one Fen's been skulking around about?"

"Dahlia!" Little Bird said aghast.

"I can see why; I can also see why you're here." She looked me up and down critically and said, "You look like a citizen."

I laughed nervously and blushed furiously with my discomfort.

"I, um, guess I kind of am one. I'm trying to understand. I don't really know how it all works, really…"

"Honey, it's okay," she said, giving me a pointed look. "First thing's first. We gotta get you looking the part." She looked over at Little Bird and asked, "What have you picked out so far?"

Little Bird laughed and said, "We haven't even gotten started."

"Oooo! Perfect! Allow me to offer my services, then."

What ensued can only be described as an absolute *whirlwind* of activity.

Dahlia asked me to find something I liked in the boots but told me to make damn sure that whatever I picked was waterproof now that the seasons were changing. Thankfully, the waterproofing qualifier narrowed things down considerably but still, there wasn't a single option for a pair of boots that wasn't one hundred and fifty dollars or more! For just one pair of boots!

I stuttered and stammered my resistance to the idea until Dahlia rolled her eyes, stuck her thumb and her ring fingertips in her mouth and let out the most earsplitting whistle imaginable. I stood there, face flaming, as Fenris stalked over and asked, "What's the problem?"

"Your girlfriend's balking at the price tag," Dahlia said and Fen frowned.

"Which pair do you like?" he asked me and I pointed, mutely.

"See, that wasn't so hard." He turned to Dahlia and said, "Get that pair."

Dahlia wrinkled her nose impishly with an exaggerated smile and gave a nod.

"Seriously, if you like it, say so. If you don't – say so. She can make this so much worse," Little Bird said with a conspiratorial little smile, her lovely brown eyes almost apologetic. I had to think that she'd had a turn at this a time or two before.

"Okay, boots are decided," Dahlia said looking me up and down. "You're definitely *not* a leather pants kind of girl so let's go look at chaps. You're definitely a chap over jeans girl."

"I-I-I'm sorry? Did you just say *chaps?*" I asked. She closed her eyes, smiled at me, opened them and just turned and walked away.

I looked at Little Bird who was laughing, confused, and she said to me, "Don't worry about it. Dahlia takes some getting used to."

"I'm not sure I'll ever get used to *this*," I muttered and Little Bird's smile grew.

I mean, *what a bitch.*

I swallowed my confoundedness and irritation and let Little Bird guide me to the next section of apparel.

By the time we were done, I had a complete outfit with an absolutely staggering price tag to match. I mean, there was easily a thousand dollars or more between the three items in Dahlia's hands. The boots were almost two hundred, the chaps, over four hundred, and the jacket that she and Little Bird had finally had to choose for me was over six hundred and fifty dollars! I didn't even spend that much buying my first car!

I was deathly pale as Fen wandered over to look everything over. He nodded in casual approval.

"Not bad for a first set, still incomplete, though. Come on. We need to get you a better lid, Leaf."

"Leaf?" I asked.

"Yup."

"Why Leaf?" I asked.

"Because you look like a little lost leaf on the wind, caught in a fuckin' hurricane, right now."

"I feel like a little lost leaf on the wind caught in a hurricane, right now. Hurricane Dahlia."

"I heard that!" Dahlia called from behind us. "I'm taking it as a compliment, too!"

Fenris chuckled and guided me over to the helmets saying, "Dahlia takes some getting used to."

"So, I've heard," I said charitably, unsure if I could or would ever get used to her brusque interactions.

"You okay?" he asked with a laugh.

"Overwhelmed," I said, and he turned me by my shoulders to look at me.

"Listen," he said gently. "Like with anything, there's good with the bad. I've been filling you in on a lot of shit in a short amount of time when it comes to my world and this was the part about it I was neglecting. Are there risks? Yeah. Are there perceptions? Yeah. Are there a lot of misconceptions?" he asked. "Fuck yeah."

He searched my face and said finally, "There's a fuckton of good things about it, too, baby. We keep each other close; we keep each other safe, and sane, and we're always there for each other. This is a family in a truer sense of the word than there's ever been. Do we always get along? No. Are we always there for each other? Without fucking question." He gave my shoulders a little shake and said, "You're with me; you're part of that family."

"I don't know what to say," I said quietly.

"You don't have to say anything right now, not even 'thank you.'" He kissed my forehead, and I felt the tension drain out of me, my eyes slipping closed. "Taking care of you has been and is my pleasure."

"You're going to make me cry," I whispered, eyes misting.

"No tears, beautiful. No need. I've got you," he said pulling me into a tight hug.

We stood like that for a solid minute while I gathered my wits, then he led me over to be properly fitted for a damn helmet.

I WAS A BIT EMOTIONALLY EXHAUSTED, THOUGH FOR A FAR BETTER reason than grief, by the time we rode back down his driveway, dusk just beginning to settle.

Fenris had insisted, as soon as our purchases were made, that the girls help me get into them so that I was safe to ride. I was still speechless at how much he had casually spent on me. Shocked didn't even begin to cover it. I don't think my ex-husband had ever spent so much at once on me the entire time we were married… and it was all in the name of ensuring I was *safe*. Cared for; and I felt so… loved.

When I'd asked Fenris to love me that first night we'd had sex, I'd meant just my body. I guess he was just an all-or-nothing kind of a man, and to be completely honest, I could appreciate that. I was finding it hard, after all of this, not to love him, too.

Too fast? Maybe.

Too right? Absolutely. It absolutely felt so *right*. The only thing I think I'd ever felt so surely that I never once second guessed it. That did not make it, in any way, less scary than it felt. Certainty, did not, in every case, negate fear.

"Penny for your thoughts?" he asked and tucked the smashed penny we'd gotten at the Ballard Locks into the palm of my hand. I smiled and laughed a little. I didn't know why, but Little Bird was absolutely enamored with the things. The souvenir pennies. She'd gotten so *excited* when she'd found the machine that made them at the Locks' gift shop that she had insisted that she get one of every design it offered.

Dump Truck had humored her without question, producing pennies and quarters from the depths of his pockets as though he kept them on hand for just such an occasion, and with her enthusiasm over them, I had to believe that was *exactly* why he held on to such copious amounts of pocket change.

"Today was a good day," I said and Fenris nodded, turning me around gently and taking my new leather jacket from my shoulders to hang it beside his from the pegs set inside the back door.

I was glad I had worn a plain, fitted white tee beneath my sweater. It had been too bulky for the jacket to slip over and had come home in a Harley-Davidson store bag in one of the saddlebags on Fen's motorcycle. That bag now hung next to our jackets as he smoothed his hands over my shoulders, digging his thumbs *just so* between my shoulder blades alleviating the tension there just a bit.

What he did next, bringing his lips to the side of my neck, was the real magic trick to make all of the tumult I was feeling drain away.

It was so simple when it was just he and I like this, in his kitchen, leaning back into his broad chest as he gently kissed my neck. His arms pulling me tight against him, rocking me gently, swaying us as though we slow danced to music that only he could hear.

"I have to go back to my mom's place eventually," I said, and the mere thought of leaving this place, this refuge, this idyllic place where I felt so loved and so safe… it broke my heart.

"So, we go back," he whispered gently. "We go through things a box at a time, chip away at the pain until it becomes some kind of manageable."

I closed my eyes and rested against him and whispered, "And tonight?"

"Tonight, I make love to you until there's no room in that pretty little head of yours to think about anything other than how good you feel."

I chuckled slightly and said, "That's a tall order."

"I'm confident I'm the man for the job," he said.

"Mm," I hummed in contentment and anticipation as he wheeled me around as expertly as he piloted his bike.

He steered me in the direction of the stairs and would receive no resistance from me. I wanted him, wanted this, everything about being with him soothed the ragged edged of my heart that'd been torn asunder by Charles. I wanted to hold onto this for as long as possible because my soul *craved it*. Craved this man who protected my tattered soul from the hurt. Holding my grief at bay and letting me clear my plate at my own pace. Feeding me tiny bites at a time, keeping me from being overwhelmed but *allowing me* to feel what I needed to feel when I needed to feel it.

He didn't tell me to stop, he didn't order me to dry my tears, or tell me I was being a drag, or say anything else that made me feel like I was somehow wrong for feeling what I was feeling whenever I was feeling it. He was like this giant tree, branches and canopy protecting me from the rain. Twisted roots plunging deep into the earth, trunk strong enough to hold me up when I couldn't seem to stand on my own for anything.

Someday, I hoped I could repay him. I didn't know how, or in what way I could ever do it. His kindness had been as immense as he was… but I wanted to. Someday.

"Don't move," he growled in my ear, smoothing his hands down my body and over my denim clad hips once we'd entered his room. He went to the dresser and picked up the long lighter, clicking it to life and dipping it into the glass cylinders to light the candles one after the other.

He returned to me, the music going, the soft glow of the flickering flames filling the room with muted light and resumed his place behind me.

"Arms up, baby," he ordered, voice a husky, sexy growl. I raised them up obediently, and he lifted my tee, pulling it from where it was tucked into my jeans, his fingertips whispering against my flanks, tickling, making me jump and giggle slightly.

He quickly got the hooks of my bra undone while he stood behind me, but not before I heard him pull off his own shirt. I covered my chest with my arms, a reflexive action, as he turned me around to face him.

"Don't hide from me," he whispered, pulling my arms away from my chest, my hands from my shoulders, and tugging me close to him, winding them around his lean waist. I looked up at him and he smiled down at me.

"You're so fucking beautiful, don't you ever hide it."

I sucked in a sharp breath as I saw the truth of everything he said in his bright blue eyes, just before he lowered his mouth to mine.

It was cool in the room, and I cuddled into his warmth gratefully, loving as his hands skimmed over my hips; half over my skin, half over my jeans.

I moaned into his mouth but he was just getting started. We kissed like that for a long time, giggling and chuckling awkwardly as he toed off his boots. Mine were too new for that to work, but he seemed in no hurry to get me undressed the rest of the way. At least not yet.

The light skimming of his fingertips, slow, up and down my spine, a ghostly erotic touch of his fingertips sent me into a fit of shivers and goosebumps, the sensation absolutely exquisite as he kissed me deeply. I clung to him, and dug nails lightly into his flanks just above the waistband of his jeans and he laughed darkly, a sound that tasted rich and decadent like no other, warmth curling at the apex of my thighs at the mere sound of it.

I broke the kiss and moaned, "Fenris, *please…*" even though I didn't even know what I was begging for precisely.

"Please what?" he purred.

"Everything." I gasped as he kissed the side of my neck in that spot. "Just… *everything.*"

"I'll give you everything and more," he promised, bending low, grabbing me by my outer thighs and hoisting me up his tall body.

I gave him no resistance, hopping up, wrapping my legs around him frustrated by the layers of denim and cotton still between us.

I held his face between my hands, kissing him fiercely as he turned me around and took the half step to the bed, setting me down on its high edge, leaning forward on his hands to either side of my hips, pressed in the furs. He kissed me for a time, then broke it just long enough to order me to lie back.

I was his obedient girl, and did just that, but only because the anticipation for what he would do to me next was too strong not to.

He stood, raising up to his full height and went for the belt at the front of his jeans.

"Play with those beautiful titties," he demanded and awkward though I felt at first, I didn't want to disappoint my man. I let my hands drift up to the sides of my neck, my arms covering me, as I made a great show for him, letting my fingertips glide from just behind my ears down my neck. I tipped my chin to the ceiling and looked up my nose from my prone position, locking gazes with my lover as I performed for him.

His nostrils flared slightly as he worked at his belt and his fly, watching me grip and massage my breasts for him at his behest, arching slightly as I teased my own nipples and waited for him to get naked, and for whatever would happen next.

My man did *not* disappoint, stripping himself in front of my eyes, for my gaze only, standing confident and sure between my still-clad knees, his cock standing high, thick and long reaching almost to his navel. He throbbed with need, a pearly drop of pre-cum tantalizingly sliding from the head of his cock, making its way over the pronounced mushroom head to his veined shaft.

Oh, that was a sight. So erotic, so raw and powerful like everything else about him. Fenris was so *organic*, salt of the earth, no pretext no assumptions to be made. The look on his face intense as he reached for my belt and slipped the leather tongue through its restraining loop, folding it back, the leather creaking, as he freed the slip of metal from the hole.

He made quick work of undressing me the rest of the way, stopping to let down the zippers on my boots, dropping them to the fur rug at the side of the bed with a soft thud, first one then the other. My jeans sliding and slithering, belt rattling and clinking to join them with a softer thump to the floor.

He stepped up and pulled me down further, to the edge of the bed, my ass barely supported, hands smoothing and massaging up and down my thighs as he looked down at me. God, my pussy *ached* to have him inside me and none of this was moving quite quick enough for my taste.

"I'm going to make you come so hard," he murmured.

"Don't threaten me with a good time," I teased, raising my eyebrows and biting my bottom lip.

He smiled and said, "Don't you dare take those hands off those titties, baby."

I giggled lightly, as he massaged the top of my legs a few more times and brought his hand to his mouth.

Making a great show of getting his middle finger lubed up, reaching down between us and sliding it inside me with no resistance, as I was quite aroused already.

Still, my hips jerked slightly at the contact, and I couldn't help my eyes closing and my head falling back as he slid that finger all the way inside me, the knuckles of the surrounding two meeting my body, the pad of his thumb slicking through my wetness and finding my clit.

He played me expertly, just the right amount of pressure, the right pace, starting me at a steady climb for the stars as he rubbed tight circles around that sensitive bundle of nerves, his eyes sharp, the calculations behind them certain as he gauged my responses.

It was like a rollercoaster that slow climb to the top, the breath held at the precipice and that wild, screaming plunge down the other side.

I bucked and writhed against his hand, but he was determined to make me overwrought, determined to make it last for as long as possible until the line between pleasure and torture became exquisitely blurred and I lost every one of my senses and faculties.

"Mm," he said, tasting me. "I can't wait to feel the way you tighten up like that around my cock."

"Mm," I echoed. "Well come here." I rose my arm, heavy with dreamy afterglow, beseeching him to come to me and he smiled with an edge of savagery.

"Oh, no, not like that. Turn over and come slide off the edge of the bed some for me."

The anticipation of what he would do to me once I was bent over the bed for him had me intrigued. I turned over onto my belly and slid back, my toes finding the floor, the bed a bit too high, but putting my pussy at the perfect height for his cock.

The furs were sensuous against my naked tits, teasing my nipples as he grasped my hips in his big hands. He pressed the head of his cock at my entrance and groaned in appreciation, pressing forward, slipping inside, as I gasped and gripped fistfuls of the furs beneath me.

I was still sensitive, but he knew that I was sure. Nothing Fenris did sexually was an accident. It was purely by design, and I loved it. How sure he was, how confident. How safe with him that made me feel.

He went slow at first, making noises of appreciation that sounded so sensual falling from his lips. His hands traveling over my ass, sweeping up my back as though he touched a fine piece of art. One that he never dreamed he would or could ever lay hands on.

"God, I love it when you touch me like that," I murmured, and he gave a dark little chuckle.

"How about this?" he asked, laying a sharp, stinging slap against my ass. My hips bucked, and he laughed and said, "Oh, that did some nice things."

I just moaned in response and wriggled a bit, trying to take him deeper. He laughed then and said, "I think she likes it."

"God, shut up and *move* already!" I cried, and he laughed some more but obliged me, rolling his hips in sure, deep, slow and lazy strokes that got me on a low-key build up.

So intense, so wonderful, he gripped my hips, driving into me, sweeping his hands up my back, pinning me to the bed with our lovemaking, until all that was left was sensation and warmth to bask in.

He took me through at least two more mind blowing orgasms before he took his own, collapsing over the top of me, and holding me close.

"God, I love loving you," he murmured with such a reverence, pressing a kiss to my shoulder.

"Are you saying what I think you're saying?" I asked, breath catching in my throat. Sometimes it wasn't what you said but *how* you said it, and this was most definitely one of those times.

"Absolutely," he said in a tone full of such fierce certainty, there was no doubt to be had.

CHAPTER TWENTY

*F*enris…

We were waiting outside the gates at the Monroe prison complex, waiting on our boy Mace to get out. We'd had the prospect, Sauley, ride Mace's bike out here as was tradition. Maverick stood by with Mace's colors, waiting to restore them to their rightful owner.

We chatted, joked, and to some extent, even though he'd only been locked up a couple of years from arrest to release, we worried for our brother. Adjusting to life outside could be a royal pain in the ass, especially if you were on probation or parole, which he would be for at least another year.

He had to keep himself clean on paper, and off The Man's radar until he was completely free and clear. That meant he damn sure wouldn't be going on any runs with us, especially if it meant crossing borders or state lines. One, he was a felon, Canada wouldn't let him cross legally, not that we did much of that, anyway. Two, he technically had to get permission from his P.O. or Parole Officer to cross state lines.

We would do what we could to find him employment, which was always a good first step to get The Man outta your ass, but tonight we cut loose, celebrated, and welcomed our boy back into the fold.

I was both excited and nervous. My girl and I had spent yesterday at her mom's and made a damn good dent in the crazy amount of shit that stuffed the house to bursting. There'd been more laughter than tears, which was a good thing, and by the end she was feeling a little stronger, a little better.

I tell you what, though. Leaving her to sleep there by herself last night was one of the hardest things I'd ever done. She had a whole mess to sort through when it came to not just the house, but her divorce, and fighting off her husband who was literally going after everything she held dear as though *she* were somehow the asshole in this situation.

I wanted to hurt him physically as much as he'd devastated her emotionally, but that wasn't my little leaf's way. She was tossed and pulled in every which direction, almost seemingly along for the ride in a lot of ways, but through it all and just like a little leaf on the wind, cast adrift, she drifted in elegance. So damn graceful, pretty to look at, and I couldn't wait to see where she settled on certain things.

"Your little lady is in for a rude awakening tonight," Tic-Tac declared and chuckled.

"Don't be a dick," Dump Truck warned him.

"Or did you forget who the fuck you're talking to?" I demanded and glared at Tic. He was like the angry little cocksucker brother that nobody could really fucking stand sometimes. Like we all just let him fuckin' hang because we all knew he ain't got no place else to go. He could be a real asshole for no reason sometimes, though and I wasn't about to let him start in on Aspen

She was too fuckin' pure. Too good. He'd better watch himself around her. I would kick his ass.

"Shit, she's got you wrapped around her little finger, don't she?" Tic-Tac grinned like my love for my woman was something to be ashamed of. A weakness. He really didn't have a fuckin' clue.

"Sorta like Dahlia has your dick in knots?" Major asked, laughing. That shut Tic down real hard, his brow dropping into a deep scowl. He didn't say anything after that.

"Tic, ain't no one ever told you not to yank an angry dog's chain?" Maverick asked, laughing. "Since you wanna sit here trying to start shit, you can be the one to give Sauly a ride back to the club."

"Aw, fuck no, man! I don't do none of that nut to butt shit!" Tic cried.

"Too fuckin' bad! Prospect, you're sittin' bitch with Tic for the ride home."

"Whatever you want, P." Sauly didn't look happy when he said it, but he was a team player and knew how this shit went.

"Oh! Here he comes!" Deacon called and we turned as the grating buzz of the gate sounded out over the parking lot.

It got rowdy really quick; Mace, a little thinner than he'd gone in, come waltzing out in the clothes we brought him. Making strides in our direction and pressing on through the gauntlet of us hugging and pounding on his back to where Maverick stood, holding open his colors. Mace grinned at our president, turned around and shrugged into his cut over his jacket, Mav grabbing his shoulders and gripping them hard, shaking our boy back and forth.

"Welcome home, Mace."

"Ain't home yet," he declared. "I need a cold beer and a warm pussy. I say goddamn, it's good to be free!"

We all cheered, and Mav gave the order, "Mount up! Let's get the fuck out of here and get our boy a decent fucking meal!"

Another burst of rowdy cheers and Mace was guided on up to his bike, at a place of honor in our pack at Glass Jaw's usual position – Mav's right hand.

Mav had an exchange with Mace up at the front. He turned around after a minute and called down the line, "The man want's a steak!"

Whoops went up, and we started up the bikes as soon as Mav started his, revving engines and peeling out, getting our boy far the fuck away from this forsaken fucking box of concrete and steel.

We rode back to the club. There wasn't any point in going out for a steak when the club had the outdoor grill in the back on 15th and we had some gourmet ass motherfuckers in our ranks, myself included when it came to meat and fire. Still, I left that shit to Blackjack. He knew his way around steaks, specifically, like nobody's fuckin' business even if he was being a princess over having to cook with gas over the charcoal grill that he fuckin' preferred.

There was a Sarr's one block over on 16th, but while the meat was cheap and plentiful and pretty much butchered on site, this wasn't an 'it'll do in a pinch' situation. This was a time for some serious celebration. That meant we took our asses further up Ambaum out of White Center and into Burien for B&E Meats. An actual fuckin' butcher shop worth something.

I preferred Green Valley Meats out in my neck of the woods. Quality was better and the prices more reasonable, but right now the club was sittin' flush again. We'd replenished the coffers since Little Bird and business at the boneyard was good. Our side hustle, sadly, was booming too, but we didn't take more than we needed to keep the supply run going. People needed those meds, and the fastest way to get busted was to get fuckin' greedy.

We were still on pins and fuckin' needles thanks to the Eastern Washington chapter's bullshit, waiting to see if any of those fuckers were going to narc that were chillin' out that way. They used to be club, out bad for killing that family. That made them somewhat unpredictable, but by the same token – they fuckin' knew what was comin' should they open their fuckin' mouths.

Yeah, I thought to myself. *You.*

Scarier than any fuckin' boogeyman the PNW had ever seen. Hell, that this club had ever seen except for that psycho motherfucker out in the mother chapter – Reaver.

He and I had gone up against each other at the last National Lake Run out to Lake Eversong and he'd won. I had the scars to prove it. Of course, I was probably a little crazier than that bastard, because given a second chance? I'd for sure go up against him again. He was a worthy fuckin' opponent. I didn't come across too many of those anymore.

When we'd gotten into the club, I'd gotten myself a bottle of IPA and headed across to the boneyard with Dump Truck. He wanted to put some work in on his latest rebuild, but honestly, I was pretty sure he just wanted to see his woman; even if it was just briefly. I knew what that was like now, and it was an odd little thorn… meaning it was really nice to have someone to feel that way over but by the same token, it was a new kind of suck. Still, I would see her real soon. It was just a new thing for me: missing someone who was still here.

"Baby, how about you run around the corner to the Saars and get us some shit to go with these steaks?" Dump Truck asked, and Little Bird smiled across the counters at him.

"Fen, you mind gettin' the phones?" he asked.

"Sure thing," I said. I went over to take Little Bird's spot behind the cash wrap and she went to her man to take the wad of cash he held out.

"Mav's sendin' Marisol over this way, meet her out front," DT said.

"Okay, love you." She leaned over and kissed her man who sat near his latest rebuild. He gave her a slap on the ass as she headed out the front door.

For the time being, the boneyard was quiet, and it was just me and him, sitting it out for a minute while things were just starting to pick up across the street in the club.

"Tic sure had a mouth on him, today didn't he?" Dump Truck said casually.

"Knock his fucking lights out he keeps it up," I said and took a pull off my beer, emptying half of the fresh bottle in one giant swallow.

DT nodded. "Got attached to this girl awful damn quick, didn't you?" he asked.

I raised an eyebrow at him and fixed him with an otherwise flat look, staring at him hard. He chuckled and tossed down one of his socket wrenches with a clink.

"I'm not the one who dropped literally fuckin' everything and went haring off to fuckin' Vegas after a woman I only fucked once as a one-night-stand."

"Touché, motherfucker. Touché," he said chuckling. "I just wanna know, you thinkin' about the long term with her?"

"I am," I said carefully.

"Think she's cut out for this life?" he asked evenly, tone a little too neutral for my tastes.

"She's different," I admitted. "A citizen, sure," I said. "But there's more than that underneath. She's got spirit. A soul trapped in there yearning for something else, wanting to be free. It's like I just gotta show her the way without letting her get too... I don't know, over-whelmed? She's been burned in the worst way. The rug pulled out from under her. Everyone she's loved either dying or straight up abandoning her when she needed them the most."

Dump Truck nodded slowly. "Club would be a good fit for her in that regard," he said slowly. I nodded. "You sure she can hang, though?"

"Worried about her citizen morals?" I asked.

"Ah, yeah. Would be lyin' if I said I wasn't. You know the rest of the guys'll be thinkin' it, too. She's awful fuckin' white bread for the lot of us."

Again, I fixed him with a hard look. Motherfucker was one to talk. Little Bird's ass had started out as a spoiled little rich girl.

The shiny had been taken off of her real quick, though. Baptism by fuckin' fire when DT had blown her husband's head off for her. Right in front of her, too. Not that she would miss that abusive rapist pig. I wished I'd been there to carve that son of a bitch up myself; *slow.*

I closed my eyes briefly against the blood on my hands, slick. The stench of death, the sound the organs made as I'd dropped them into the toilet, the flush, watching them spool out of the SOB's body cavity as they went down the fuckin' john.

It'd taken several attempts and cutting his insides up into smaller pieces to get it all down the fuckin' toilet. It'd been worth the time and effort.

I got 'em Lacy. Every last fuckin' one of those assholes.

The first kill was the hardest and had stuck with me the longest. The one I still flashed back to. The one where I saw red, every time, and wanted to do it all over again. The one I'd done on my own. The rest, my pops had joined me on.

While there was guilt, it was misplaced. I didn't feel guilty for killing any of them. I felt guilty that I'd done each and every one of 'em too quickly for what they'd done to my sister.

"How many times I got to tell you not to fuckin' go there, boy?" I heard my dad demand in my head.

He was right. Those ghosts were dead and buried. A worthy sacrifice to the gods.

"She is," I agreed. There wasn't any denying it. "I guess you all are going to have to trust me that there's more to her than meets the eye."

Dump Truck eyed me critically and then said, "I believe you. She and Little Bird are two peas in a pod."

"Nobody except Tic had shit else to say about LB," I mused and Dump Truck nodded.

"She was bruised to shit with a wild fear in her eyes. Not many men can get around the desire to fix that shit. Your girl hides her hurt a lot better in mixed company," he said. "She's reserved. Watchful. The rest of our brothers are going to find that unsettling, except for maybe Mav."

"You think?" I asked, turning over his observations about my woman in my head.

"I know. She's smart, and Mav'll see right through her. It's what he does."

I nodded slowly and the front door of the boneyard burst open, Mace coming right on through with Glass and Cipher with him.

"Was wondering where you two fucks were hiding!"

"Not hiding, just chillin'," I declared.

"Alright, alright, so what's knew with you? Other than I hear Dump Truck's got a woman?" Mace asked, hoisting himself up onto the countertop.

"Little Bird's legit," Glass Jaw said. "I'm more interested in meeting the citizen chick Fenris has supposedly picked up."

"Yeah, man. You been scarce the last few weeks," Cipher agreed and Dump Truck and I traded a look.

Tic-Tac, I thought. Or Dahlia. I couldn't really imagine Dahlia having much to say, though. She wasn't like that. Dollars to doughnuts, Tic had already had some shit to say and was bitchin' about my little leaf being too outsider, too *other*, too *normal*.

"Yeah?" Mace asked. "What's the deal, man?" He gave me a punch in the shoulder and I grunted. He may be skinnier, but he hadn't lost any of his strength in there. If anything, maybe he'd leaned out some. Maybe 'skinny' wasn't the right word.

"She's a good woman," I grunted, and left it at that.

"Cipher?" Glass Jaw asked as a joke.

"Don't look at me, man. When it comes to Fen and DT, there ain't no decoding these two assholes and their way."

"So, when do we get to judge for ourselves?" Mace asked.

"In just a bit," I said, looking at the time. "She's coming up this way after she gets off work."

"What's she do?" Glass asked, dropping onto one of the two old bench seats from an old 60s era pickup that were against the low wall that served as the boneyard's waiting area.

"Owns her own business," I said.

"Doing what?" Cipher asked, when I didn't volunteer any additional information.

"Stuff," I said with a shrug.

"Wow," Mace said with an incredulous laugh. "You're serious about this one."

I scowled.

"He's right, man," Cipher declared. "The less you talk about something the more you're into it. That's always been your way."

"It's like a tell at poker," Glass Jaw grunted.

"Fuck you guys," I growled, my mood beginning to sour. "Maybe I just don't like to be interrogated."

They all busted up laughing at my expense at that and my mood darkened further. I was gettin' fuckin' irritated. The door opened up, and I looked over, my pops comin' through.

"Well, there you are," he grunted, but he wasn't talking to me. He was talking to Mace.

"Hey! Vyking!" Mace and my dad embraced heartily, pounding each other on the back.

"How's life on the outside?" my dad asked him.

"So far so good," Mace said grinning. "We were just trying to talk to Fen about his girl."

"Closed-mouthed bastard," Glass Jaw said with a laugh.

"Aw, yeah? I like her. Aspen's a nice girl."

A chorus of "Oh?" and "Ooo!" went up around us followed by a song of laughter.

I shook my head, a passage from the *Havamal*, specifically *Odin's Rune Poem.*

I know, if a modest maiden's favor and affection I desire to possess, the soul I change of the white-armed damsel, and wholly turn her mind.

Looking at the pack of assholes in front of me at the moment, I had my work cut out for me on that last part – not that it had been wholly difficult to turn Aspen's mind thus far. Maybe I worried about it too much. *I don't know.*

What I did know, was that in order for the rest of my boys to see in Aspen what I did, they need to see Aspen. They needed to talk with her and learn for themselves what I had.

I tuned back in to the conversation in time to hear my pops say, "I've always been proud of my boy, but the way he is with her? Proudest papa I've ever been. Quit giving him a hard time, boys. I think she's the one."

I met my dad's eyes, and he met mine. We were alike in that it was just like staring into the future in some ways. Wanted to know what I was gonna look like? Just look at my pops. Twenty or thirty more years and I'd be there.

I could see it. The pride shining in his gaze. For all that we could be a pain in each other's ass and butt heads, pretty spectacularly I might add, we had an accord on some things. This was definitely one of those things. He knew. I knew.

Aspen was the one for me.

CHAPTER TWENTY-ONE

$\mathcal{A}$spen...

It was dark by the time I pulled up outside the address in White Center that Fenris had given me. It wasn't precisely what I'd expected. There weren't any fences. No razor wired gates. There were no loud dogs, and though it was set back from the road with a parking lot out front, it wasn't desolate by any means. There was an O'Reilly's auto parts store closer to the main drag and to the right of the building, a Subway even closer to the road sharing the same parking lot.

Across the narrow street behind the O'Reilly's was a grocery store, and on the other side of the Subway, a tropical fish and aquarium supply store.

The club was a two-story building and looked as though its prior incarnation had been some kind of a bar. The building was black in front, a riot of spray-painted mural on the long, cinderblock wall down the side. There were no bikes parked out front, but there were picnic tables occupying three of the four spaces out front. Poles cemented into old tire rims with heavy old chain strung between them suitably roped the picnic tables off from the rest of the parking lot. I parked off to the side, in one of the vacant spaces in front of the large, spray-painted mural of the club's logo, the only artistic license taken was a motorcycle bursting from the sacred heart.

I turned off my headlights and with a sigh of trepidation got out of my car.

Loud music was blaring from inside the club. Classic rock. Bob Seger, I think. Vyking detached himself from the front corner of the building, cherry of his cigarette flaring in the dark as he came over to me.

Relief washed through me, because even though I didn't know Vyking well, I at least knew him enough that he was familiar in this looming wave of unfamiliarity I was about to be washed away by.

"Hey, darlin'," he said and stopped in front of me, opening his arms.

I laughed, caught slightly off guard and gave him the hug he asked for.

"Boy's in a mood," he warned me. "They've been pickin' on him all day over you."

"Oh, no…" I said, heart sinking.

"It's nothin' on you, girl. They don't know you yet," he said, taking a step back and holding me by the elbows to look me over. "Word to the wise, don't take nothin' personal, and whatever you do, don't take nobody's shit."

"I'll do my best," I promised, but his words left a knot of dread in the pit of my stomach.

"You'll do fine," he said. "Let's take you in to see Fen. I guarantee just the sight of you will put him in a better mood."

"Okay," I said pasting on a brave smile.

"You're a shy girl," he said, looping his hand into the crook of his arm. "Somehow I knew that about you." He gave my hand a pat and led me around to the club's front door which was standing open to let a cross breeze through. The moment we stepped in, I could see straight through and out the back door.

"Oh! Your cigarette!"

"Private club, baby. Don't you worry about me," Vyking grated.

We threaded our way through a pretty crowded and smallish barroom, a living room setup just inside the front door to the left, two black leather couches and two leather loveseats around a black area rug and a thick glass and wrought steel coffee table. To the right, immediately as you walked in, was a bar. Only six stools perched under it, five of them featuring a man. A happy, portly, older woman behind it wearing a black and orange tiger print caftan serving up drinks.

Vyking stabbed two fingers into the shoulder of one man hunched on his stool and it was only when he straightened did his blond, ponytail consisting of its many interwoven braids slipped back over his shoulder. That made me smile.

My smile only grew when Fenris' dark expression seemingly evaporated the second he laid eyes on me.

He twisted on his seat and reached out, taking my hand and pulling me between his knees, his hand going one to my hip and the other to the side of my face, fingers curling around the back of my head, thumb caressing my jaw as he dragged me in for a kiss.

And boy what a kiss it was.

Fiery, passionate, possessive, and fierce. He tasted of the hops from the beer that he'd drunk and vaguely spicy. He definitely tasted all male and as I melted into his embrace, happily, while the music blared deafening around us, I dropped my hand to his thigh and accidentally where his erection was growing in the prison of his jeans.

He broke the kiss and put his lips beside my ear and growled, "If I thought you'd be into it, I'd fuck you right over this bar to let every one of these motherfuckers know you belonged to me."

He brought his head up, pulling my forehead to his chest to help me hide my vermillion blush and yelled back at his dad, "Thanks for finding her, Pops!"

"Don't mention it!" his dad yelled waving us off and heading down the hall toward the back door. I leaned my temple against Fen's chest and watched him go, thankful that he'd waited for me. That he'd seen fit to escort me to his son and tell me what he had.

"How was your day, babe? You hungry?" Fenris asked low beside my ear. I smiled, the boisterous activity around us falling away as though it were just, he and I in the room.

"Long, and I'm starving," I answered him.

"There are some things laid out in the chapel to nom on and we got steaks going on out back on the grill. Let's go get you something to eat."

I nodded and smiled and he let me go enough to step back so he could slip off the stool. He had me precede him in the direction of the hall and touched doors as we went down it, telling me what they were. The first two doors on the left were bathrooms, the first on the right he said led up the stairs. The third on the left was Maverick's office, and then the last door on the left what he called the chapel.

It resembled a very cramped boardroom, the table draped with cheap dollar store plastic tablecloths and laden with big salad bowls, with a variety of things – fruit, a garden salad, and what looked like a Caesar salad in another.

Fen swept me past the room onto the cramped little back landing among other men clad in black leather and asked me, "How do you like your steak?"

"Um, medium-rare?"

"Blackjack, one medium-rare! You already know what I like!"

"Yo! Got it!" a man called up from down below where he manned a barbecue gas grill.

"Thank you!" I called down, and the man raised his beer in an almost salutation before looking up.

"Hey!" he said. "Fen, is that your lady?"

"Yeah," Fen called down. "Aspen, Blackjack. Blackjack, Aspen."

"Hi." I curled my fingers in a shy wave.

"Nice t' meet you, Aspen. One medium-rare steak, coming right up!"

"Hey, girl!" Dahlia came up the steps and shouldered between two of the men. She was dressed in a pinup dress and looked out of sight. She was so beautiful, and I was envious of her confidence.

She grabbed my hands and kissed air beside each of my cheeks. "Glad you made it."

"Thank you," I said with a smile.

"Grab some food, get a drink, and stay a while!" she called out, pushing past Fen and into the narrow hall beyond.

I laughed. "I will!"

"Hi, I'm Major," a tall, thin ebony man said, his pencil-thin dreadlocks held up in a spray that resembled a crown.

"Aspen," I said and held out my hand.

Phew, what followed was a small flurry of introductions. The other two men on the little back landing were Nine and Squatch, which there was no mystery on how the latter man got his name. He looked like a Sasquatch with all his black wild beard and hair.

Back inside, Fen led me into the boardroom that he called the chapel. It wasn't a stretch of the imagination to say this is where they held their club meetings when it wasn't being used as a buffet.

I fixed myself a plate, and we chatted a bit, the only two making our way around the table. He'd waited for me to eat, and I felt a little bad about that but warmed at the same time.

"What do you like to drink, babe?" he called as we got to the end of the table.

"Cider?" I asked.

"You got it; we'll stop at the bar on the way out front.

"Okay."

That's just what we, did. More introductions shouted along the way. There was Derry and Deacon as well as a couple of men that Fenris said were from the Eastern Washington chapter and new in town. There were men from Western Oregon and Eastern Oregon in attendance, too. However, I would not likely encounter them again.

We took a seat across from one another at one of the picnic tables out front and he yelled out, "Prospect!"

One came running, and he said, "Sauley, Aspen. Aspen, this is our prospect Sauley."

"Hi, nice to meet you," I said and Sauley gave me a nod.

"Hi, how's it goin'?" he said distractedly and looked to Fen, wiping his damp hands on the seat of his jeans. "What's up, Fen?"

"Bring me and IPA and a Cider for my lady," he said. "Then go on out back and check with Blackjack on our steaks. If they're done, bring 'em to us."

"You got it." The prospect, who seemed harried, bobbed his head and took off like a shot.

"Momma Kat! I need an IPA and a Hard Cider!"

"You got it, honey!" the woman behind the bar yelled out.

I smiled and shook my head in amazement as several men on the other side of the front door burst out laughing and one passed a joint to another.

"Doin' okay?" Fenris asked me.

I nodded, silent, just looking around and taking it all in.

"Seems to me she thinks we're some kind of a freakshow," a voice behind my man declared. My head shot up, and I looked wide-eyed at the speaker as Fen turned, scowling.

It was Tic-Tac. I'd met him on Sunday. Dahlia had been with him at the Harley store, but he'd mostly stayed with Fen and Dump Truck. We'd barely exchanged pleasantries when we'd left and parted ways.

I didn't understand… I hadn't thought I'd done anything offensive.

"I'm sorry," I called. "It's just—"

"You ain't gotta apologize to him, babe. Tic's just an asshole," Fen said and turned back around to face me with a wink.

The prospect came back out with our drinks and said, "Steaks are coming right up!"

"Thank you," I said to him while Fen just grunted.

I was mollified. I felt as though Tic's glaring daggers at me behind Fen's back wasn't warranted. I wasn't doing anything wrong. I was just existing, spending time with Fen and here at Fen's behest to meet his people. I didn't know what I'd done wrong – and then Vyking's words came back to me.

Don't take anything personal and don't take anyone's shit.

Okay, I would try. I took a deep breath and a drink of my cider and just ignored Tic and ate my meal.

"So, what did you do today?" Fen asked, returning the subject to me and my day.

"Mm, made several raw serving platters to teach an underglaze decal class the middle of next week. They're fast and easy to make, but kind of a pain in the ass to fire. They have to be done in batches, but with the decals, you have to do them before the first firing otherwise they don't quite work. So, I try to make an excess since with greenware breakage is bound to happen."

"I don't know how you keep track and do it all, babe."

"You have a lot more to keep track of on your farm than I do in my little shop," I said with a laugh.

"I don't know about that," he said. "Greenware, earthenware, bisqueware, slurry, scoring, glaze, underglaze, decals, you got all these things and I can't keep up on which shit is which."

I smiled. "I kind of miss the days where it was just making things, start to finish. Doing farmer's markets and the like on the weekends. I don't miss working what was essentially two and three jobs to get where I am but there was a certain simplicity to it all." I shook my head and speared a bite of salad. "With everything going on, keeping the shop going is becoming exhausting and I'm not really wholly turning a profit now."

"Ever consider just doing what makes you happy?" someone behind me asked. I startled slightly and looked up into a handsome face shadowed with afternoon growth, deep indigo eyes sparkling over a million-dollar smile.

"Rare," he said, setting a plate in front of Fenris. "And medium-rare." He set a plate down beside the one I was working on.

"Thank you," I said.

"Mav, you didn't have to do that," Fenris declared.

"Of course, I did," Mav declared and took a seat next to me.

"Aspen, this is my president, Maverick. Mav, I'd like you to meet my girlfriend, Aspen."

Girlfriend. I didn't know why the title surprised me. I mean, wasn't that what we were? Still, it had, and a pleasant blush crept into my cheeks as a giddy riot of butterflies took off in my stomach, tickling the underside of my heart that took off in a rapid succession of beats.

"Hi," I said with a bit of an unsteady laugh. I wasn't used to being the center of attention. I was used to Copper, who was the absolute ham of the family and my mother's favored only son, getting all of the attention, which had suited me growing up. I much preferred hiding on the fringes and the shadows and I absolutely hated being the center of attention in this application.

At work, it was different. At work, I was almost performing a role, and I loved teaching what I so loved to do and sharing that with the world. It was the only time I really did feel comfortable with people. When I was selling or teaching. The scrutiny with which Maverick raked me from head to toe with his gaze had me shrinking in my seat.

"Nice to meet you, Aspen," he said kindly and gave me a nod.

"Nice to meet you, too," I murmured.

"Gotta admit, Fen's been keeping you quite the secret and now I see why," he said.

"Oh?" I asked, slightly intrigued. I mean, I can't imagine why Fen would.

"Uh-huh, you're a knockout."

I choked on the swallow of cider I'd been taking, coughing and sputtering as Fen looked on concerned and Mav pounded me on the back.

"Um, thank you," I said and wouldn't look at either of them, embarrassed.

"Shy, too, I take it."

"Um, yeah," I said, slightly uncomfortably.

"She is shy," Fenris said and smiled at me. His smile was every-thing, telling me that I was alright.

"And a citizen through and through," Tic grumbled behind him.

"Disrespect my woman one more fuckin' time, see what happens," Fen growled.

I froze. I'd never heard him like that before. His whole face changed into something frightening and I bit my lips together, my stomach turning leaden.

"Easy now, big dog. You know how it is," Mav said.

"I don't," I said softly.

"Just takes a while to get to know you, is all," Maverick said kindly.

"It would be nice to be given the opportunity," I said pointedly.

"It seems as though some of you have already made up your minds."

I stared past Fen, pointedly at Tic, Vyking's words playing over and over in my head, *take no shit, take no shit, take no shit.*

I wasn't a mean person. I didn't have that in me, but I would and could stand my ground if the occasion called for it… which apparently, it did at the moment. Tic laughed in my face, practically, took a drink out of his glass and said, "Look at her trying to be all hard and shit."

"Mav, he don't quit it. I'ma knock his fuckin' ass out."

Maverick looked nonplussed, but thankfully, he was looking at Tic and not Fenris.

"Not sure what crawled up your ass and died, there, Tic, but I'm inclined to agree with our enforcer here. Keep it up, I'll sanction that fight."

Tic scoffed like a sullen teenager and muttered, "Whatever."

"I don't know," Mav said leaning back. "Dump Truck, what do you think?"

Dump Truck sat up, rising like a leviathan from the deep, much like Fen had off his couch that first meeting. He was sitting at the picnic table on the other side of Tic's from ours.

"I say Tic is fixing to have his ass beat. There ain't nothing wrong with Aspen. Spent all day with her on Sunday. Little Bird and I happen to like her just fine."

"You're seriously going to take the side of some citizen trash over your brother's?" Tic demanded.

"I told you, you disrespect my woman one more time I was gonna knock your ass out. I meant it. Get your ass up."

"Fen, please," I said, frightened. Not for Fenris, but for Tic. He wasn't any match for Fenris in size and I'd been insulted much more heartily than someone refusing to trust me because of my background. "It's alright," I said. "I'm not that fragile and I can take it."

"Not how it works with us, baby," Dump Truck called out. "Tic is disrespecting you, you're Fen's property, for all Fen hasn't made it official."

"That means that shit cannot stand," Maverick said with a wink at me.

"Please, I don't want anyone fighting because of me," I said.

"Ain't fighting over you, hon," Dahlia said from the front door. I turned to look at her. She blew a plume of fragrant smoke into the air and handed a joint over to one of the men there looking on in interest.

"They're fighting over Tic being a royal fucking disrespectful dumbass." She gave Tic a flat, unfriendly look and turned on her heel, reaching behind her and grasping one of the men's hand.

"Mav, I'm going to borrow your office if you don't mind," she said lightly. "Pool table is occupied."

Tic looked murderous, and she gave him a meaningful look before towing the guy whose hand she had a hold of into the club.

"Help yourself, Dahlia," Maverick said, but his expression was thoughtful. Thoughtful and, dare I say, disappointed somehow.

"Fenris, please. Give him one more chance, for me?" I asked.

Tic made a disgusted noise and got up, stalking around our table and going in the front door to the bar.

Fen sank down, staring holes in the other blond man's back.

"He needs to figure his shit out," Fen growled.

Mav, who was staring after Tic as well, said, "I don't disagree. He opens his mouth again in your lady's direction, I got no problem with you settling things the good old-fashioned way.

"Should I just go home?" I asked softly. "I really don't want to cause any trouble."

"No," Maverick said unequivocally. "It's nothing on you, honey. It's all Tic and whatever issues he's got going on in his head. We don't do drama, Tic knows that. He's just asking to get his ass kicked."

"I'm gettin' happy to oblige," Fenris declared, cracking his knuckles.

I sighed and nodded.

We ate the rest of our food in relative peace and had a nice conversation with Maverick – one that Dump Truck and Little Bird joined us for.

Maverick asked a lot of questions, but I got the impression he was genuinely just trying to get to know me for himself and his own peace of mind, and so I did my best to answer them honestly and truthfully… even if some of them did happen to feel quite personal or strayed into uncomfortable territory.

They weren't very trusting. I understood that. I also understood that I was wholly an outsider. A law-abiding citizen, through and through… even if or when I disagreed with a particular law. It wasn't because I was any sort of particular goody two-shoes, I just had always been raised to follow the rules. Not just follow the rules, but to not make waves. I had always been raised to worry incessantly about what other people would think if I did this or that. My mother had always been hard on me, extremely judgmental, while Copper being the male of the family had been allowed to do whatever he wanted.

I hadn't been lying when I said my mother and I had a contentious relationship. I had never been good enough, really. Had never stood up straight enough, had never been pretty enough or thin enough, a million little flaws of mine and more pointed out at every turn. Not thankful enough, not gracious enough, not appealing enough… very rarely had I made my mother proud.

In short, I was used to being a disappointment. I was certain that no matter what I did, no matter who I encountered, I would always in some way be disappointing.

Which is why I had worked so hard to be precisely what Charles and wanted and needed me to be. Which was why his betrayal had been all the more devastating. I'd done everything right. More than right. I knew that to the bottom of my soul. It had, in its own way, been a sort of revelation.

Then there was Fenris, who lifted me up, who looked at me as though I were some sort of queen, and I have to admit… I loved that despite the feeling that I'd done nothing whatsoever to deserve it.

"Hey." Fen looked up and Dump Truck too, beside him. I looked up myself and turned to find one of the other bikers standing behind me.

Mav's smile lit the night as he asked the man, "You doin' good brother?"

The man rocked slightly on his booted feet, eyes glassy and bloodshot with too much weed and drink.

"Good food, good booze, and even better pussy. Dahlia hooked me up. I'm right as rain now, man!"

There was laughter around the table and I realized this was the man Dahlia had led into the club by the hand.

"Good fuckin' deal, bro," Fenris said, grinning, his mood much lighter for the conversation and the distance put between himself and Tic.

"And who might you be?" the man asked me.

"Oh, hi. I'm Aspen," I said blushing cursing my shyness and inability to be under any sort of scrutiny without doing so. "I'm with Fenris."

Throughout the conversation, it had become increasingly apparent that there was some sort of unspoken rule that if you weren't with anyone, you were sort of here for everyone so it was important to quickly establish just who you'd come with to avoid any misunderstandings.

"Hi Aspen, I'm Mace. I'm the birthday boy," he said, laughing at his own joke which most of the other guys laughed too, but there was some confusion in their eyes.

"Um, happy birthday?" I supplied.

"Thank you!" he cried, rocking back on his heels. Mav reached out and grabbed him by the front of his jacket and vest to keep him from going right onto his back.

"Easy there! Bro, how about you take a seat with me and Aspen here?"

"Don't mind if I do," Mace said.

"And who're you?" he asked Little Bird who was cuddled into Dump Truck's side.

"Kestrel," she answered. "But everybody calls me Little Bird. I'm Dump Truck's Old Lady."

"Yeah?" Mace asked. "Congratulations, bro!"

Dump Truck chuckled. "Thank you."

Mace said, "All you guys went and got yourselves some real hot women while I was locked up."

It dawned on me; this was the man who the entire party was for. A strange sort of tingle went up my spine and I wondered why.

The only answer I had was that it was a visceral reaction to knowing that not only had he been imprisoned, that he'd been imprisoned recently and for a very serious assault. I immediately felt a wave of shame for even reacting that way, even though no one knew it. I had kept a smile on my face the entire time, hadn't missed a single beat, but still… I had judged this man unfairly with just that little bit of information.

Maybe, in turn, that meant Tic was right to judge me. Maybe I wasn't good enough to be among them. Maybe I was just another hopeless citizen that could never belong…

"You doing alright, babe?" Fen asked.

"Oh, yeah, I'm just getting tired. It's been a long day for me. What time is it, anyway?" I asked.

"Ten o'clock," Little Bird answered.

"The night's still young," Mav said, and I laughed.

"Then I'm too old," I said. "It is way past my bedtime. I have to open tomorrow and six am comes early. I still have to drive to Tacoma."

"What's in Tacoma?" Mace asked and I smiled a little sadly.

"My mom's house."

"You live with your mother?" he asked, looking confused.

"No, my mom died a few months ago. I'm just living in her house."

"Oh. Oh, man… I'm sorry," he said.

"It's okay, you didn't know."

"Come on," Fen said, hoisting himself to his feet. "I'll walk you to your car."

I smiled.

"I'd like that."

Fenris came around the table and held his hand down to me. I took it and let him help me to my feet. I traded goodbyes and farewells with the people at the table and led Fen back to my car just around the corner. He leaned me back up against it, hands on my hips, dipping his head to meet my mouth with his.

I kissed him, and the tension and apprehension I felt in my shoulders eased marginally.

"I love you," he said, and his eyes held… worry.

I smiled, and it felt brittle. "I love you, too," I murmured.

"Text me when you get home, baby. I need to know you're safe."

I nodded.

"Okay," I whispered.

He kissed me again and opened my door for me.

"I'll see you soon," he said as I started my car and rolled down my window for him. I nodded and smiled.

"Okay."

He rapped twice on the roof of my Prius and stepped back to allow me to shift it into reverse and back out of the parking space. I smiled and waved through my passenger window steering my little, environmentally conscious, boring car choice out of the lot.

I couldn't help but feel that keenly… that I was utterly boring, especially after leaving the gathering. All of these doubts about whether I could or would be good for Fenris almost immediately started crowding in.

I just didn't know if I was cut out for 'the life' as he called it. I certainly didn't feel entirely welcome.

I felt tears well in my eyes as I took the freeway on-ramp onto I-5 South.

Maybe, just maybe, it would be the wiser course of action to end things now… if I waited much longer, it could hurt so much worse when things ended badly, and right now it really felt as though it wasn't a matter of 'if' but when.

I had a lot to think about.

CHAPTER TWENTY-TWO

enris…

"She good?" Maverick asked quietly when I got back to the table.

"I dunno," I said. "I think so." Truth was I didn't think so. Something in her eyes… a little too wide as she'd looked up at me, her posture a little too stiff. I was thinking that she maybe was letting her insecurities get to her.

"I like her, she seems nice," Mace said, but bro had definitely overdone it. Of course, that level of drunk implied a certain amount of truthfulness.

"It'll be fine, bro," Dump Truck assured me.

"If it's any consolation, and she asks, I like her, too. She seems like a damn fine lady," Maverick said.

"Not to talk too out of pocket," I said, giving Little Bird a quick, side-eyed glance. "She's an angel in the streets and a little wild in the sheets."

Maverick grinned. "Knew it had to be something to catch your interest."

I grinned back. "I don't think y'all got the best impression tonight. She's shy, and it takes a bit to get her out of her shell. Tic fucked all that up."

"You know Tic," Maverick said with a sigh. "Always got some kind of sand in his man pussy."

Mace, Dump Truck, and a few other guys in the near vicinity had a laugh at Tic's expense.

"Where'd he fuck off to, anyway?" DT asked.

"Dahlia collected him after she got done with me," Mace grinned.

"Ah." Dump Truck nodded.

"No idea what those two got going on, but it's something," Maverick said.

"Don't fuckin' care," I declared, and I didn't. "All I fuckin' care about is that he stays in his goddamn lane where my woman is concerned."

"Have to agree," Dump Truck said with a sigh and I was grateful my brother had my back.

❧

THE NEXT DAY, MY POPS AND I WERE BUSY AROUND THE FARM. I WAS distracted, shot a few texts back and forth to Aspen, but didn't really fully absorb that she only sent back one to a few word answers to everything until it was too late to call her and actually talk.

She was probably in bed and asleep already, and with keeping her out late the night before, I didn't want to do that to her.

I called her the next day, in the morning, just before I went out to feed the goats.

"Hey," I said when she picked up the phone, hating that I sounded so eager. I mean, I missed her. I missed her a lot.

"Hey," she replied and her voice was soft, somber… a little too somber.

"You alright?" I asked.

"I'm okay," she said quickly, her voice warming at an artificial rate. Something was up. I just didn't know what.

"Talk to me, baby. What's going on?" I asked.

She let out a big breath. "My lawyer and my ex-husband's lawyer are trying to reach an agreement. Charles wants half my business, but that would mean closing down, liquidating, and giving him half of everything."

She sounded down, and I scoffed. "No," I said. "Sounds like you maybe need a new lawyer."

"No, I can't afford that," she said with a sigh. "I don't know… maybe it's for the best?" She sighed again and said, "I'm just so tired… of all of it."

"I know, babe," I said, gripping the phone tight, trying not to see red. I swallowed hard and said, "Maybe I can come by tonight."

There was a long silence, a pregnant pause, and finally she said, "No, I think maybe I just need to be alone for a while."

I didn't like it, but this was a tough decision.

"You know, I talked to the club's lawyers to see if I could get a rec for a good divorce attorney. I could maybe help you—"

"No," she said and the finality in her tone both took me aback and honestly made me kind of proud.

"I'll be okay. No matter what happens."

"I know you will, baby," I told her. "You've been handling your business just fine for a long time. I just hate to see you hurt," I said. "I'd pretty much do anything to take that off your shoulders. You're a good woman, and you don't deserve the year you've had."

Silence on the other end of the line and finally, "I've got to go."

"Okay," I said. "Maybe call me—"

The line went dead.

The fuck?

I scowled and put my phone away. Maybe she was just overwhelmed and needed a minute.

I went about my business, feeding the animals. The next day or two was going to be busy. It was finally cool enough for the slaughter which with just me and my dad, that meant *a lot* of work between the slaughter itself and the butchering.

I sent Aspen a text.

Me: I love you, woman.

I didn't get anything back right away, which wasn't completely unusual. Maybe she had her hands dirty, elbow deep in a mound of clay.

Still, something was niggling at me, doubts eroding my confidence that we were alright. I didn't like it, but I'd had my interlude and I needed to put some work in before I could take another.

It took a lot of effort on my part to resist the urge to drop everything and ride out to see her and get some answers.

By Friday things had not improved with my woman. She was *definitely* dodging me, and I didn't like it. I was sitting at the bar at the club nursing a beer and feeling sorry for myself with Mace when Dump Truck sidled in and dropped onto the stool on the other side of me.

"What's his fuckin' problem?" he asked Mace.

Mace had started working the farm with me and my pops. Offering his services in butchering for a steady paycheck until he managed to get on with a local meat packing plant, butcher shop, or grocery store. My dad and I kept the farm all legal and above board, so it hadn't been much to hire Mace on and keep his parole officer happy.

"Aspen's been dodging his texts and calls."

"Oh, yeah? Why d'y'think?" DT asked frowning.

"Started right after Mace's coming home party. I have to imagine it was partially Tic puttin' ideas in her head that she'd never fit in here."

"Well," DT said in his infinite wisdom. "Maybe it's time my girl cashed in on you, or did you forget you owed her, Marisol, and Dahlia that paint night thing."

"Yeah, well, they *better* cash in," I said. "Her ex might be forcing her to shut her business down."

"The fuck?" Dump Truck scowled.

"Exactly. She might be forced to liquidate and give him half."

Mace started laughing.

"What's so funny?" I demanded.

"She should sell you the lot of it for four cents and give him two pennies."

"Wait," I said. "Could she do that?"

"Dunno, would have to talk to a lawyer," DT said.

"Or Mav," Mace suggested. "I bet he'd know."

"Huh." The wheels were turning, now.

"Listen," Dump Truck said. "I like her. You let me deal with that paint night thing, I'll get the girls on it. You talk to Mav and see what kind of devious fuckin' shit he can come up with to ruin her ex's fuckin' day – all on the right side of the law. I think that'll be the only way to win her over. She's a sweet girl," Dump Truck said with a nod. "I like what she does for you."

"Yeah, me too," I said.

"I like her, too. What I can remember of her," Mace said with a laugh and we shared in the chuckle.

"Man, you were fucked up," I agreed.

"Totally worth it, though." He sighed.

"What?" I asked.

"Had a long time to just sit and think when I was locked up," he answered.

"Yeah." I nodded.

"I think I want what you guys have. A woman, a real one, the only one. You know? A life, settle down. Kids?" he shrugged. "Maybe, who knows? I do know I'd like a house. Some land, like what you and your pops got going on."

"Find you a woman who likes to garden," Dump Truck said. "Knows how to can. Y'all would be set come the zombie apocalypse."

We all laughed. "You're not wrong," I agreed. Then started really thinking about something Aspen had said.

"You know, Aspen said she was getting tired of running her place with everything else she had going on."

"Yeah?" Mace said.

"Yeah, said she missed the days she worked out of her garage in addition to her day job, selling her stuff on the weekends at Farmer's Markets."

"Shit, she'd probably make a killing at some of the ren faires and SCA events around the area," Dump Truck said.

I nodded.

"I thought about that."

"Go talk to Mav," Mace urged. "Let DT do whatever he was gonna do with the girls. The way she looked at you, man? This is imminently fixable for all you feel like shit right now."

"Swear to God, next time I see Tic, I'm fixing to punch him right in the mouth if that's the problem," I said.

"Little Bird'll let me know."

"Thanks, bro," I said slipping off my barstool.

"What am I? Chopped liver?" Mace asked, brown eyes twinkling under his mop of black hair.

"Fine," I said. "Thanks, *bros*."

"That's better." He slapped me on the back of the cut. "Go get 'im, Tiger."

"Man, fuck you," I said, shaking my head.

He gave me a cheesy grin and the finger and I went off in search of Maverick.

CHAPTER TWENTY-THREE

---

*A*spen...

I was in hell, but it was sort of a hell of my own making. I didn't know what to do. I wanted so badly to keep Fen in my life, *but* not at the cost of his club pestering or bullying him over it. Yes, I knew he was big, yes, I knew he was strong, but the thought of him fighting someone to defend my honor worried me. Did I worry about him getting hurt? Partially. Did I worry about him hurting someone else? Most definitely, and I didn't want it to be because of me.

Besides, who was to say things didn't get out of hand? That weapons didn't come out or get involved? Fen could be seriously hurt, and for what?

It just wasn't worth it, but I didn't know how to talk to him about it, either. So, I threw myself into my work, trying to get as much done as possible considering I was on the precipice of losing it all.

I felt like I was going insane, but I also felt as though I had already relied on Fenris too much.

I needed to figure it out on my own now. Do this for me, as much as for him.

The phone rang, and I picked up. "Clayrity, this is Aspen speaking, how may I help you?"

"Hi, I'd like to book a private paint night for me and my two girlfriends."

"A private booking for three?" I asked.

"Yeah."

"I can do that," I said.

"This week?" she asked.

"Oh, um, when were you thinking?" I asked. Jesus, talk about short notice. Still, a private booking was good. It was listed on my website, three minimum and a minimum of X amount of dollars. I would double check she knew, but I should be able to handle this – even with the short notice. Double-edged sword, the perks of being the boss but also its downfall.

"Any time between tonight and Friday," she said. "I know it's short notice, but we really need a break and it sounds so much fun. Cost is no object."

"I can do tonight," I said, "It's really the only time for a private session that I have between now and Friday. I do have regular classes on Thursday, Friday, and Saturday nights. Are you sure you don't want the Thursday night regular class? It's my least crowded," I said.

"No, we're sure, we want a private class, just the three of us."

"Okay, can I get your name?" I asked.

"Marisol," she said, and the name tickled my memory but didn't quite click. It sounded familiar. Maybe if I had a last name?

"Last name?" I asked.

"Vasquez."

"Okay, Miss Vasquez, I have you and two others down for tonight. Does seven pm work for you?"

"Absolutely."

"Perfect, I'll see you then."

"Uh-huh, sounds good."

"Bye now!"

"Bye."

I hung up and let out an explosive breath.

"Shit," I muttered.

I picked up my phone and texted the truth…

Me: I wanted to see you tonight but I just had a private party book for a paint night and I could really use the money.

I tossed down my phone and sighed, leaning back in my desk chair in my little office.

"Amber!" I called out.

"Yeah?"

"Set out the glazes for a private party of three, they're coming in at seven!"

"On it, boss lady!"

I put my head in my hands and fought not to cry. That was going to be the hardest part of losing my business, to be honest – letting Amber go.

She didn't deserve it, and I seriously *hated* Charles for putting me in this position. I was beginning to hate my lawyer, too – for not returning calls and, for seemingly brushing me off to the side. I understood that my divorce wasn't particularly lucrative for her, however, it felt like she was doing the absolute bare minimum here, and that just added to my stress and my heartache in several ways.

While it was good news that Charles couldn't touch my inheritance from my mother, I needed to figure something out there, too.

With Copper gone, my sister-in-law, who was a stay-at-home mom, couldn't keep their house. She was going to lose it, and I couldn't let that happen. My mom's house was paid for, and while I could sell it and give my sister-in-law half the money, I couldn't bring myself to do it. Besides, half the money from my mother's house wouldn't be enough to buy her and Silver a home of their own.

I needed to talk to her, but for a while, we might be roommates after a fashion, which was going to be tough on me. While I didn't dislike my sister-in-law, she didn't exactly like me. It wasn't about me, though. It was about my nephew, Silver, and making sure he had a secure future.

The only thing I had going for me was that the clean-out of my mother's house was going pretty well. We'd made a good dent on

Monday, and I'd gotten a little further every night since the party, too.

I hadn't gotten to see Fenris, and that was okay. I was making progress, and I knew he was busy at the farm. I honestly didn't want to be around for the slaughter of the goats, and they were in the thick of it, apparently, so I had begged off seeing him over the weekend. Now, it was Wednesday. I hadn't seen him in a week, and I knew he was starting to worry and things were starting to strain. I hated that it was all my fault but *a private party.*

The timing both sucked and was fortuitous. I really was hanging on by a thread, here.

I stared at my profit-and-loss statement and willed the numbers to move into a healthier position, but it wasn't going to happen.

Not overnight.

Dammit.

"Decisions, decisions," I muttered.

"You know, you don't have to make any right now, right?" I jumped and yelled, pressing my hands over my heart.

Amber burst out in a fit of nervous giggles as I had scared her just as hard as she'd just scared the hell out of me!

"I'm sorry!" she cried, laughing, doubled over and looking at me with wide, sparkling eyes. "I thought you heard me."

"No," I said. "God, you scared the hell out of me!"

"Tis the season?" she asked meekly, and I rolled my eyes.

"Ha, ha!" I declared.

"Speaking of, we're almost out of the greenware pumpkin tea set. I know it's not ideal but do we have it in us to order some more or are we sunk?"

I looked back at the profit-and-loss statement and sighed.

"I wish we did, but no. I think we're going to have to move to plan B for any further autumn-related sales."

"Leaf plates and platters?" she asked.

I nodded. "Glazed in fall colors," I agreed.

"They got some great maples lining the street on the other side of the soccer fields," she said.

"You want to take the walk, or shall I?" I asked.

"I think you could use it, boss. You've been back here fretting for entirely too long. Get some fresh air, take some time to think."

"You are wise beyond your years, Amber," I said, leaning back in my chair with a dejected sigh.

"I know," she said and smiled. I laughed slightly and shook my head.

"Find me a box with handles?" I asked.

"On it, boss."

"Thanks," I murmured, but she was already back near the greenware shelves in the storeroom, rooting through the discarded fruit boxes we tended to collect for those clients that preferred to take greenware home to work on and bring the pieces back to be fired.

While she found a suitable box, I found my jacket and scarf. I looped the infinity scarf in greens around my neck twice and hefted down the leather jacket Fenris had bought for me. It was way too much for me not to wear it, plus it *did* suit me, was warm, and I liked it.

I took the box from Amber and scooted out the back door, calling out to her I would be back before dark to let her get home. I took a deep breath of the crisp, damp, October air and set off to scout for suitable leaves. I tended to roll out some clay flat so I could press the leaves into the surface. I could make plenty of things using the method. Things like platters, serving plates, trinket trays, and spoon rests. Of course, I could do much more than just that with a bit of damp earth and a fallen leaf, but that was just the start.

A good start. Plus, it didn't cost me anything but time and energy rather than the money I would otherwise spend for already molded pieces from a supplier. I didn't have enough of a facility here to just buy the molds and mold things myself.

The walk *did* do me some good. The somewhat mindless task of gathering leaves that were still pliable enough to use for my purposes took my mind off my other troubles for a time. All too soon, dusk foiled my nice time, and I needed to make the walk back to my shop. I went in through the back door and called out to Amber that I was back and that she could clock out if she needed to.

"Thanks," she said, coming back and using the computer to do so.

"No problem," I said, hanging my jacket.

"Store is all yours," she said. "Everything is set up for tonight."

"Thank you, honey."

"Sure, I'll see you tomorrow." She pulled down her own jacket and hefted her backpack and went out through the front of the shop.

I set to work making things for the hour and a half or so that I had before the private party arrived.

I was out front when the trio showed up at my door, smiling, laughing, and waving and I opened it to them bewildered. Suddenly, the name Marisol clicked when I saw her with Dahlia and Little Bird.

"What?" I cried. "What are you doing here?"

"We wanted to come hang," Dahlia said, hugging me fiercely. Little Bird was next, and Marisol didn't hesitate.

"I would have met you at the party, but my little brother got sick and I had to stay home and take care of him," she said. I stood back and let them into my shop, turning the sign to 'closed' and locking the door, pulling the chain on the neon 'open' sign so that it would go dark.

"You didn't have to book a private party for that!" I protested.

"Nonsense," Dahlia said pointedly. "You have to make a living."

"Oh, well, um…" I was disoriented for sure but not so much I couldn't do my job, I'd like to think. I tugged on my apron and said, "Grab your aprons and I'll take you on a full tour before we begin. We can choose which projects you want to paint and go from there."

I gave them the tour starting out front with the neatly lined shelves of bisqueware and finishing in back with the more fragile greenware and the raw clay.

"What are you doing with these?" Marisol asked, picking up one of the leaves out of the box I'd carried them in.

"Oh, I'm making these." I went over to the shelf where several platters and plates were drying.

"Oooooh, those are going to be so neat!"

"Can we make our own?" Dahlia asked.

"Sure, but they won't be ready to paint until after I've fired them and that takes time."

"So." Marisol shrugged and grinned and said, "We come back and book another time to paint them."

Little Bird clapped excitedly and I just sort of stood there stunned and said, "I can't possibly charge you!"

"You can," Dahlia said, steering me to the worktable taking up the center of the room, "and you will."

"Okay, what do we do?" Marisol asked.

"It's really easy, actually…"

We set about making each girl a set of three serving platters, each successively smaller than the one before, using some of my wooden forms, to curl up the edges of the leaves to hold pooling liquid when they were finished.

It didn't take terribly long to accomplish. I mean, roll the clay flat, press the leaf, roll it into the surface to get all of the delicate spines and veins into the impression, cut around it with an X-acto knife, mold it over the wooden form carefully so as not to obliterate the design and take a damp sea sponge to the bottom and around the leaf's cut edges to round and smooth them.

"How long you been doing this?" Marisol asked, smiling as she worked. I'd given them all the plain black student aprons I kept around the shop to protect their nice clothes.

"Since I was young," I said. "My mother taught me. She was exceptional at it."

"So, what's the deal?" Dahlia asked, getting right to it. "Why are you avoiding Fen?"

I startled and blushed with guilt.

"I'm not a-avoiding him," I stammered, and it was, of course, a lie. I had been, and I knew it.

Marisol took one look at my face and snorted, laughing indelicately and Little Bird said, "As Dump Truck would say, you can't bullshit a bullshitter."

I felt my face drop, and I shook my head unwilling to look at any of them, "I don't belong," I said quietly. "I don't want to cause Fenris any trouble with his brothers. You all are very important to him."

"Tic," Dahlia muttered, and put her hand on her hip. "Well, he'll be lucky to keep all his teeth when Fen finds out, and he *will* find out, eventually."

"Girl, you need to talk to him!" Marisol chided.

"I've never seen him so happy or at peace than when I've seen him with you," Little Bird declared.

"Truth is," I murmured, taking a seat in one of the metal folding chairs back here, "I've never been so happy as when I'm with him, either."

"It's like they see you, no pretenses, no bullshit," Little Bird said and I looked up sharply, knowing my emotions were raw and naked on my face.

"Yeah."

"Honey, you can't let this fall apart just because of Tic," Marisol said, rolling her eyes. "Tic isn't the whole of the club. I wouldn't be here otherwise. Honestly, Mav *liked you*. He wouldn't have said anything to me or let me hare off with these two to convince you to come back and give us all another try if he didn't."

"So, you're Mavericks…" I trailed off.

"Old Lady, and damn right," Marisol said with pride.

I made a face. "You can't be more than twenty. A little young to be calling yourself *old*," I said.

The three of them laughed.

"It's just one more terminology out of the biker vernacular you need to learn," Dahlia declared.

"So, since you were with Tic does that make you…"

Dahlia made a face. "Oh, God no! I'm just a club slut, and proud of it!"

I blinked stupidly, not sure what to say to *that*.

"Okay," Marisol declared. "Crash course time…"

CHAPTER TWENTY-FOUR

*F*enris...

I was sitting at the bar and nursing a hard cider, feeling like my ass was being held to the flames of hell while I stared at the black, blank screen of my phone waiting for it to fuckin' *do* something.

Maverick and Dump Truck were to either side of me, waiting with me.

Finally, the phone lit up with an actual notification that I *wanted* instead of the bullshit news or whatever.

A text came through.

Dahlia: You can come down and talk to her.

I felt my shoulders and back loosen up with relief.

Me: What was the problem?

"I can go talk to her," I said, getting up.

"Good," Dump Truck said with a nod.

"About fuckin' time," Maverick said. "What was the problem?"

"Tic, probably. I haven't—" My phone buzzed against the bar top where I'd tossed it back down after shooting back to Dahlia.

Dahlia: Tic and his mouth.

Maverick leaned over and saw it and gave a nod.

"Yeah, that's worth at least a punch in the mouth the next time you see him."

I scowled. Mav had to give me the go-ahead for at least that.

"I'll see how bad it is and get back to you," I declared.

"I hate fuckin' drama." Dump Truck rolled his eyes. "Bylaws dictate an ass whoopin', he keeps this pansy ass shit up."

"I know what they say," Maverick said sharply, giving my boy some side-eye.

"Right, I better get down there while the invitation stands open," I said. "I'll catch you two on the flipside. Pretty sure the girls will head this way when I get there."

"Good deal," Mav declared.

"Good *luck*," Dump Truck shot at me. "Go easy on her." I gave him a look like, *no, shit*, and he gave a nod. "You got this."

"I fuckin' better," I grumbled, and I went for the back door and to cross 15th where my bike was parked at the boneyard.

I rode down the hill toward Georgetown, across the 1st Ave S. bridge. It was maybe five minutes of travel time from the club to her shop, which was damn convenient. I parked behind it, and before I could even get off the bike, the back door opened, Dahlia standing in it in one of her 40s style dresses. Black with white polka dots this time.

I took the steps up to the back door of the building and she stepped out in her red peep-toe pumps and sighed.

"I don't know what his fuckin' problem is," she muttered dispassionately, and I shook my head.

"You," I answered. "You, and the fact you don't see it."

"See what?" she demanded and jerked her head back, an ugly scowl on her face.

"Talk to him and find out. Just do me a solid, don't tell him shit about how he's gonna get punched in the fuckin' mouth for this."

"Oh, for Christ's sakes," she muttered irritably and threw up her hands.

"Don't believe in him," I said honestly. She rolled her eyes, and I grinned and added, "Better to be a wolf of Odin than a lamb of God."

She sighed looking tired and shook her head saying, "I can't argue with you there."

"There a reason we're out here and not in there?" I asked.

"Yeah, I just wanted to warn you, she's had a good cry and the girl's an ugly crier. Don't be too hard on her. She really loves you and thought she was doing what was best."

"Not a chance," I said. "On either account."

"Then let me collect my ladies and let us get out of your way," she said and slipped back in. She left the door open, and I got a view down the worktable at Aspen red faced and sniffling as Marisol stood up and gathered her purse. Little Bird, who was consoling my girl, smiled in my direction and stood up as well.

The three of them cleared out, hugging Aspen in farewell. Before they left out the back door I asked, "You want I should walk you around out front to your car?"

Aspen's had been the only one out in the back lot, so I had to assume they were parked out front.

"I can let you out the front," Aspen said, rising.

"Nah, we got it," Dahlia said, waving us off.

"We're tough bitches," Marisol added.

"Holler if you need to," I said.

"Will do," Little Bird said with a smile.

The door shut, and it was just me and my girl, and despite the sadness that painted her face in blotchy red and white, making her green eyes stand out all the more. She was beautiful and an absolute sight for sore eyes.

She sniffed, her eyes welling again, and I went to her and pulled her in tight against me, resting my chin on the top of her head and murmuring to her that everything would be alright… and it would. As soon as we talked.

"Come here," I murmured, hooking a boot under the rung on her chair and pulling it closer. "Sit down," I said.

She took the seat, her hands never leaving mine as though terrified if she let go, I would leave. I hooked my boot in the chair Little Bird had been in and sit my ass down, and no – I didn't let go of her, either.

"Talk to me," I said, steeling myself for whatever would come next. Afraid she was gonna say she couldn't do it. That she couldn't hack it in the life and that this was going to be goodbye. I dreaded it. So much. I still needed her to have her say, though. I couldn't fix it if I didn't know what was broken.

"I just don't know that I'm right for you," she finally said, defeated, and her shoulders dropped and my heart sank.

"Why?" I asked, needing to hear it.

"I'm just not like those other girls. The loud music and all those people. I'm so… *boring* and I don't want anyone thinking *badly* of you for being with someone like me."

I smiled a little sadly, sighing, weighing my words carefully. I looked at her and I saw a beautiful woman who when she smiled, I couldn't help but smile myself. When she wept, I fully expected the rain to fall outside, and when she was content, made me content by default. I hated seeing her go through this storm of emotion but I couldn't fault her for it.

She'd been through so much; *too much,* and the way she'd been brought up? The piece of work her mother had been, always criticizing, nothing ever having been good enough, that was a lifetime of indoctrination and conditioning to work through in the short time we'd been together.

While she wasn't weak; far from it in fact, she had her weaknesses and thinking badly of herself? Going to the first negative foregone conclusion in any given scenario where she was concerned? That was part of a conditioned response that would take another lifetime to eradicate.

And the only way to do that? Patience. Consistent love, commitment, and care. Talking it out when shit like this went wrong. There were no shortcuts. There was no end run to be made around it. This was part of who she was, and none of the flaws she imagined she carried was in fact true.

Being blind to her wonder and her worth? That was her greatest flaw, and a deeply ingrained one at that.

"First of all," I said gently, "your biggest mistake here is thinking I give a *fuck* what anyone else thinks. The only one you gotta impress is me, and you've already done that in spades." I raised the back of her hand to my lips and pressed a kiss to it.

"Second of all," I continued, "the only person who thinks you can't be trusted, or that you're *boring*, or what the fuck ever, doesn't even *know you*. To be honest, I don't think he even deserves a chance. The flaw in the design here is that he didn't give you one. He's acting more like a citizen than you are being all judgy and shit. That ain't supposed to be what we're about."

She sat mutely, staring into my eyes, the wheels in that pretty little head of her's turning, chewing through what I was saying.

"I don't want you to get hurt," she said, and I barked a laugh.

"I'm not the one who's gonna be hurting," I said. "Look, I'd be lying if I said this life didn't come with its fair share of cuts, bumps, and bruises… but they heal. The kind of broken I'm faced with, you walking away from me, even now, even after so little time?"

I shook my head. "I don't want to hurt like that, baby. I honestly wouldn't be able to sleep at night wondering, not knowing how you're doing, scared you'd be out here getting steamrolled by life because let's face it. It's run over you more than a couple of times lately."

She nodded and gave a choked, bitter laugh.

"You're not lying about *that*," she said and closed her eyes sighing.

"I think it's time you stopped thinking and worrying about everyone else," I said and tried to keep my voice soothing, knowing how anathema to her that very statement was. A complete opposite to her entire being. "I think it's time you took time to worry about yourself. To take care of *you* and find the things you love. Get back to some of that, move forward with something new… on *your* terms and nobody else's."

"I don't know how to do that," she whispered, crystalline tears falling from those emerald eyes of hers.

"I do," I said with a half-smile. "Can teach you what you need to know on that front easy."

"Yeah?" she asked softly, her gaze a little eager.

"Yup. It's all about the subtle art of not giving a fuck."

She laughed, an abrupt but good sound.

A silence stretched between us and I took a cleansing breath and asked her, "So, what do you want? What do you *really* want?"

"I want my divorce to be over," she said. "I want Charles and all of his bullshit out of my life once and for all. For good."

"Could kill him for you, if you'd like," I said casually, lifting one shoulder in a shrug.

"Ha, ha," she said and her voice was laden with sarcasm. Must have been the look I gave her, because it was like I'd stolen the very air she breathed from the room.

"You're not joking," she said quietly, and I kept my gaze steady.

"I'm only *half* joking," I said, and she swallowed hard.

"That scares me," she admitted honestly.

"Why should it?" I asked. "Club charter has a rule, no women and no children. No exceptions. You're as safe as can be."

"It's not that," she said a little helplessly, and I cocked my head.

"Then what?"

"For as awful as things are right now, and as awful as he's been… Charles didn't mean for my mother or my brother to die. He didn't mean for me to discover his cheating the day after my brother's funeral. He's just angry, wants to talk to me, and he thinks by pouring the pressure on, he'll get me to crack… none of those things should be execution worthy."

I nodded slow. "Does make him a monumental asshole at least worth an ass whoopin'," I said.

"Okay," she conceded. "I'll give you that, but I don't want that either."

"Why not?" I asked. "Easy enough."

"Because that's not the way *I* handle things!" she cried. "Everything Charles has done so far is on *Charles,* is a reflection of who *Charles* is. I don't want or have to do bad things because that would just be a reflection of *me* and I don't want to be that kind of ugly when I look into the mirror."

I bowed my head and nodded carefully, unsure how to bridge the gap here because I *was* the type of ugly she was talking about here. My soul was stained, I wasn't above getting dirty, and I didn't know what that meant for her.

"Is it a dealbreaker that I am?" I asked.

"That you're what?" she asked, and the confusion was clear in her green eyes.

"That I am that type of ugly. That I can look in the mirror just fine most days with the man I am."

Her mouth dropped open in a little 'o' of surprise and she protested, "You're *not*, though."

"You don't know the things I've done, baby. You can't know."

She took her hands from mine with an inarticulate cry of frustration and covered her face with them.

"What was the last bad thing you did?" she demanded firmly, taking her hands from her face and fixing me with a diamond hard look.

"Broke a man's arms," I said, without any preamble.

"Why?"

"He broke into the club's property and stole from us."

"I'm not even going to ask why you didn't call the police," she said and her face set into lines of grim resignation.

"Yeah, pretty pointless. They'd take a report and fuck right off never to be seen or heard from again. They don't care." I gave a little shrug.

"What did you hope to accomplish, hurting him?"

"Well," I said with a sigh. "He'll never steal from us again, that's for sure. By extension, we'll get our shit back, and maybe he'll be scared straight. Get himself clean."

She stared at me, eyes bouncing back and forth over my face. She sighed.

"How do you know I won't go to the police?" she asked.

"I trust you," I answered simply. "You go to the police; I'd probably be fucked. Likewise, you tell anyone in the club I told you club business? I'd get my ass royally handed to me and it might not be no pair of broken arms."

"Then where would your father be?" she asked softly. "With the farm?"

"Royally disappointed in my ass, that's for sure," I said with a chuckle. "And not for breaking the dude's arms."

She sighed and her shoulders dropped in defeat. "I understand it," she said softly. "I just don't know if it's something I can ever condone."

"Not asking you to, baby. None of us really do, I don't think. We all know it's between us and our maker when the time comes. Every man among us has our demons. We all know what rejection feels like as we try to make our way through this life. Hell, some of us know rejection so hard that's why we're here. So we can know what it's like to have one place where we belong."

"That breaks my heart," she murmured.

I nodded.

"Mine too, since I'm being honest. That's why I'm here. A part of the club, I mean. It's a strange way to balance my scales, but it's worked for me… They also accepted me when no one else would."

"There's a good and a bad to everything, I suppose," she said softly.

"That's the truth, Little Leaf," I said.

"We might be rough around the edges, we might be the kind of thing most normal people fear, but they only fear what they can't understand and the thing most people could never understand about us? Is the depths of love, loyalty, and brotherhood we'll go to for one another."

She bit her lips together and regarded me and finally confessed, "I am so tired of being alone, and afraid, and of not having anyone I feel like I can trust. There's none of that when I'm with you but…"

I sniffed and nodded, "I'm right here, baby girl. You can trust me, and I'm telling you right now, any motherfucker tries? He's going to have a lot more to worry about than a pair of broken arms. As for the rest? Tic is an outlier. Maybe some of the rest of the boys don't trust you yet, but trust comes with time and unlike Tic? They're willing to give you that."

"I don't want to lose you, I just thought—"

"I know, baby. I know. And you ain't lost me. I'm right here." I opened my arms, and she leaned forward, resting her head against my shoulder and crying softly, letting the last of whatever it was holding her back go… and I was here for it. Right here.

CHAPTER TWENTY-FIVE

spen…

Maybe it was foolish of me, I don't know… maybe it was impulsive. Crazy. A bad idea… but I went home with him. I didn't even take my car. I rode with him to his place, frozen to the bone after the chilly ride and shivering even despite the warm leather jacket.

He took it from me, inside the back door, and hung it on the line of pegs in the mudroom before shucking out of his own.

"Upstairs, babe. Let's get you warm," he murmured, and I nodded.

We went up the stairs and I paused, unsure which direction. Bathroom or bedroom? He touched my shoulder gently and went past me to the bedroom, taking my hand to pull me after him, closing the door behind us.

Wordlessly, he went and lit the candles and put on the deeply primitive yet healing Nordic music that he preferred and that I was growing to adore.

He came back to me, reaching past me, clasping a hand on my hip and pulling me tight against his body, his mouth finding mine. I melted into the safe and familiar place of solitude that his kiss brought to me. The storm in my mind of mixed emotions falling silent. The surety that this is where I belonged, in the circle of his arms, crashing into me, sweeping over and through me, twisting me around and showing me that all my doubts were utter *bullshit*.

God, I was like a trained damned *monkey*. Constantly trying to live up to the shifting expectations of a woman who was dead and my ex-husband who had very likely never even cared for me from the beginning… only for what he thought I could do for him.

With Fenris, everything was different. All pretenses stripped away, no nonsense. No expectations, no more bullshit.

Just, *this is me and how I live my life and I hope you can accept me.*

Which wasn't that what I wanted? To be loved, to be wanted, to be allowed to exist as I was?

I held onto Fenris tightly and kissed him back fervently and with passion. His grip on me tightened, his other arm joining the first to wrap around me, and I had to think, his notion of warming me up was right on target. The fire of my desire stoked, the low burning coals sparking, flame licking up from low in my belly and tickling me just beneath my breastbone. Nipples tightening with my arousal, my breath stolen, my body responding to his touch like a night-blooming flower whose petals had been touched by the moon, unfurling and perfuming the air sweetly.

Our hands worked without conscious thought, plucking at buttons, lifting fabric, and lowering zippers. Cold hands against warm skin, teeth nipping, tongues licking, fingers grasping and through it all the panting. The feral little grunts of need and frustration as we both tried to meet one solitary need – to be fitted to one another as intimately as possible in as short amount of time as possible.

He picked me up, once we were both nude, and I put my arms around him. He laid me back on the bed and crawled up behind me, fitting himself between my legs, his mouth back to mine, his arms tenderly around me as we made out, ravenous for one another.

He thrust his cock against me, rubbing against my pussy lips, not penetrating, not yet, but the sensation of his velvet length against my clit was amazing, driving me wild. I grasped his face between my hands, his beard rough against my palms

He felt so good against me. Strong, capable, and fiercely protective. I gave in. I wanted to. I needed to. To feel this kind of savage love felt like a once in a lifetime opportunity and I didn't want to cast that aside. Not when I had been desperate to feel this loved for so long.

I wrapped myself around him like ivy. Holding onto him as fiercely as he held onto me. Crying out into his mouth when he found purchase and sank into me. I wasn't quite ready, but my body quickly adjusted.

He thrust deep inside me, and I clung to him. Both of us moving against each other in perfect synchronicity. I don't know how long we were like that. How many songs passed through the shuffle of his playlist, or how far the candles burned down. I didn't care. He didn't care. It was just *us*. Both he and I existing, breathing hot and heavy the same air, the dew of sweat cooling our skins, his gods watching for all I cared as we loved each other deep into the night.

I don't know how many times I came – a gentle rolling ebb and flow of wave after wave of pleasure crashing onto my shore.

Likewise, I didn't know how many position changes he took us through. Always careful of me, that nothing grew too tired.

My back, my knees, my stomach, on top of him. Each transition fluid and at the perfect time. Gazing down at him in the firelight from all those flickering candles… I didn't know who was worshipped or who was doing the worshipping. Perhaps it was both of us. Perhaps neither. Perhaps, the old gods he sometimes spoke of watched.

I had no doubt in my mind of their approval.

~

WE LAY IN THE CANDLE LIT TWILIGHT. CLOSE; ME NESTLED INTO HIS SIDE a leg over his and my head on his shoulder. He traced spirals on my back, his other hand a warm weight on my thigh as I stared unseeing and vacant, my mind barely lucid as I drifted in the calm waters of afterglow. He kissed the top of my head suddenly, as though he'd just woken from a dream himself and asked, "You doing alright?"

"I'm good," I said dreamily, and he chuckled and kissed my hair again, his hand trailing fingertips up my spine and burying in the back of my hair, massaging the base of my skull, causing me to groan in a completely different pleasure.

"You ever think about what kind of life you want to live?" he asked.

"A simple one," I answered immediately. "One where I can make my pottery and glaze it. I wish I could go back to selling it at markets… I don't want to close down my shop, but I do at the same time."

"Yeah?"

"Yeah. It feels like my old life. It's not making money, and I *really* just want my divorce finalized. I hate giving Charles what he wants, but I just can't do this anymore. I'm… I'm tired."

I let the defeat creep into my voice and I hated that, to some effect but that was what it was. I couldn't hide it anymore. I couldn't keep pretending that I was strong, or some kind of a badass. I wasn't. I was just tired. Tired of Charles, tired of grieving, tired of struggling, and tired of having to be the one to make all of these complicated decisions.

I took a deep breath. Fenris had trusted me implicitly earlier tonight, and I felt the least I could do was return the favor.

I trusted him back and spilled my guts about all of it. About exactly how I felt, and he just squeezed me a little tighter and kissed the top of my head again. "What if I told you there might be a way to have your cake and eat it, too?" he asked

"How?" I asked, sniffling, an errant tear dripping down my nose.

"You need to liquidate your assets in the business, yeah?" he asked. "To give him his half?"

"Yeah, but they were all bought with my money, it's hardly fair," I said.

"They're yours, and ain't nobody said you have to sell them for what they're worth."

"What?" I asked.

"Sell the whole fuckin' lot to me for a buck, then when your husband wants his half, give him a check for fifty cents and tell him to fuck off. Of course, one of my boy's suggested selling for even lower than that. He said do four cents, so that when it came to giving him his half, you could hand him your two cents."

I laughed. Oh, God. I actually liked the sound of that!

"I mean, I don't know… could I *do* that?"

"Mav is the smart and devious mind when it comes to the law. Let me run it by him?"

"Sure," I said softly.

"How much you got left on your lease?" he asked me and I hadn't even thought that far ahead.

"Um, I don't know," I answered. "I didn't even think about that and I can't remember dates and times for the life of me right now. I mean, if it's not right in front of my face and on some sort of fire that needs putting out, I don't seem to have a head for anything.

"That's okay, baby. That's okay."

"There's just so much…" I said. "Not just with Charles but with my brother's widow and my nephew, Silver."

"What's going on with them?" he asked.

"I think they're going to have to move in with me at my mom's before too long. Christen can't keep up with the house payments. My brother had life insurance, but the policy won't cover the remainder owed on their house. Not even close."

"Not sure how that's your problem, babe."

"My sister-in-law and I may have no love lost between us, but I can't do that to my nephew. I would never do that to my brother's son."

"That's fair," he said. "You're a good woman, you do know that, don't you?"

"Eh, I'm alright," I tried to joke, but he wouldn't let me get away with it. He tipped my chin, and I looked up at him.

"You're a good woman, Aspen, and it's only one of the many reasons why I love you."

I think I forgot to breathe. The sincerity in his eyes was something that I didn't think could be matched.

"We're gonna get you all sorted out, baby. One complication at a time. You just tell me where to start."

"Um, getting my mom's house in order and cleared out," I said, and he nodded.

"Okay. We stay there until it's done."

"What?"

"You heard me. We'll get up first thing tomorrow, head over there so you can get a shower and a fresh change of clothes and take you to work. When you're done for the day, we'll stay there chipping away at it 'til it's done."

"You're serious," I said.

"I am."

"You would do that? Uproot your entire life just to make mine better?"

"In a heartbeat," he affirmed.

I fell mute and lay my head back down.

"Okay?" he asked.

"Okay," I murmured.

"Okay."

IT'D BEEN A FEW DAYS, AND WE WERE EXECUTING FEN'S LOOSE PLAN through a bit of trial and error. There honestly wasn't a whole lot we were able to get done the next few nights. By the time I got home, it was *late* and I could only maybe go through one or two boxes or fill a trash bag.

Still, slow progress was better than no progress, I guess.

On Saturday night, Fen rode from his farm to my shop and came in just before I flipped the sign to 'closed.' Several of the ladies from the class that evening eyed him like he was a side of beef as they walked by, and I fought down the urge to say anything.

"Hi," I murmured as he bent to kiss me.

"Hey, gorgeous."

"What brings you here?" I asked as I locked the doors.

"Wanted to see my baby," he murmured and reached over to pull the cord on the lit 'open' sign higher up in the window.

I couldn't help but smile and said, "Well, here I am."

"Club's having a feed tonight. Thought we could grab dinner on the way home versus cooking."

"Oh, you know what?" I said. "That sounds really good. Are you sure I'm invited, though?"

"Babe, you're mine, you're with me, you're invited. The girls'll be there and it won't be nearly as crowded as Mace's thing."

"Yeah?" I asked, moving around my shop, picking up.

"Yeah, just the local chapter. No out-of-towner's."

"Okay." I nodded. "Just let me finish closing up."

"What can I do?"

"Nothing!" Amber called from the back of the shop. "I got it! Go on and get outta here, boss!"

I smiled and laughed a little. She knew now that I would eventually be closing down. That had been a hard conversation, but she'd declared herself in to the bitter end.

"Naw, we'll help," Fenris declared. "It's dark as fuck out there and no way I'm letting you go out with no one here to have your back. Safety in numbers, kid."

"I'm not a child," Amber said, stepping out front with us and rolling her eyes for Fen's benefit.

"You're just a damn baby," he argued.

"Fen's right, Amber. It's getting sketchier and sketchier out there."

"Yeah, well, gentrification hasn't *quite* taken a firm hold around here just yet."

"I know."

"Double-edged sword," she said breezily.

We made quick work of cleanup, and I declared the rest could be done on Tuesday morning when I came in.

"Okay, boss. Whatever you say."

We went out back and Fen made sure Amber was shut safe in her car. We waited for her to pull out and I turned to him. He gathered me up and kissed me for *real* this time, hand on my ass and everything.

"Mm, I like it when you do that," I said.

"I like that you like that I do that," he said with a smile.

"Riding with me, or?"

"Naw, I'll see you up there. Park out front."

"Okay, see you in a few." He opened my car door for me and I got in. He had a habit of knocking on the roof of my car twice after I shut the door before walking away enough for me to be sure I wouldn't run over his foot or something as I pulled out of the gravel lot.

The drive up to the club was barely enough to get my car's heater blowing warm air. I parked in the same spot I had last time, around the corner of the building, and killed the engine, my lights, and what have you. Making sure I had my phone and tucking my purse under the seat.

I got out of the car and was just coming around the front of the building when who should I *almost* run into?

Why, Tic, of course.

"Shit," he muttered and feeling much stronger than I had last time, I took a deep breath, let it out and looked at him square in the eye.

"Got something to say, citizen girl?"

"No, but I do." Tic turned, just in time for Fen's fist to crash into his jaw. Not even *I* had seen that coming!

"Fen!" I cried as Tic wheeled around and put some distance between me and Fen. I stood in front of my man; hands splayed across the cool leather on his chest.

Fen pointed at Tic and called out. "You disrespect my woman or me again, I'm going to whoop your fuckin' ass!"

Guys came pouring out of the club.

"The fuck's your problem, man?" Tic demanded, spitting blood and touching his lip gingerly. "Ain't you ever heard of bro's before ho's?"

"Oh, shit," I heard someone say as Fen literally passed me off into someone's arms beside us and went after Tic.

I actually suddenly didn't care. Tic was asking for it with that one.

Tic went low and rushed Fen, tackling him and I surged forward instinctually. Arms went around my waist and hauled me back.

"Whoa, there, darlin'! Let the men folk sort their shit out!" whoever it was called, and he started laughing.

I shit you not, money came out and the other men started placing *bets*.

Of course, the favored winner was Fen.

I covered my face with my hands and leaned back against Mace, who was the one who had a hold of me, when Tic cracked Fen in the face with a closed fist and a meaty 'thwack!'

"Oh, God!" I cried, peeking between my fingers.

Of course, it's all fun and games until the cops show up, which they did. A King County Sherriff's SUV whipping into the parking lot off the main drag, red and blue lights sparking to life in the dark.

My stomach turned into lead as groans and boos erupted all around me.

"Shit, gotta go," Mace muttered and disappeared inside the club while there was still enough confusion and the cops had yet to get out of their vehicle. Maverick stepped up beside me, taking Mace's place, a hand down low, reaching back to clutch my wrist.

"The only thing you say is 'I don't answer questions' period. Okay?"

"I don't answer questions," I said, and he turned his head, flashing a feral grin at me.

"Atta, girl."

"Whoa, what's going on out here?" the first officer demanded.

No one said anything.

"Alright, everyone get your IDs out," the second one ordered. I looked to Mav, and he gave me a nod. I extracted my phone with its little silicone wallet on the back that held my debit card and ID for when I didn't want to carry my purse around.

I swear, it was like the cop made a beeline for me to check mine first and I frowned slightly.

"Aspen Lawson," he read, and I said nothing. He eyed me critically and asked, "What are you doing out here Ms. Lawson?"

"I don't answer questions," I said firmly.

"Really now?" the cop asked.

"I don't answer questions," I repeated, and I gave him a look that told him he might as well stop trying, I was not going to be that bitch.

Fenris fixed me with a look across the open ring of people and sniffed, wiping at the blood under his nose.

The cop caught the look between us and went over to Fen, snatching his ID roughly out of his hand and squinting at it. "Okay, Mr. Lars Elstad. You want to tell me what's going on here?"

I blinked, realizing that this was the first time I had actually ever heard Fenris' legal name. My next thought being he didn't look like a Lars or an Elstad. He looked like a Fenris.

"I don't answer questions," he said with a smirk.

"What about you?" He pulled Tic-Tac's license out of his hand but didn't say his name.

"I don't answer questions," Tic declared and spit on the ground at the deputy's feet.

"Well clearly somethin's going on out here."

No one said a word. We all froze them out.

Another Sherriff's office vehicle pulled into the lot.

"Anyone inside?" the first deputy who'd spoken, an older man going soft in the middle demanded.

"We don't answer questions," Maverick declared. "As for inside, you got a warrant?" he demanded.

"No, no we do not."

"Then inside ain't none of your concern," and with that, Ms. Momma Kat came around the bar and shut the door.

"Get all their IDs, run 'em for warrants," the older officer ordered.

"Get comfy, baby, this is gonna be awhile," Maverick said out of the side of his mouth.

He wasn't lying, it *did* take a while. The better part of an hour.

"It's your lucky day," one of the deputies said, handing Fenris his ID. "You're coming with us."

"On what charge?" Maverick demanded, scowling as the hair stood up on the back of my neck.

"No charge, yet. He's wanted for questioning."

"Yeah, fuck that. You can go through our lawyer," Maverick said.

"You don't want to come voluntarily?" the deputy asked, and it was the young buck from the first car.

"I don't answer questions," Fen said in a low growl of irritation.

"Here's our lawyer's number," Maverick said handing a card over. "You tell whatever detective to call them. Now, if you're not arresting any of us or charging us with anything? Do us a solid and go the fuck away. This is private property, and as you can see, we aren't doing anything illegal."

"I don't see that at all," one of the cops from the second car grumbled.

"Then charge one of us or off you fuck… *sir*," Maverick said. "We all know our rights."

"You sure you wanna get mixed up with the likes of these fellas?" the fat cop asked and held out my ID to me.

"I don't answer questions," I said firmly with a tart little eat-shit-and-die smile.

"Your funeral, little lady," he said.

"I'll take that bet and win it," I shot back and a few of the guys from the club laughed at the man's expense. He gave me a flat, unfriendly look, and I stood my ground, even though I felt my cheeks flush and my heart race in my breast.

"We'll see, now won't we?"

I wrinkled my nose impishly and reiterated for the umpteenth time, "I don't answer questions."

That got more laughter out of the guys still milling around.

"Best quit while you're ahead, son," Major said and laughed, his tongue ring winking in the light from the front of the club, which had several lights under the overhang running the length of the front of the building.

"Y'all have a nice night, now. Keep the peace," one of the other guys said, tipping an imaginary hat.

"Alright, boys. Let these fine deputies get to more important things out there tonight," Mav ordered.

They got in their cars and drove off and I practically sagged with relief.

"That wasn't nothing," Maverick said dryly. "We're lucky they didn't line us up and frisk us."

"Naw, man. Why should they care? We were only beating the shit out of each other this time," Fenris said, and I slightly jumped. I hadn't seen him move up. I put my arms around him and hugged him gratefully.

"Yeah, well, it's gonna be a hurry up and wait now to see what the fuck they want to talk to you about," Maverick said. Fen just grunted noncommittally and sniffed.

"Let me get you some ice?" I asked softly, and he nodded down at me, whipping a black bandana out of one of his back pockets and wiping at his nose.

I looked over at Tic and murmured, "I'll get you some too, on account of I'm not an asshole."

Fenris laughed and gave me a squeeze, while Tic just scowled and gave me a solitary nod. I would take it, for whatever it was worth.

"You did good," Maverick declared and hoped I didn't glow outwardly from the praise. I would much rather keep that shit to myself on the inside.

Fenris, thankfully, let me fuss over him a little. I gave him two ice packs that Momma Kat and I put together. One for his nose and one for his swelling knuckles. When I had a stiff drink in his hand and him seated on one of the love seats I sighed and said, "One down, one to go."

"What do you mean?" he asked me.

"You catch more flies with honey. I'm going to check on Tic if it's all the same to you."

"You're a good woman," he said, and it was something that he'd said before.

"I should hope so," I murmured. "I'm *your* woman and you only deserve the best."

His blue eyes flickered up to mine, and I saw some surprise in them, then a warmth flooded them that made me smile like some sort of madwoman, and maybe I was? I mean, I'd just seriously stood up to the cops out there. *Yikes.*

Tic was in one of the two bathrooms, running cold water over his hand and looking at himself in the mirror. I leaned against the doorway and sighed asking, "Can I get you an icepack?"

"Yeah," he said, nodding and solemn.

"Need more than one?"

"No."

I went and made him up an ice pack and brought it to him.

"Thanks," he said tersely, and I nodded.

"You're welcome. This does not make us friends."

At that, he cracked the first smile in my direction that wasn't shitty or a sneer.

"You're alright," he said with a nod.

I smiled but didn't say anything. I just went back to Fen. The pizza was delivered just a few minutes later.

There wasn't a whole lot to the rest of the evening. Eventually all the guys started leaving by ones and twos. Some with girls, some by themselves or with each other until it was just me, Fen, Maverick, and Momma Kat, who was going around cleaning up the place like some sort of den mother.

"Hey, Mav," Fen said.

"Yeah, what's up man?"

"Got some sticky legal shit I wanna ask you for my little leaf on the wind, here."

"Shoot," he said.

Fenris asked about the divorce and liquidating my shop, then asked about my mom's house and the half of my brother's inheritance.

"Shit, I'd need to see some things. Like the wills, and your lease, that sort of shit to get it all sorted out. Can you get a hold of those things?" he asked.

"Of course," I said.

"Would you mind me having a look at 'em?"

"I don't see why not," I said with a shrug.

"Good deal. As soon as I have all the documentation, I'll look over everything and let you know what I can come up with."

"Thanks," I said softly.

"Thank *you*," he said. "You did real good under a tense situation out there with the cops."

"I don't feel like I did anything to be honest," I said with a laugh.

"You did plenty, trust me. Now if you ever encounter any cop for any reason, them's the magic words," he said.

"I don't answer questions?" I guessed.

"Those are the ones."

I smiled, he smiled, and with a nod at Fen he hoisted himself to his feet.

"I'm about to get back to my girl and get myself laid," he said.

"I'm going to take him home and probably do the same," I said with a grin and Maverick laughed out loud.

"We'll make you one of us, yet," he said.

Fenris smiled at me and I smiled back.

"I told you so," my man declared and it warmed me down to my toes.

CHAPTER TWENTY-SIX

*F*enris...

Her sister-in-law was a bitch, had fucked around, and the bitch was about to find out.

Time had gone by in a bit of a blur over the last couple of weeks and Halloween was right around the fuckin' corner. Aspen and I had been busting our asses around her mother's old place clearing out old furniture and a lifetime of her mom's shit only for this bitch right here to spit on her fuckin' efforts in one of the rudest, most self-entitled ways I had ever seen in my fuckin' life.

"You're selling the house, you're giving me half, and that's final. It's not my problem what you do after that." Christen was a literal fucking ice princess. She fucking *radiated* cold, from her glittering flat blue eyes, to her pale, overdone makeup, to her blond hair that was more than likely out of a bottle.

We were at some coffee place near Aspen's shop. Her brother's widow – I now knew why Aspen had phrased it that way since there was definitely nothing sisterly about her, was glaring daggers at her across the table. Her arms crossed over her chest.

"Christen, I'm trying to help you," Aspen said. "I'm trying to help us both!"

Christen scoffed and looked at Aspen with utter disdain. "You're trying to cheat me and Silver out of what's rightfully ours!" she cried.

"Hold up, let me stop you right there, princess," I said, holding up a hand.

Aspen was ashen, quiet, and swallowed hard, but didn't say shit about me addressing her brother's widow that way. She'd warned me it might go down like this and I'd warned her, I wouldn't be anything other than myself about it.

"Did you actually sit down and read the wills?"

"My lawyer did," she snapped imperiously.

"Might wanna have a talk with him about that," I said.

Mav had found grounds for Aspen to keep everything from her mother, even though her brother had died after her. It was stipulated in her mother's will that should either Copper or Aspen die, the whole of her house and belongings would go to the surviving sibling. Even though Copper had died after her mother, he'd died before her mother's will could be officially discharged making everything Aspen's. She didn't have to give this gold-digging whore one red cent and with the way Christen was acting right now? I didn't care how nice my girl was. I wouldn't let her be a doormat.

"What do you know about it?" Christen demanded, raking me with her gaze and leaning back in her seat slightly, clearly reviled that the big, dirty biker would deign to even open his mouth in her direction.

"I know that the provision in my mother's will dictates that if either I or Copper are deceased before the will is discharged, then the remaining sibling gets it all." Aspen sounded somber but there was some steel in her voice.

"You're lying," Christen said, voice low and savage.

"Talk to your lawyer," Aspen said calmly, shaking her head. "I honestly don't know what else to do. I've bent over backwards to get you to like me, and I'm over it. I'm done." Aspen stood, and I stood with her.

"I'm tearing a page out of your playbook, love," she said, putting her hand in mine and looking up at me.

"The not-so-subtle art of not giving a fuck?" I asked.

"That would be the one," she said, and she looked tired and not at all happy about it, but you know what? That was okay. Slow progress was better than no progress. I knew she was likely to knuckle under when Christen came crawling back for help – which she would. She would have to, and that was going to be okay too.

Aspen was right. It was about *her* but in this case and more importantly, it was about what was best for her nephew, who was an innocent child in all of this.

We left the coffee shop; Christen looking so pissed she was about to cry and honestly, fuck her. Again, she wanted to fuck around and now she was finding out. Hopefully when she did come crawling back, it would be with some fuckin' humility but I doubted it.

I put my arm around Aspen as we made the walk back to her shop. She was in the middle of pricing things to sell and making more to come up with the money to break her lease so she could close down.

Her landlord had been good to her all this time, she said, so she wanted to at least do this right and I was all for it.

Turned out, she was a go for selling all her equipment and shit to me for a stupid low price. It wasn't going to be a dollar, there was a minimum threshold that would be acceptable according to the courts, but her hubby wasn't going to get near what he hoped out of it and that was going to be one hell of a shock and surprise.

We went in the back door and she called out to Amber that she was back before hanging her coat in the office and lifting down her apron, green eyes sightless and far away as she lost herself in thought.

I took a seat on one of the metal folding chairs and watched her as she moved around her shop, unwrapping a wad of clay, taking it over to the slab roller against the wall between two shelves. That thing was, by far, the biggest piece of equipment aside from her kilns.

I let her find some peace and solace in her work. I didn't need to be front and center in her attention all the time. It was just enough that I was here in her presence.

"I don't understand why I'm just so unlikable," she murmured.

"It's not you, babe. It's them," I said.

"How can you be so sure?" she asked, rolling the clay flat, turning the great wheel on the slab roller, making adjustments to it to get things the thickness she wanted, all automatically without thinking. I smiled a little to myself. She was a well-oiled machine when she created her things.

"Just going to have to trust me on this one, baby. I think I may have a little clearer perspective," I told her.

She stopped and stared at me and nodded slowly. "Maybe you're right," she said quietly.

"Not always," I promised her, "but on this one, yeah."

"God, we citizens are so fucked up," she said and came over, dropping into a seat around the worktable. Her hands hung limp between her thighs in the hammock made by her clay stained apron.

"Just starting to come around to that fact, huh?" I asked with a grin.

She looked up at me and shook her head and let her breath out of her lungs in a woosh. "They sit there acting like spoiled entitled brats all the while looking at you with disdain like *you're* somehow in the wrong and I just *don't understand it*." She stood up forcefully and went back to the slab roller to collect her clay.

"It's sheer madness," she muttered. "The whole world's gone mad."

"So, fuck 'em," I said. "Let 'em go crazy. Let 'em try and live up to unattainable expectations, constantly running the fuckin' rat race tryin' to get where they're going without even knowing what the destination actually *is*."

She turned around and looked at me and I smiled. "You know better, Leaf. Don't fall into their fucked-up rat trap."

She sighed. "Well, I feel like I am stuck in it for as long as it's going to take me to clean up this damn mess of everything."

"We'll get through it," I promised.

She brought her slab of clay over to the worktable and laid it over one of her wooden forms. She put her hands on her hips and looked at me, an appreciative little smile curving her lips.

"I don't know what I would do right now without you in my corner, cheering me on."

"I do," I said, and she cocked her head.

"Oh, yeah?"

"You'd manage just fine without me, it would take a while, but you're stronger than you give yourself credit for. You'd get through."

She came over to me and put her hands on my shoulders, straddling my lap and her lips against mine.

"I'm glad I don't," she whispered.

"Don't what?" I asked softly.

"Have to muddle through without you. I can't imagine what it'd be like, but I can imagine it would be very uncomfortable and unpleasant."

"Baby, your whole life is about to change," I murmured, smiling, looking into those beautiful green eyes of hers.

She smiled back and said, "I like the sound of that."

~

"WHAT YOU STARING AT, BOY?" I LOOKED DOWN THEN UP FROM THE bales of hay I was stacking in the lower part of the barn, part of getting ready for winter and over to my pops.

"I want Aspen to come live here," I said without any preamble. "I was thinking about turning the upstairs loft into a sort of studio for her, was thinking about what it would take to run better electricity out here and where to put her kilns and shit to where we could plug 'em in and they would actually work."

"Not out here," my dad said with a dubious laugh. "One malfunction and the whole barn could go up. I think upstairs could work as storage, but as for a studio space?" He looked thoughtful. "Could always build one out back of the house, out near the tree line. One of them she-shed deals. Kilns could go up against the back of the house on the outside, wouldn't take much to put the plug in out there for 'em."

"No complaints?" I asked. "No telling me I'm nuts or that it's a crazy idea?"

My dad shook his head, and heaved a big sigh, leaning on his pitchfork he'd been using to lay down new straw in the birthing stalls.

"I like her," he said with a shrug. "She's one of us."

I nodded slowly. The first was my father talking, the second? Vyking. Club brother, through and through.

"Guess there's only one thing left to do," I said.

"Ahhh, uh-uh," he said. "There's gonna be a metric fuckton of shit to do around here to make this place ready for her arts and crafts."

"Guess we better get on it, then."

He laughed at me. "Ha, ha, fuck you. I'm happy to have her around, but I ain't up for all that."

"Fine," I said. "Can you at least call around for me for the relevant work dudes to get some of this shit done? I don't know shit else about electrical."

"Now that," he said pitching a forkful of straw, "I can do."

CHAPTER TWENTY-SEVEN

*A*spen...

"Thank you for doing this for me," I murmured and looked around my mostly emptied shop. Today was the day. A rainy November morning outside the front windows matched a little how I was feeling on the inside about closing down and moving all of this stuff out to Fen's barn.

I missed the farm. I hadn't been in a couple of weeks and I was looking forward to the lush green pastures, the old wooden shake house, and the welcome sound of the bleating goats.

"Hey." Fen's voice snapped me out of my reverie and I dragged my eyes from the leaden gray outside and the falling rain.

"Hey," I said softly, smiling.

"You doing okay?" he asked.

"Yeah! Yeah, why?"

"You just seem a little out of it, that's all."

"Just saying goodbye, I guess." I sighed unhappily. "I don't know what I'm going to do next."

He hooked a hand behind my neck and pressed his lips to my forehead.

"Ain't gotta worry about any of that right now," he said and I put my arms around him and cuddled into his chest.

"I know," I murmured, but I did. I still felt so… detached. Like everything was up in the air, and I didn't like the feeling. I had always been one to crave roots. Maybe it was a byproduct of my name? Aspen was a kind of tree, after all…

"I got you, baby girl," he murmured and kissed the top of my hair.

"And I am so grateful for it," I murmured.

The U-Haul pulled up out front, blotting out the rain bouncing in the street and I took a deep breath and let it out slowly.

Fenris had asked the club to help with the move promising barbecue, beer, and mead a plenty at the farm in exchange for their efforts. Nearly everyone had volunteered, so long, they said, as Vyking did the cooking.

Vyking was back at the farm, manning the firepit. Little Bird and Dump Truck were out there with him, along with Dahlia and Momma Kat fixing sides and making sure there was a dry place to eat.

It was the absolute worst weather to be doing any of this in, but that was Washington for you. You couldn't plan anything by the weather here or you would never get anything done.

"Okay!" Maverick called, Marisol coming in the front door behind him. "Let's rock-and-roll, people!"

I smiled and mouthed *Thank you* at him as Fenris let me go.

"Hey, boss?" Amber called from the office.

"Yeah?"

"Need you a minute, please."

"Sure, sure!" I went in to find out what she needed.

"Well?" she asked, and I shook my head in confusion.

"Well, what?" I asked.

"How did he react?" she asked, eyes clear, bright, and curious.

"He didn't really," I said. "It was all very strange. He just stared at me like he didn't know who I was and signed the papers."

Amber fell into the desk chair laughing, her hands clutching her belly as I looked on even more confused than I'd been the moment before.

"That's great!" she cried. "You shocked him so bad he didn't know *what* to do!"

I smiled then and blinked as it sank in and I realized, *she was right.* He'd honestly expected me to just roll over and show my belly, and probably for the first time *ever,* I'd shown him some teeth.

I started laughing too, and the bikers that passed the shoebox of an office door just looked bemused, eyebrows raised in curiosity, but this was mine and Amber's secret inside joke. For now, at least. There was too much to do to stop and explain.

It only took an hour and a half to empty the shop of its kilns, the slab roller, its worktables and benches, and all of its industrial shelving. I swept and cleaned as soon as things were moved out of the way and when the last of it had gone, Fen came back to me and hugged me tight.

"I didn't think it would be like this," I said, surprised at how I felt. "I thought I would be relieved more than anything, you know?"

"Shh, I know. I got you, babe."

"It's okay," I said, letting him hold me. "I don't think I'm going to cry."

He chuckled and took a deep breath letting it out slow and said, "I'm so proud of you."

"Proud? Of me? Why?"

"You're getting stronger every day," he said, and I nodded.

"Yeah," I agreed.

"Let's go home," he said, and I nodded and put on another brave smile.

"Okay."

Fenris drove my Prius, and it felt just a little strange being a passenger in my own car. Not because I *was* riding shotgun, but because I felt strange for not feeling strange about Fenris driving at all.

Everything about being with him was so *easy* and I was a little sad, I realized, that everything I loved about this new life going forward was going to be at the farm and I would be in my mother's house… all alone.

It felt crazy to me, but it was what it was in some ways. I just couldn't bear to ask to stay. I don't think it was a matter of pride. I don't know what it was. Fear of rejection maybe? That fear had led me to make some really poor choices lately, I thought to myself, running fingertips over the rough and dirty patches on Fenris' vest in my lap.

He refused to wear it in a car. I guessed it was some kind of rule about respecting the vest and the patches on it. Something about refusing to cage something that was meant to be free. They had a tendency to call cars cages, too, and I understood that one. Especially after riding with Fenris.

We tried to only go out during good weather. Or, at least, he only took *me* out during good weather. He rode no matter what the sky was doing. Rain, shine, mist or even hale, he was out in it. Said he wasn't a fair-weather rider, but I would be lying if I said that didn't scare me a little. Not that I was worried about him and his riding capabilities. I was more concerned with all the utter fucking brainless *assholes* on the road.

He reached over without looking and threaded his fingers between mine, raising my hand to his mouth and kissing the back without taking his keen blue eyes off the road. I smiled, my heart swelling with love and commitment in my breast.

A feeling that turned into a bit of *'wait, what?'* when we pulled down the long drive of the farm behind the U-Haul, several more trucks and bikes bringing up the rear behind us. I got out of my car and stared across the expanse of grass at the new, but still rustic looking shop building that had been erected next to the barn, the sliding barn doors on its front standing open as Derry and Sauley went in and out, working on something.

"What's this?" I asked, looking over the roof of my car at Fenris.

"Something I've been meaning to talk to you about," he said with a wink in my direction.

"Yo, Fen! Where you want this stuff?" Maverick called from the back of the U-Haul, unlatching the roll-up door and sending it rocketing to a sky that was lightening. The rain had finally stopped out this way.

"Gimme just a minute, Mav!" Fen called back and all the guys were looking at us, me standing there, mouth hanging open, breath fogging the air, Fen's cut draped over my arm with reverence as he shut the driver's side door and came around to me. I shut my car door and stepped back. He took his cut gently from my hands and put it on.

"Come this way," he said and led me under the built-out roof section of the house, over the back patio.

I trailed along, my heart beating fast and faster against the inside of the cage of my ribs.

"Here, here, and here, are the plugs for your three big kilns. We figured they'd be safer out here than anywhere and the roof'll keep the wet off."

He led me down the flagstone walkway that had been put in from the patio leading to the new shed.

"Out here, is your studio. We're still working on getting it wired for electricity, but I figured your potter's wheel could go in this corner where it gets the light from both windows. You could have workbenches here, here, or there and the slab roller could go against that back wall. You still got plenty of shelves, and you could set those up wherever else there's room as soon as we finish getting it drywalled and painted in here."

I stared up at him open mouthed and he smiled down at me with an edge of shyness I'd never seen in him before. It took me a second to realize it wasn't *shy* but *nervous*. He was *nervous* and I couldn't for the life of me understand why…

"Now, as for storage for pieces waiting to get fired and that, you could keep those down here but the rest of your shelves can go up into the loft in the barn. Come this way." He towed me back outside and down the new path to the foot of the stairs outside the barn. We went up those stairs and he led us both in to the doorway at the top and into the freshly swept and cleared out loft at the top with its windows and high ceilings.

"I figured you could keep finished pieces up here, maybe do the online shipping thing for a while. You know, still work for yourself but on a smaller scale with little overhead. No rent, no mortgage. Just supplies… Little Bird likes taking pictures. Maybe you could set things up all artsy on the old stump out back. Could look really nice for like an Etsy shop or something. You could sell local on the weekends to build a following – hey! Hey, hey, hey, what's wrong?"

I covered my mouth with my hands as my eyes spilled over and I stared at him speechless.

"No, no, no, babe! Don't cry!"

He folded me against him as I let myself be overcome with *all* of the feelings.

"You did all this for *me?*" I asked, and he held me tight, smoothing a hand over my hair.

"Yeah, of course I did. I want you to be happy but more important, I want you to *be with me.* Here… I want you to do whatever the fuck you wanna do."

I clung to him and looked up at him and he smiled down at me, caressing the side of my face.

"I don't know what to say," I murmured.

"Say yes. Although, I want you to keep your money. Build yourself a 'fuck-off fund.'"

"A what?" I asked laughing.

"A 'fuck-off' fund, a big enough chunk of money that if shit goes sideways for you in any way. If this… stops working," and he almost visibly flinched at the idea, "you can take yourself anywhere in the world if you wanted to."

I shook my head. "There's no place in this world that I would rather be, than right here with you," I said fervently.

He looked me in the eyes and asked, "Is that a yes? You'll move in with me?"

"That's a yes," I murmured. "There's no place I've ever felt so at home than here."

He swept me up into a big bear hug and I shrieked, laughing as he spun me around.

"Oh, my God!" I cried, and he said to me, "Not yet. That's later tonight. Come on, let's get this part of the move over with.

"Okay," I said, hushed, and I led *him* down the stairs, excited to start down this new path in life. With him.

It took considerably *more* time to unload and set everything back up where it needed to go than it had to load everything up. By the time we were through, it had started to rain again and we were all crowded around the two picnic tables under the shelter of the back overhang. The food had been unreal, the mead and home brewed beer had flowed a plenty, and I had thoroughly enjoyed the mead part of things.

I'd never had it before and especially liked the variety where they'd added fresh blackberries from bushes surrounding the farm. It'd enhanced the honey flavor with a tart berry richness and I was easily drunk by my second glass. Nobody warned me that mead could be so potent, but then again; I was home, so who cared?

I sat straddling one of the picnic table benches, leaned back against Fenris, his arms around me as he casually rocked me back and forth. The guys were all varying stages of intoxicated around us, all telling stories that had every one of us in stitches. No one would be driving home. Some would be on the couches or up in the guest bedroom on the second floor, that I hadn't known was there, which made me smile now.

Some would likely be passed out in the barn by morning. All in good fun, until the hangovers hit.

"You ready for bed, baby girl?" Fen growled in my ear and I smiled.

"Mm-hm."

"K, come on."

He got up and helped me to my feet and both of us slipped off into the house, no one paying us any mind.

Up in the bedroom – *our* bedroom, the candles were lit, the music playing softly, and once again, Fenris pressed himself to my back, his lips to the side of my neck after pulling the collar of my thick sweater away.

"You are so fuckin' beautiful," he growled sweetly in my ear before lightly kissing the shell.

I spun in his arms and put my arms around his neck.

"And I love you," I breathed. He smiled and dipped his head, his mouth meeting mine in a gentle kiss that grew in urgency.

"Oh, baby," he whispered impassioned when I slipped to my knees and kissed the crown of the head of his cock. "Yes, please, *gods.*"

I took him into my mouth, eyes closed, listening to him gasp, relishing in the sensation of him gathering up my hair, loving the feel of him sliding across my tongue, touching the back of my throat. He grunted every so often, trying to hold back, and I was okay with that. Finally, he jerked his hips back, the hold he had on my hair tightening, preventing me from following him.

"Enough!" he cried hoarsely. "Enough. Get up off your knees," he ordered.

I got up off my knees and he kissed me savagely. I loved it when I riled him like this. When he got excited like this. It excited *me* and when he threw me down on the bed, I was both elated and giggling.

"You drive me crazy, woman," he said with a grin and I smiled.

"Good."

He kissed me, all the way down my body and I arched beneath him, into his touch... and as I stared at the ceiling, at the wavering patterns of golden light across it, I had one thought.

It was good to be home...

EPILOGUE

*M*ace...

"Another?"

I looked up, squinting at the plucky bartender chick that was serving 'em up.

"Yeah," I murmured and nodded and she gave me a look that was somewhere between empathetic and sympathetic.

"Okay, but this is going to have to be your last one, man. I don't need to get busted for overserving you, no matter how good looking I think you are."

I gave her a watery smile and swayed a bit on my barstool and nodded as she poured me another whiskey.

I was at this shithole bar in White Center, probably a quarter mile or so from the club. I honestly needed a fuckin' break from the fuckin' lovefest going on over there for a minute. Guys were gettin' girls and settling down left and right and shit if I didn't want that.

I was a jealous bastard. Weren't no bones about it.

"What's your name?" she asked me as she tipped the bottle back up and set it just out of reach.

"They call me Mace," I said and took a sip of the smoky amber liquid in my glass.

"Oh, yeah? Why's that?"

"Not supposed to ask me that, sugar."

"Well, I apologize then."

"'S no worries, you didn't know."

She was quintessentially Pacific Northwest. Her clothing organic, a mix between steampunk and hippy tree freak. Her top was a tank top looking thing with lacing like a corset in the front. Her shoulder tattooed with a Raven, the rest of her arm crawling with lush ivy vines.

Her hair was a brownish blonde, and in thick, ropy dreads down past her waist. Wood and metal beads with runes on them decorating her thick locks in irregular intervals.

Her skin was on the pale side, a scattering of light freckles over her nose and cheeks, barely there and almost unnoticeable in the dim light of the bar. She was thin, but wiry. I didn't think she was weak, but she certainly was willowy – almost looked vegan but that could have just been the Burning Man style she had going on.

Burning Man was popular up here, even though it was a big musical festival, rave, party thing that happened down in the California desert. A lot of people from up this way went down that way and partied hard for like a week or two every year – pitching tents, a bunch of crazy art installations – you name it.

"What's your name?" I asked her and she smiled at me with a wry twist of lips.

"Most of my friends call me Raven," she said.

"Nice to meet you, Raven."

"Nice to meet *you*, Mace."

A few guys came into the bar. Frat types. Asshole types and Raven gave me a wink.

"Duty calls," she said with a breezy sigh and she moved away from me, carrying her herbal scent down the bar with her. I smiled and thought through the haze of my drunk that she probably used essential oils for all the things.

She was pretty, and I liked the sparkle in her light eyes, but she probably wasn't the girl for me. I mean, she was a lover not a fighter type and probably couldn't hang or go my speed. Her speed was probably saving the spotted owl on the weekends or something. Spending forty-nine days camped in a tree so the man couldn't cut it down.

I chuckled to myself and shook my head. I could respect sticking it to the man every which way, but I needed somebody that could stick with me. This life wasn't for everyone. Still, I thought to myself, looking down the bar where she was at the opposite end talking to some old barfly regular; I could tap that.

Her legs were encased in tan leggings that looked like leather, a bunch of bronze zippers along her hips and thighs, but there were definitely no pockets. The way the material clung to those long stems of hers left nothing to the imagination. Her tank boots finished off the look she had going quite nicely.

I heard laughter and muttering behind me and turned a bleary eye on the three frat lookin' motherfuckers. They were sizing me up, and I turned back forward again.

Little shits could fuck off into oblivion for all I cared. It happened a lot, two or even three guys getting it in their heads that they could take on a Sacred Heart. That we weren't nothing. That was, until they lay on the pavement broken and bleeding, or until we fuckin' caught up to their little asses later – whichever came first.

They burst out laughing about something and high-fived each other and I didn't care except they were ruining my peace and damn quiet.

"Hey, hey yo!" one of them called out, and I knew it was to me. I just ignored them. I was on parole for another year and I had absolutely no desire to go back to the state pen and finish that bid off, fuck them very much.

"I'm talking to you!" he shouted, irritated.

"Hey! Knock it the fuck off, boys, or you can get the fuck out my bar," Raven told 'em.

"Shut up and just keep pouring the fuckin' drinks, sweetheart," one of them called out. I turned, just in time to see him grab his crotch and tell her, "I'll deal with you later."

Nice.

"Some people's fuckin' children, man," I said slowly. "You kiss your mother with that mouth?"

"Man, fuck you!" the dude's buddy, some Asian kid, said laughing.

"I don't swing that way," I said, turning back to the bar. "More power to you if you do, though."

I have no fuckin' idea what happened next. I heard something snap, shouting, and a white light flared through my vision as the back of my head erupted in pain. Next thing I knew, I hit the sticky barroom floor, face first and next, my ribs exploded in fire.

I managed to get up, more shouting, as I groped blindly and spilled out of the exit and onto the front sidewalk.

I couldn't get air, I couldn't breathe and I had a second to think through my drunken haze, *goddammit! They got the drop on me.*

What came next was probably the most brutal ass kicking of my life, and that's including the one I took in that yard fight when I was locked up.

I took a sneaker to the face and grimaced, immediately tasting blood as kicks and blows rained down on me.

Boom! Boom! Boom!

Three deafeningly loud rapid reports sounded. I heard some muffled shouts and screams, the thudding of rapid footsteps down the sidewalk and then the smell of essential oils assaulted my nose.

"Come on Mace, you gotta get up! Cops are coming for sure and we need to not be here when they do."

I struggled, but things didn't want to quite work. My eyes were swelling shut and every time I breathed in, it was like breathing so much bitter broken glass. I spit and tasted nothing but copper.

"Come on, Mace! *Help me!*" a woman's voice cried, and I struggled to my feet. My head swam with liquor and a beatdown. I don't remember shit else after that.

ALSO BY A.J. DOWNEY

The Sacred Hearts MC

1. Shattered & Scarred

2. Broken & Burned

3. Cracked & Crushed

3.5 Masked & Miserable (a novella)

4. Tattered & Torn

5. Fractured & Formidable

6. Damaged & Dangerous

The Virtues

1. Cutter's Hope

2. Marlin's Faith

3. Charity for Nothing

4. Stoker's Serenity

The Sacred Brotherhood

1. Brother to Brother

2. Her Brother's Keeper

3. Brother In Arms

4. Between Brothers

5. A Brother's Secret

6. A Brother At My Back

7. A Brother's Salvation

Indigo Knights

1. Her Thin Blue Lifeline

2. His Cold Blue Command

3. A Low Blue Flame

4. His Wild Blue Rose

5. Her Pained Blue Silence

6. A Cold Blue Call

7. Her Reluctant Blue Cavalier

8. Forged Under Fire

9. Under A Blue Moon

Sacred Hearts MC Pacific Northwest

1. Over the High Side

2. Wind Therapy

Paranormal Romance (with Ryan Kells)

1. I Am The Alpha

2. Omega's Run

3. Hunter's End

Standalones

Synchronicity

ABOUT THE AUTHOR

A.J. Downey specializes in writing real and relatable contemporary romance stories. She's from Seattle, WA and loves the Pacific Northwest. She finds inspiration from her surroundings, through the people she meets, and likely as a byproduct of way too much caffeine. An avid reader all of her life, it's now her turn to try and give back a little, entertaining as she has been entertained.

Stalker Information:

Website
www.ajdowney.com

Sign up for her newsletter at
http://eepurl.com/dkQiIH

Facebook Group - AJ's Sacred Circle
https://www.facebook.com/groups/authorajdowney/

facebook.com/authorajdowney
twitter.com/authorajdowney
instagram.com/ajdowney
bookbub.com/authors/a-j-downey